T. GEPHART

DEDICATION

To Karen – That inbox was priceless.
Sharing it with me is what started this whole ride. Thank you.
To Sally – Thanks so much for
checking in on me and talking me off the ledge.
No books will be left behind,
even if there are tears while questioning our life choices.
To Gep – I couldn't have done it without you. I know
it's my process but I need the reminder and you by my side.

White Trash Circus will be taking an extended break and won't be playing any time in the foreseeable future. Please lodge all your complaints to my guitarist—and my ex best friend—who I found *inside* the girlfriend I've had since high school. I will pull the freaking knife from my back and continue—without either of them—when the time is right. With enough hate and anger coursing through my veins to keep me in therapy for life, I'm going to save my cash and let the music heal me. Prepare all your bleeding hearts to be tormented with the most righteous, heavy and cataclysmic tunes to ever come out of me. So there's that to look forward to. Thank you for all the support over the years, the gigs, the love and most of all memories. Don't trust anyone and stay metal—Vaughan.

PS. Connor, you left your guitar and rig at my house so I took the liberty of relocating it to my front lawn. I might have dropped it on the way out the door. In your own words, *brother*, "Sometimes stuff just happens."

PPS. Our drummer spontaneously combusted and is no longer with us.

WhiteTrashMegaFan - Whoa! Is this real?

VaughanLover4Eva - I love you Vaughan, you were too good for her anyway. I want to have your babies.

HeavyBrad69 – So rock and roll!! Can't wait for the new stuff, it's going to be metal AF!

Nico – Ummm, Vaughan, what about me?

LicksNStick - LOL awks

White Trash Circus – No one cares about the bass player, Nico.

Vaughan

Fuck.

Pretty sure my soul had checked out of my body twelve hours ago with my liver about four hours before that. I didn't much care what the hell happened, except I was starting to sober up and that just wouldn't do. Everyone knew the best way to beat a hangover was to stay drunk, and I was on a bender that had no expiration date.

My head lifted off the bed only to be hit with the smell of stale beer and sweat floating up from my shirt. Screw that, my eyes squinting shut as I immediately lowered it. Why the hell was there banging on the front door? Wasn't the whole idea of being in the fucking woods so that everyone left you the fuck alone? It wasn't my boss, that much I knew. The asshole who ran the Get Go gas station I worked at, called and fired me on the spot for not turning up for my shift. And surely the other two cocksuckers weren't dumb enough to come crawling back.

The cocksuckers in question were my ex-girlfriend and my ex best friend. Those two shitstains had been fucking each other behind my back for who knows how long, which meant they not only killed their relationships with me but the only other thing that I loved.

My band.

Damn it.

I was positive we were on the edge of greatness, just waiting to be discovered when it all went to shit. And while we might have survived losing our drummer—his exit completely coincidental—there was no way I was going to play with a dude who could stab me in the back so freaking hard.

"Vaughan, open the door." The knocking had graduated to shouting, my head not fond of the new progression. At least it wasn't Connor or Lindsey, meant I wouldn't end up in a jail cell before the end of the day.

"Vaughan! Open. The. Fucking. Door."

Wow.

Who knew he had it in him?

"Go away, Nico," I yelled, not in the mood to hear his bullshit. Fine, I probably should have consulted him before pulling the pin and posting the status, but it was my freaking band and I'd do what I wanted.

Before I could add that while my comment about "no one giving a shit about the bass player" might have been harsh but undeniably true, a boom vibrated through the room. The door that had been locked shut had flung open, separating from the splintered jamb.

Old door, not great lock and a solid kick would do that.

"What the fu—" I didn't even get to finish the sentence, six-foot-six of pissed off coming through the hole where the door used to be, only stopping short when he saw me.

"What the hell happened to you?" Nico covered his nose, taking a step back. "It smells like something died in here."

Ha.

Wasn't that the truth.

I felt like I'd died too, and couldn't remember when I'd last taken a shower. My eyes were probably so bloodshot I was going to need a gallon of Visine, while my long hair had started to form dreads. Not that personal hygiene was running high on my list of priorities.

Nico had about four inches on me, and I was a respectable six-two. He also carried at least ten to fifteen more pounds because he got beat up a lot as a kid. I didn't have the same problem, which meant I stayed just under two hundred.

"What happened?" I asked, wondering if Nico was actually stupid or just playing the part real well. "Connor fucked Lindsey and—"

"Ok, look, that's not why I'm here." He cut me off, waving his hands and taking a step forward. "I need to talk to you about something important."

Great.

I wasn't drunk enough to hear him bitching about whatever it was he needed to say. "Nico, if this is about the fucking status—"

"Can you shut the fuck up for a minute and listen to me?" His voice boomed, echoing off the walls. "The status went viral, Vaughan. It's been liked and shared over three hundred thousand times. It's been what? Two days? Closer to three if you counted the extra hours. There are more comments than anyone can read and my phone hasn't stopped buzzing."

"Huh?" My hand scrubbed the front of my face trying to understand what he was saying.

We had maybe a thousand fans on our pages, and some of those were family and friends who didn't give a shit about the band but were just being supportive. Which was why I put up the status in the first place, made it easier to tell everyone that Connor was a dick, Lindsey a whore, and the band was done.

Not wanting to see either of them—or anyone else—I headed to my grandpap's cabin in Nemacolin where I could drink myself into a stupor and connect with nature or some shit. My grandpap swore the place had magical fucking powers, and while the old dude was a drunk and had been dead ten years, I didn't have anything else to do. Not like I had a job or anything, my life pretty much in the toilet.

"Viral," he repeated, not telling me anything more than he had the first time. "A few people shared it and then it sort of exploded. Facebook, Twitter, Instagram—likes, shares, comments. Phone calls, people knocking on my door—I'd been trying to get a hold of you for six hours before I finally went and saw your parents. They told me that you grabbed the keys for this place and took off."

The room swayed, or maybe I was, my head feeling weird as I shuffled back and found a seat. "Three hundred thousand?" I swallowed, not even being able to visualize what that number would even look like. "What the hell are they saying?"

It felt like a crazy-ass dream. And I wasn't sure if it was my blood alcohol level, the fact I couldn't remember when I'd last ate, or that Nico had grown a set of balls all of a sudden, but none of it made sense.

Three hundred thousand—so many zeros my head hurt— over a fucking status about the band being over?

What did that even mean?

"Radio stations looking for interviews, people wanting to hear from us—and considering *no one gives a shit about the bass player*," the sarcasm thick in his voice, "I figured I'd come here and get your sorry ass."

He pulled his phone from his pocket, swiping up my original post, and thrust the phone in my face. Even with bloodshot eyes and blurry vision, I could see the counter clicking over live as that *three* hundred thousand moved closer to *four*.

"Holy shit." I grabbed my own phone and brought it back to life. I'd switched it off when I'd left my apartment in Swissvale and hadn't even looked at it since. The minute it found a signal, the thing buzzed, beeped, vibrated and flashed like a slot machine spitting out a jackpot in Vegas.

Love you, Vaughan. Keep fighting the good fight —
Luda92

Hey Guys, you need a guitarist? I can play AND keep
my dick in my pants. DM me—SiTheShreddingGuy

Is this for realz?—LolliPop8

Fuuuuuuuuuuuuuck. Condolences Bro, don't fade into
the darkness, we've got ya back—DOA

This is Kasey Blackwell from KDP News, can you
please check your inbox and email account for our
messages. We'd love to get a statement.—KaseyBKDP

How can you do that to your boy, Connor? I hope you
get herpes and your dick falls off. PS your guitar work
sucked ass. Vaughan was being held back IMHO. Rise
above, brother!—RitchM

"See, told you." Nico smirked, tipping his head to my phone which seemed like it was going to explode from the activity.

Message after message appeared, new ones popping up faster than I was able to keep up with. And my voicemail was full too, texts not being enough for some, the need to call me too overwhelming.

"I need to get back." I tried to stand, my body swaying as I unsuccessfully tried to get upright. To be fair, I hadn't spent a lot of time vertical in the last few days so I was probably out of practice.

Nico grabbed my shoulders, putting that extra muscle to good use as he kept me on my feet. "Maybe we get you some coffee and sober you up a bit first. And for all our sake's, I hope there's a shower in this place too."

The old water heater still had some life in it and I was able to wash away the stench of bad decisions and cheap beer with the help of a bar of Irish Spring. Thankfully, I had some clean clothes stashed in a gym bag in the back of my truck, because the ones I'd been wearing were going to need an exorcism and about a gallon of Tide if they stood any hope.

After downing three cups of coffee, a bag of beef jerky with a questionable expiration date, and two Advil, I was as close to being human as I was going to get. Not sober enough to drive though, which meant I had to leave my beat-up Ford pickup at the cabin and hitch a ride with Nico in his Nissan Altima.

The two-hour drive back to Swissvale gave me time to try to weed through some of the comments and get a handle on what we were dealing with. Sure, there were assholes who called me a crybaby for airing my dirty laundry. Or others who assumed Lindsey strayed because she wasn't getting enough satisfaction at home. But for the most part, they were supportive. Of course, it would have been nice if even one tenth of these people had shown any interest in our music or turned up to a gig. Not that it mattered now.

"Fuck!" Nico slammed on the brakes, skidding to a stop as we pulled into my apartment complex. There were people everywhere, hanging out on their phones, banging on my front door and trying to peek through my drapes.

"Jesus, who the hell are they?"

There had to be at least thirty people in the parking lot, most of them faces I didn't recognize.

VIRAL

"Fans?" Nico shrugged, slowly reversing out of the complex and onto the road. No one seemed to notice his Altima, probably expecting my Ford truck.

"Fans? Dude, our last gig there were fifteen people in the bar. We don't have that many *fans*." I scoffed, wondering how the hell I was going to get back into my apartment. "Look, just go to Johnny's place."

Nico hesitated, continuing down the road with no real conviction. "You sure, man? You think he's going to want to see us?"

"Well if he doesn't, he'll be the one person in Pittsburgh who apparently doesn't. Just go to Johnny's."

Johnny Cash—legit, his name—was destined for rock stardom. How could he not be? If you were named after a legend, you had to follow in their footsteps—it was like an unwritten law. But instead of taking up guitar like his namesake and becoming a superstar, Johnny decided drums were more for him. Suited me fine though, because we needed a drummer and no one else was interested.

But as far as talent went, he drew the short straw. He could keep time—barely—but you could tell his heart wasn't in it. It wasn't until two weeks ago that he sat us down and *came out* to us as a band. Confessing he'd been living a lie and it was eating him alive.

No, he wasn't gay.

Gay would have been awesome. He could have sucked as much dick as he wanted to and I would have been his number one supporter. Because I didn't give a shit what anyone's sexual preference was, and truth be told, it meant there was less chance of him screwing Lindsey like Connor did.

But nooooooooo, he couldn't be fucking gay and make us all happy. Instead, he *came out* as a fucking circus freak. You know the kind that wear one-piece white leotards that show

7

off your junk. And maybe it would have been easier to take if he did something cool like breathe fire or scare people as some demented clown. But unbeknownst to any of us, he was a fucking acrobat.

Flips through the air like it's happy hour at Cirque du Soleil.

And you think you *know* a guy.

So he packed up his sticks, told us he was joining the freaking circus—like an *actual* one—and that we were going to be less a drummer.

For a second I thought it was some sick, perverted joke and then I saw his costume. Yeah, the joke was on me since I'd been the dick who'd named the band. And yet, like I'd been a freaking crusty old Greek dude sprouting a prophecy, one of our members legitimized our name.

No way in hell I was fessing to that truth, which was when I decided I'd turn to *Spinal Tap* for inspiration. I mean, he might as well have died. As soon as he took off with the carni folk, he was as good as lost to us. It was worse than a cult.

We pulled up to Johnny's place and thankfully it was a ghost town. His parents had retired to Florida—or left from the shame—leaving their only son their two-story aluminum-sided house in Munhall.

"Vaughan?"

Before we'd even knocked on his front door, he'd pulled it open and was staring at us from the other side.

He looked so fucking normal, still dressed as a regular guy in a pair of jeans and a tee, keeping his junk as well hidden as his dirty secret.

"I'm here too, asshole." Nico rolled his eyes, pissed that despite being right beside me with his fist ready to knock, I was the first one who was acknowledged. Pfft, bass players—they just didn't get it.

Johnny shook his head, pulling open the door a little wider and welcoming us inside. "Yeah, I know. But you aren't the cocksucker who told the world I fucking died."

"C'mon, man," I scoffed, still not sober enough to be less honest. "There wasn't a chance I was writing the truth. This way, you got a dignified exit. Everyone is happy."

"Tell that to my parents who have been fielding calls from concerned friends and relatives ever since you posted it." He pointed to a couch and I was more than happy to take him up on the offer. "And next time you decide to post something like that, how about you give me a heads up."

If my head didn't hurt so much, I would have rolled my eyes. And had I not been so pissed at Connor and Lindsey, I'd have probably extended him the courtesy. "Yeah, yeah fair call. You want to rail me a little longer or can I have a minute to work out what the hell is happening?"

Johnny might have traded drumsticks for a big top but he'd been a friend for a long ass time and had always had my back. I was willing to overlook his recent indiscretions on account he'd given us a safe place to hide out.

Huffing out a breath, he parked his ass on the armchair opposite us and opened up a laptop that was sitting on the coffee table.

It seemed absolutely impossible, that in the time between driving from the cabin to civilization that the likes, comments and shares had multiplied so much I couldn't even process the number. How many zeros were there? And where the hell did these people come from?

Will fuck you so hard you'll forget her name—AnnieGee

Disseminate them in lyrics! They deserve each other—TulsaTodd

9

Blowjob will make you feel better babe. Slide into my DMs—TawneyM

"Jesus." I scanned over the comments, unable to focus as the screen blurred. "It doesn't look like it's slowing down."

Johnny barked out a laugh, cracking his neck to the side like he was enjoying himself. "Yeah, that ship sailed, brother. And no offense, but you're not hiding out here. I leave to go on tour next Tuesday."

Didn't think there was anything that could manufacture a laugh, but that statement made me chuckle.

"Dude, stop saying you're going *on tour* like that's what it is. You're joining a traveling freak show and roaming through the country like fugitives."

Johnny raised his brow, not finding the same humor. "Says the asshole who has wanted fame his whole life and now that he has it, is hiding out in my house."

Touché.

The man had a point.

I'd waited my whole life to have their attention.

It was time to think about what I wanted to say.

2

Vaughan

It seemed like everyone in the city was looking for me.

A few local news stations had picked up the story, knocking on Connor's door, looking for a statement. Unsurprisingly, he chose not to answer it, leaving reporters to make up their own BS as they crossed back to their studios while putting his address on blast.

My lack of sympathy was also unsurprising, guess there were only so many fucks I had to give and I was all out.

It was only a matter of time before they tracked down Johnny, the story of his untimely demise debunked by his crazy Uncle Earl who ran a trailer park out in Jeannette. So rather than wait until they smoked us out like criminals with a list of warrants, I decided the best thing to do was face the music—pun intended.

The lack of wheels—my truck still at the cabin—meant Nico was acting as chauffeur, but it was me who was firmly in the driver's seat. Metaphorically of course, we weren't sitting on each other like a couple of clowns ready to join Johnny's circus.

While Nico drove, I dialed, waiting as each passing second felt like an eternity.

"This is Amy at WJVE, the station that rocks and never sleeps, how may I direct your call?"

"Hey, Amy, it's Vaughan Hale. How's your day going?" It wasn't the first time I'd called the station, but I had a hunch she wasn't going to shoot me down like she usually did.

"Vaughan? Vaughan from White Trash Circus?"

"Awww you remembered me." I smiled, trying not to see the irony that it was exactly two weeks ago since we'd last spoken. She'd told me they didn't take unsolicited calls to get music played on air and then laughed at our name saying she'd never heard of the band.

And yet, there we were.

"Of course, I remember you." Her voice so sticky sweet I was at risk of developing diabetes. "You're my favorite person in the world. And I'm so glad that you called me, you want me to patch you through to Jasper on the air?"

Yeah, I thought so. She might be lying through her teeth about giving two shits about me, but she knew dollar signs when she saw them.

"That would be grand, Amy. I'd *love* to talk to Jasper."

Love might have been too strong a word considering he wouldn't have been my first, second or third choice. But all the good DJs didn't come on until drive time so it was either chat to Jasper or hide out in the parking lot of a Giant Eagle until then.

Not happening.

"Great. Now don't hang up, okay. I need you to stay on the line," she warned, the sweetness gone and in its place a FBI negotiator trying to secure the release of hostages from a terrorist. "I'm going put you through in just a minute."

She'd over estimated, the pop of my call being taken off hold exactly thirty seconds later.

"Vaughan Hale, this is Jasper and you're on the air. How are you doing, buddy? People are turning over the city looking for you."

"Yeah, I was out of cell range," I lied, rolling my eyes. "And I am doing . . . okay."

That might have been a lie too considering I hadn't had time to evaluate exactly how I was feeling. Still, I wasn't calling in for a therapy session, so my feelings weren't really the point.

"Anyway, I just wanted to say that I appreciate all the messages and likes on the post and I want the fans to know that this will not end me. I'm going to come back heavier and harder than ever, and rest assured I'm going to shake the 'Burgh to its foundations."

"Wow, sounds great. Have you spoken to Connor or Lindsey?"

"Those two ass—"

"Oh, hey, Vaughan, we're live. Can't have you saying things that are going to get us shut down by the FCC," Jasper laughed, cutting me off before I could finish my colorful description.

"Right. Yeah, maybe it's best we don't talk about them then." I coughed, not having it in me to find something nice to say.

"Probably for the best." He chuckled. "Hey, why don't we talk about your plans for the future? You going to hold auditions for a new guitarist? We could run a competition for you? Find you the best one in the state."

"Dude, I'm not interested in becoming a fuu, I mean, *freaking* reality show." There'd be a cold day in hell before I'd do that.

"You're kidding, right? You know what an amazing opportunity it would be? How many bands would kill for that kind of exposure?" I heard the disbelief in his voice, like he couldn't believe I'd had the stones to decline.

"Yeah, not going to happen."

There was a beat of dead air where I wasn't sure if I'd lost connection. But I could hear the squirrely little bastard still breathing so I guess he just wasn't used to being told no.

"Okay, well fine." He tried to recover. "Hey, why don't we take some callers? Hear what the people have to say."

The "sure" I was about to say got stuck in my throat, the hesitation something that seemed new to me.

It sounded like a bad idea.

So incredibly bad that the only part of my subconscious brain that had anything smart to say was screaming at me to say goodbye and hang up.

"*End the call, Vaughan.*" I heard it echo in my head, reinforcing what I already knew.

"*Vaughan!*"

My head snapped, the voice so loud I'd assumed someone else had said it. But when I looked over at Nico—the only other person in the car with me—he was squinting at me like he had no idea why I was suddenly giving him attention. He'd pulled over, letting the car idle in the abandoned parking lot of a closed strip mall. And it was clear I was either hearing voices in my head or he'd become a ventriloquist. And let's face it, Nico wasn't that talented.

"Hey Jasper, got to go." I killed the call, not bothering to give him the chance to say goodbye or convince me otherwise.

"Well, that went different from how I imagined it." I shrugged, feeling no better for it. "Can you believe the nerve of that guy suggesting we hold auditions with the station? Like that wasn't the worst idea ever."

Nico grimaced, weighing his words before he spoke them like he knew I wasn't going to be a fan. "I didn't think it was a totally bad idea, they'd have more reach than we have. Might have been a good way to find—"

He didn't get to finish his sentence, my ring tone breaking the silence with the caller ID displaying an unidentified number.

It was probably Jasper, no doubt pissed I'd hung up on him without letting him get in the last word. Well screw him, and his shady idea.

My chest expanded, the smile on my face not allowing him the courtesy of a greeting. "I'm not sure why you think I'd suddenly want to turn my band into an episode of *The Bachelor* to boost your ratings, but it ain't going to happen. So why don't you save us both the time, because honestly, you asked me twice and I said no and now it's just embarrassing."

"Are you done?" A female voice I didn't recognize responded. "Or do you want to keep going with your one-sided conversation a little longer?"

Wow, what? She didn't sound mad but she wasn't amused either. Her voice steady and controlled with so little emotion I had no choice but to pay attention.

"Good, I'll take your silence as a sign you're finished. My name is Gillian, and I'm assuming you're Vaughan Hale."

"Yeah, I'm Vaughan."

"Great, nice to know I haven't wasted a complete morning tracking you down. I'm from Domination Music Group, and we'd like to have a conversation."

Domination Music Group was a progressive label, who, unless you'd been in a coma for the last ten years, you'd have heard of. While the big boys out of New York were recycling same-ole-same-ole, Domination took chances and signed new acts no one would give a second look to. And a phone call from them was akin to a nod from the capo of "the family."

No one was ever the same after it.

They either made you. Or broke you.

"You want to have a conversation?" I repeated, stalling while I tried to find something more intelligent to say.

"Yes, other than the one we are currently having on the phone. In person is preferable."

She was ice cold, almost impersonal and to the point with such a snap that I wasn't sure if I should be impressed or annoyed she didn't seem to give a shit. But I wasn't an idiot either, and while my judgment was still questionable, there wasn't a chance I was telling Gillian from Domination anything but yes.

"Okay, sure. Where do you want to meet, and when?"

"We have a room at the Westin on Penn, you know where that is? Let's say two o'clock. We'll leave your name at the front desk."

"Downtown? You're *here*, in Pittsburgh?"

If it had been any other label I might have been able to hide my surprise, but Domination was like the hot girl in high school. You showed your interest, and if fate was smiling on you and she found you worthy, you were summoned. She never chased, and sure as shit didn't come down from her ivory tower to slum, or in this case, leave NYC.

"Yes, we'll expect you at two. Goodbye." And just like that I was listening to dead air, the call ending almost before it had a chance to start.

Whiplash.

All I could do was stare at the cell in my hand and wonder if I hadn't hallucinated the whole thing. It had been a strange morning so nothing seemed out of the realm of possibility.

"Who was that?" Nico asked, confirming if nothing else, I had been on the phone with *someone*. Well, at least I wasn't totally losing it, always a plus.

"Domination."

My one-word answer was all I was capable of giving, still not entirely sure what they wanted.

Nico whipped his head around, his face screwed up in confusion. "That bondage shop on South Side?"

"No, the music label, dumbass. They want to meet."

"Why?"

Well wasn't that the question of the fucking day.

Who knew why? Considering I no longer had a band, it wasn't likely to hand over a wad of cash and give me a deal. But then I wasn't ruling it out either. I was a solid singer, maybe they wanted to see what I could do solo? I had promised to write the most epic music of all mankind.

"Not sure, but I'm going to go and find out."

Beats the hell out of driving around in Nico's Altima all day, and it was clear I couldn't go back to my apartment right now. Not like I had a lot of other options. Unless I wanted to take up Jasper's offer and hand out roses to guitarists and pick the one that didn't get voted off the island. So yeah, no others worth considering.

Nico tapped the steering wheel, putting the car in gear. "Okay, well I'm going to have to drop you off somewhere because I need to be at work soon."

Even if I had a job, I'd be blowing it off, the situation demanding attention. Granted, that was why I was probably currently unemployed, but still—it was like an emergency.

"Work?" I shook my head. "You're not seriously thinking about going to *work* are you?"

First he was pissed I hadn't included him in the decision to end the band, then he was blowing off a meeting with Domination. Seriously, he was worse than a child.

"Yeah, Vaughan, work. I can't afford to lose this job, I just started getting health benefits and the hours are good. Look, I'll drop you off at your parents' house and then we can catch up tonight after your meeting." He didn't wait for a reply, pulling out of the parking lot and onto the main road.

The dude worked in the mailroom at PNC Bank, it wasn't like he was scheduled to do heart surgery, but sure, whatever, I'd go on my own.

"Fine. Go punch a clock and collect your health benefits." I threw my hands up in disbelief. "It's probably better you didn't come anyway."

I wasn't entirely sure that was true, but I wasn't going to act like a pussy and beg him to come hold my hand.

Nope.

Fuck. That.

I would do this on my own.

Well, at least I would once I got to my parents' house, and asked my dad to borrow his car. I'd probably have a lot of explaining to do, which would take more time than I wanted but it wasn't like I could avoid it.

After that, then it was all about me.

3

Vaughan

The room was stock standard for a fancy hotel. Heavy drapes, carpet your boots sunk into when you walked, and walls that looked so freshly painted I was surprised I couldn't smell the fumes. No Holiday Inn for these folks, it was a flashy penthouse with a living room bigger than my whole apartment.

"Something to drink?" A woman wearing glasses and a scowl directed me to a chair. She didn't sound like the lady I'd spoken to on the phone, but her attitude was definitely on par.

"Coffee would be good." I decided to go the safe route, figuring my caffeine levels hadn't caused tachycardia just yet so I was good.

She turned, giving me a view of her unremarkable ass as she went to the bar area and poured me a cup. She wasn't unattractive, but her vibe was decidedly unpleasant.

I accepted the cup she handed me—no sugar, no cream and no fucking smile—and shot her my best attempt at charm. "So now you have me here, Gillian, what do you want to talk about?"

If the ice queen was capable of surprise, she didn't show it. Best I got was a raised eyebrow, the corner of her mouth twitching into what were the makings of a grin. "Oh, I'm not Gillian Duzan, I'm her assistant. *Mr*. Duzan will be with you shortly."

Well *that* was interesting.

Her name was Gillian *Duzan*.

It was probably no coincidence she had the same last name as the head honcho. Warrick Duzan was not only the founder of Domination but the CEO. And while he was a shark in business, he had a Baskin Robbins approach to marriage and liked to *thirty-one flavor* his wives. Hey, not that I was one to judge but by my limited knowledge, he'd been divorced like five times, which would probably make Gillian lucky number six.

Fucking perfect.

Just when I thought the conversation might be for something legit—not sure exactly for what considering I didn't have a band but still—a whole heaping load of realty was dumped into my lap.

Gillian no doubt had seen the noise online when she was busy Instagraming her morning latte and decided she needed a new plaything. Nothing like a bored rich wife who wasn't getting enough attention at home to stoke a fire under her husband's ass. She got a younger, more agile model to keep her happy and he got to do whatever he wanted to do without interruption. At least that was the way I assumed it worked, I'd seen enough movies to figure it out.

And while I wasn't on the cover for *GQ*, I knew I was a decent-looking dude. I worked out, kept myself in shape, and was never hurting for female attention. Whether it was random numbers stuffed into my pockets or more direct propositions, I wasn't stupid enough to think it was my stellar personality that turned heads. Nope, girls liked what they saw even though for the most part I turned it down on account I had a woman. That had probably been my bad, keeping myself monogamous when it clearly hadn't been a requirement. But even though I was obviously single, turning into a whore for some asshole's wife hadn't been the plan either.

I was half way through my debate when old man Duzan walked in, he was alone—and unlike his wife's assistant—he was grinning ear to ear.

"Vaughan, thank you for joining us." He strode through the room with a confidence that came with either a big dick or a fat bank account—I was guessing the latter—and extended his hand with no hesitation.

Despite the urge to leave, I accepted the handshake, giving him my best I'm-not-going-to-fuck-your-wife smile.

It wasn't about me taking a moral high ground either. I wasn't committed to anyone nor did I have an issue with fucking around. And lord knows, I could use the cash. But if I ever wanted to graduate from singing in seedy bars, then screwing Duzan's wife didn't seem smart. Last time I checked, I wasn't Julia Roberts and I wasn't going to end up with a fist full of cash—or in my case, a record deal—after it was over.

"Hey, no problem. Happy to chat."

That *wasn't* a lie. I was genuinely happy to chat; it was whatever else he might propose that I had a problem with.

We both took a seat, him opposite me, and with a flick of his wrist he made the nameless assistant disappear. Probably better for all concerned if there were no witnesses.

"Do you know who I am?" He tilted his head, waiting for my answer.

Ordinarily, a total jerkoff thing to say but it seemed like he was asking honestly. Like, do I have to go through the whole saga of telling you my life story or can we just cut to the chase. Have to admit, I liked the man's efficiency.

I nodded, because as much as he probably didn't want to do the whole song and dance about who he was and all that shit, I didn't want to hear it either. No point. Didn't serve any purpose and I wanted us to move to the part where he told me why I was sitting in the hotel room at the apparent request of his wife.

"Good. So, Vaughan, Gillian brought your post to my attention." He unbuttoned his jacket, relaxing into his chair. "And to be honest, I was skeptical. But she likes what she likes and I can't really reason with her."

"O-kay." I measured my response, pretty sure where it was heading but shocked that he was actually going to say it.

He nodded, seeming to appreciate my lack of chatter so he could continue. "And while I'm happy for her to have her fun, I want you to know I'll be making the decisions when it comes to how this plays out. My money, my rules. You got it?"

Awesome, because it wasn't bad enough this dick wanted me to fuck his wife, he wanted a say in *how* it happened. Was he going to watch, jerking off while calling out suggestions from the sidelines? Film it for posterity? Or perhaps he was going to give me a contract, letting me know what I could and couldn't do and then threaten to string me up by the balls if I didn't follow it.

And why the fuck hadn't I told this idiot I wasn't interested? My ass hadn't moved from the chair, mouth shut as I listened to him, curious to how much cash he was talking about.

Jesus.

What the hell was I doing?

Was I actually considering it?

"Dude, no offense but I'm not sure I'm cool with this agreement." *Thank you, Jesus.* And while I might not have turned him down flat, I was hoping he was reading between the lines that I wasn't about to become a plaything for the Mrs.

His eyebrow rose, like he was surprised I hadn't pulled out my dick and asked him where he wanted it. "Really? Without even hearing my offer?"

Yeah, asshole, we haven't even heard his offer yet.

"Doesn't matter." I wasn't sure if I was arguing with myself or him. "There isn't enough money," *at least I didn't think so,* "you could offer me to fu—I mean, scre—I mean, sleep with your wife."

There.

A freaking line in the sand.

He looked at me in silence, his eyes narrowing like he couldn't believe I'd said it out loud. And truth be told, I was a little surprised I'd said it too.

Might have taken me a while to get there but I'd made my choice. And look at me taking the highroad.

"My wife?" He leaned in, like he hadn't heard me properly the first time.

Lord, and to think the man was supposed to be some kind of business genius. And here I was, dropped out of my first year of college and having to draw the man a diagram.

"Gillian, the one who saw the post, brought it to your attention and now you're happy for her *to have her fun*." I couldn't be any clearer, using the exact words he'd said to me when we'd sat down.

His face hardened. "Gillian is my daughter, not my wife."

Not sure if the sudden gasp of air I took was audible but my chest actually felt tight. There was an odd stirring in my pants too, with my cock taking an interest. And it took me a minute to evaluate if it changed anything, my lips hesitating before asking A. how old she was and B. if he had a picture.

My hands were slightly sweaty as I rubbed them down the front of my jeans, my heartbeat kicking up a notch or two as I continued to debate. And really, since when did I get on this high fucking horse, being so judgmental? If he wanted to pull some strings and help his daughter—she had to be at least twenty-one though—get a date, as long as it was all consensual, what was the freaking problem?

If the tingling in my crotch was anything to go by, I'd say there was no freaking problem at all. Hmmm, sure not as clean cut as I first thought.

"You thought I was asking you to sleep with my wife?" he baited me, daring me to confirm that I'd accepted Gillian's invitation and sat down with him on that assumption.

"No, not initially." I tried to salvage the situation. "It was just . . . there was a wire crossed in the communication, no big deal. And to be fair, I already told you I wasn't interested." That had to count for something, right?

Before either of us had time to clarify our position, the door burst open. Dressed like she was ready for a raid at midnight in head-to-toe black, her dress and jacket giving no clues as to whether she was hot or not. Standing around five-seven, with a mess of dirty blonde hair that had been pulled back, her whiskey-colored eyes looked at us with suspicion.

It wasn't that she was ugly, because she sure as hell wasn't, but there was something about her that was so understated it messed with my head. She couldn't have been any less remarkable if she tried, almost like her body was just a vessel. An alien life form taking up space in the chamber and she was going to shed her shell when it was no longer necessary.

A shiver traveled up my spine and I had no idea why. It was something else, like an energy force—maybe she *was* an alien—that made it almost impossible to look away. Those eyes were hypnotic, her stare was addictive and her mouth so pink and perfect.

But other than that, she looked so . . . normal, so ordinary I could have been standing next to her at a club and she probably would have faded into the décor. And not going to lie, I wasn't sure if I was relieved or disappointed. I was already reconsidering my stance on being a Duzan-sanctioned gigolo, if she'd walked in looking like a Victoria Secret model not sure I'd have been able to say no.

"Sorry I'm late, I had some loose ends to tie up." Her voice commanded the authority her body hadn't but her face did, striding into the room like she owned the place. "I'm Gillian Duzan, so glad you could make the time, Vaughan."

It took me a minute to notice her hand was extended, her eyes not dropping from mine while she waited for me to get with the program. There was no hesitation on her part, gripping my palm firmly and shaking it when I finally offered it up. And without waiting for me to say something—what exactly, I hadn't worked out—she dropped it and took a seat on the couch separate from her father.

Being speechless around women wasn't my usual thing. I'd been in enough clubs to see all kinds. Pretty, beautiful, sexy, plain—take your pick, so while I appreciated the scenery, it didn't usually render me mute like a rookie. Which was why I wasn't sure why I was rocking the silent routine as I retook my seat.

Say something, loser.

"Ah, thanks."

Great.

Should have just kept my mouth shut.

She raised an eyebrow, waiting for me to go on while those golden-colored eyes stayed locked on me. That intense stare she had going on was lethal, it was like she could see directly into my soul.

Ignoring my lack of chatter or elaboration on the greeting, Gillian immediately turned to her dad. "There's a signed contract on your desk, how are things going here?"

Warrick coughed, no doubt trying to find a diplomatic way to frame it. "We. . .we hadn't really got into it. I was just about to put the offer on the table."

It was funny, the conversation in the room being about me while they clearly were talking to each other. I fought the urge to wave my hand and let them now I was still there.

On cue, appearing to having mindreading abilities as well as seeing into my soul, Gillian's eyes swung back to me. Their heavy weight traveled up my body like she was scanning it for information to take back to the mother ship.

"I see."

What? What do you see? I was tempted to look around and see if there was something else I was missing. Like a camera crew ready to jump out and tell me it was a big joke.

"Vaughan, let's cut to the chase, shall we?" Warrick took over, his mouth moving even though my attention was still on his daughter. Damn, she was like a riddle, and I couldn't seem to leave it alone. "I want White Trash Circus."

Well that did it.

Whatever trance I'd been in was blown apart with that little bombshell, but a record label telling you they *want you* will do that to a man.

"Err . . ." I stalled out, trying to not freak the hell out.

I'd waited for this opportunity my whole life, and now that it had presented itself I was struggling with the English language. *Not cool, asshole.* "I don't—" *have a band anymore,* I finished in my head. Sure, I still had a bass player if I wanted—Nico probably happy to stay on—but without a lead guitarist and a drummer it was kind of a moot point. "I'm going to need some time to find new band members."

How hard could it be? It wasn't like Connor was a reincarnation of Jimmy Hendrix and Johnny was adequate at best. So I hadn't planned on reforming so quickly, but I could roll with the punches.

"No, no new members." He shook his head. "I want White Trash Circus. As is. The original line up."

And here I was thinking I'd been the only one drinking.

The laugh that bubbled up my throat was unable to stop as it was pretty much confirmed the whole thing was a joke. Maybe it had been Jasper, pissed I'd blown him off on the radio, or some other asshole trying to bait me. Fair effort though, I'd believed it for about a second.

My hands clapped, applauding their performance both physically and figuratively as I continued to chuckle. "Yeah, I'll get right on that. Tell me, are you even the real Warrick Duzan? Or just some cheap look-alike in an expensive suit?"

To be honest, I had no idea if the suit was expensive but judging on appearance I'd say at least that part was authentic. As far as him being the real deal, I'd never been close enough to know.

"Not a joke, Vaughan, and this is a real offer." He didn't seem to share my amusement. "And Gillian has assured me the internet buzz from your post spiked on some matrix and people are interested. So what we're going to do is give them what they want. And what they want is the band—and all the drama that comes with it—on a stage."

Speechless.

And if I hadn't already been sitting on my ass I probably would have been knocked off it.

I opened my mouth, all ready to tell both of them there wasn't a chance in hell, when Warrick held up his hand to stop me. Obviously, he hadn't finished sprouting crazy talk and needed more airtime.

"I know your situation." He waved his hand around as my eyes widened. "And we're not asking you to reform long term. This is a one-time thing. One show. An arena. And we give you twenty thousand dollars. Then you can walk away, reform, sit in your basement and be emo, or do whatever it is you had your heart set on."

"Twenty thousand?" It was more money than I'd see in a long time, but I still wasn't sure it was worth the effort. "You know, split four ways it's only five K." Was I willing to sell myself for five grand? It was only one time, and it would be easy money. Nope, not worth it. Not to mention that I would have to get the others to agree.

"Twenty thousand each. Eighty thousand even," he clarified, my face unable to hide the shock.

Twenty.

Thousand.

Dollars.

All I had to do was get on stage—something I'd have paid for—and play a set.

One.

Time.

Oh, and I was still unemployed which meant it would pay rent for a while too.

While every fiber inside my body screamed it was a bad idea, my head nodded. It was probably going to end up the biggest disaster of all mankind. But hey, what else was new.

"What if Connor or Johnny don't agree?" I asked, not sure on where either of them stood on the issue.

"They'll agree." He chuckled to himself like he had some kind of insider knowledge. "But just in case they don't, we'll allow for additional variables in the stipulations."

I had no idea what those variables or the stipulations would be, but it sounded like a conversation for another time. Besides, he was probably right. Who in their right mind would turn down twenty grand for a one-night show?

Nobody.

"You've got yourself a deal." I held out my hand, ready to shake on it.

Warrick's eyes dropped, a smirk spreading across his lips while his might-be-hot-might-be-not daughter looked on with expressionless eyes. "I'm happy to shake your hand, Vaughan, but we do things a little more officially in New York." He accepted the shake nonetheless. "I'll have a contract drawn up by the end of the day."

"Sure, whatever." I shrugged knowing for twenty K I was going to probably sign it no matter what it said. "I guess that's it then."

Not sure what I expected, but it wasn't the low-key affair we had going on in the room. Yeah, there had been some fireworks when he mentioned I'd be getting on the stage with the cocksucker who was supposed to be my best friend. And there was the misunderstanding of me thinking he wanted me to be a gigolo, but other than that . . .nothing. We'd barely even talked.

"Looks like you were right." He turned to Gillian, smoothing out his suit jacket. "Glad to see you didn't disappoint me."

4

Vaughan

When Warrick had said the meeting was over, he meant it was over. Done. No fucking lingering in the room making small talk, no finding out about my hopes and dreams. He couldn't have cared less if he tried, leaving without so much as "see ya around."

Gillian—who had been surprisingly silent—stood, giving me a once over as she stuck out her hand, waiting a little longer after her dad had left. "I'd assumed you would have said no."

Pretending I wasn't freaking ecstatic she had stuck around, I was trying to play it cool. "Oh really?" I coughed out a laugh. "Should I have asked for more money?"

I wasn't sure if they were good cop, bad cop'ing me but it felt like a weird game I didn't know the rules to. Still, the more I looked at her, the more I was intrigued.

Her eyebrow lifted, giving me the bare minimum, like she was rationing out the fucks she'd give in any one particular day. "I'll let my personal assistant, Melanie, get your details. Enjoy the rest of your day."

"Wait." I fought the urge to barricade myself in front of the door to stop her from leaving. "Hey, why don't we have a drink or something."

I'd clearly been out of practice because as far as asking a woman out on a date, that had been terrible. Worse than bad. I'd have turned myself down. But like a lot of hotheaded front men, my mouth and brain worked at two different speeds and there was something about her that was so goddamn compelling.

She tilted her head, the edges of her lips twitching a little. "A drink? You're not asking me on a date, are you?"

"No, of course not." I scoffed, lying through my teeth. "I just thought seeing as we're going to be working together, it might be fun to get to know each other. You know. Be social."

Not my best effort, but I appreciated I hadn't made a total fool of myself. And while she probably had better things to do, I had to at least ask.

She didn't leave, instead leaning in, closing the distance between us, the space almost nonexistent. I wasn't sure if it was her perfume or her shampoo but she smelled clean and fresh without the cloud of toxic fumes most girls wore. "Vaughan, you seem like a decent guy, but we can't have a drink. I don't socialize with the talent." Her tone was different, softer around the edges. Maybe it was pity—likely—because deep down we both knew we had no business having that drink.

"Yeah, you're right." I rubbed the back of my neck awkwardly. "Guess I'll see you."

Or not, not like I was planning on heading to NYC any time soon and she didn't look like a woman who'd stick around in a city she didn't live in. And what the hell was I thinking anyway? She was nothing like a girl I'd usually be interested in, so clearly I'd fried my brain or something.

"Great. Bye." Then just like her dad had done, waltzing out of the room with so little fanfare I wasn't sure any of it had actually happened. Or at least I would've had Melanie not been glaring at me with the same amount of displeasure she'd had when I'd walked in.

"Okay, Mel, just me and you, I guess." I took a seat, trying to thaw her frostiness with a smile. No idea why everyone seemed to be in a bad mood, but usually no one was immune to my stellar personality. I'd win both her and her boss over, it was just a matter of time.

"It's Melanie, *not* Mel," she corrected me, sitting in front of me with her open laptop. "Now let's start with each band member's name and their information."

And hell, she wasn't kidding as she rapid fired questions I needed to answer. It felt more like an interrogation than anything else, giving Melanie everything except our blood types. I was almost positive a prostate exam would've been less invasive, and probably more enjoyable.

When she was satisfied, or bored—could have been either— she handed me an NDA explaining I couldn't discuss the deal with anyone until they announced it. There was also a list of numbers I could call—Gillian's wasn't on it—letting me know that someone would be in touch soon.

Like I was on a mission, I was sent away with my file of information, waiting to be summoned. I had no idea when the gig would be or even where, just a promise that there'd be one, with a contract likely to be in my hand by the end of the day. Not an idle threat either, the contract arriving at four in the afternoon while I sat eating cereal in my mother's kitchen.

I had contemplated going home, but decided to veto that idea when I remembered the crowds. One of the reasons I gave my mom and dad's address to the label as well. Last thing I needed was some asshole going through my mail and finding the contract and ruining the element of surprise.

Dad used the time while we collected my truck from the cabin to tell me how disappointed he was in me. Not that I'd taken to social media and called out my guitarist and ex-girlfriend, or that I'd been MIA for a few days—he knew I was at the cabin. But because I didn't want to waste time and money getting a lawyer to go over the contract. Why go to all the trouble? It was one gig, and all I had to my name was a used car and an apartment full of mismatched furniture. Nope, it was bad enough I was going to have to surrender some of it to the taxman, I wasn't going to give any more of it away. Instead, I'd take my chances and believe that Duzan was on the level with me.

It was shortly after dinner when my cell lit up, the name of the caller flashing across my screen as I pulled the phone from my pocket.

"What do you want?" I barked into the phone. He was lucky I answered so politely, the "go fuck yourself" I'd contemplated only switched out a second before I'd opened my mouth.

"Vaughan, I know you're pissed, but seriously, it just kind of happened. Neither—"

I cut him off before he had the chance to continue. "Connor, all I give a fuck about right now is if you're going to step on that stage and play your guitar so we can get paid. You think you can do that, or am I going to have to tell Duzan you're being a pussy?"

"Don't you think we should talk about this shit *before* we get on stage? How the hell we supposed to play a gig?"

"Not interested in talking, or an apology. And we do this the same way we've done it for the last few years. The songs aren't new, and the cord progressions are easy enough that even you could play them in your sleep. We all get paid and then we walk away."

The more I thought about it, the clearer it seemed to be in my mind. With technology making it possible for a doctor in Norway to operate on a patient in Uganda, I didn't have to see the asshole who played guitar in my band. We could converse by email, text or freaking send smoke signals for all I cared. And when the time came and I had to see him face to face, we'd stay on opposing ends of the stage. Oasis did that shit for years, Noel and Liam playing arena after arena while they publically hated each other's guts. And if those English bastards could do it, then I wasn't going to have a therapy session and hug it out.

"So that's it, we see each other on stage, no rehearsal, no nothing?"

The man was a genius.

"Just play the fucking songs and keep out of my way."

And that was the end of the call. No further extrapolating on what was going to happen, no more discussion on how I felt. Connor could unpack all his feelings and sensibilities, and discuss them until the end of time, but it wouldn't be with me.

As for Lindsey, well unless I wanted to start drinking again, that was just going to have to be sidelined for another time. I'd stayed mostly offline, avoiding the mountain of texts on my phone and was deliberating whether or not to head back to my apartment or crash in my old bedroom upstairs when there was a knock at the front door.

Mom and Dad were creatures of habit—dinner, television, then in bed by ten. They said it was because they both liked to wake early but I once walked in and caught them fucking. Scarred me for life. Which is why I don't ask and keep away when their door is closed. So anyone after ten was persona no grata since they never had visitors.

Which meant it was safe to say the knock—and the guest— was probably for me. It was even less of a surprise to see Johnny and Nico standing on the other side of the door.

"If this is some bullshit intervention, you can save it." I cracked open the door a little wider, allowing them to both come inside. "I'm not interested."

Connor no doubt had been a whinny dipshit and went crying to them about how unreasonable I was being. Because *I* was the asshole in the scenario.

"Not an intervention." Johnny rubbed his hands together nervously. "But I have an issue."

Well wasn't that just the theme of the day. And judging by the pacing of our bass player, I had a hunch I wasn't going to like it.

"What kind of issue?"

"No one can know about my career change. I play this gig, we fade to black and then you don't mention me again. As it is, I'm probably going to have to get a day off, and then head back to the tour."

I laughed, actually laughed, which I hadn't thought was possible. "Dude, I was happy to let people think you'd died. Why the hell would I tell them the truth now?"

Johnny nodded, his face more worried than it should be which prompted me to ask, "Why?"

"Because if the guys at the circus find out I used to be a drummer in a heavy metal band, it's going to kill my credibility. They're a tough crowd to crack, and if there is even a sniff of me not taking it seriously, they'll toss me out for sure. I don't need the extra scrutiny." His eyes leveled me with a hard stare.

Was he shitting me right now?

He had to be, which of course made me laugh again, wiping tears from my eyes as I glanced up at him and saw he wasn't sharing my sense of amusement.

"You can't be serious?" I shook my head, wondering when I'd tumbled into an alternate universe and he was worried about his street cred while wearing a unitard.

"C'mon, dude. This is important."

Johnny was a good man, clearly messed up in the head but other than that he'd been a decent and loyal friend. So while I didn't understand this latest madness, I wasn't going to shit on his parade either.

"Fine. Jesus, do the set, take your twenty grand and then go buy a truckload of freaking tights. Just be sure to squirrel some away for when they need to deprogram you and join the rest of civilization again. If anyone hears anything, it won't be from me."

"Thanks, buddy, I owe you one." He clapped me over the shoulder, relief bleeding from his face.

"What about you?" I turned to Nico, ready to hear whatever his problem was. "Seems like everyone has a list of demands, might as well get it out in the open."

Nico shrugged, his big-ass body taking up most of the room on the couch as he sat down in the living room. "Nope, no issues here. I'm just happy to play."

"Well, thank God for that." I tossed him a smirk, sitting opposite him in an armchair. Johnny joined us as well, parking his ass on the other two-seater.

"Soooooooo Gillian is super nice, can't wait to meet her." Nico grinned as he settled into his seat, the conversation taking a turn I hadn't been expecting.

Gillian was no doubt a lot of things.

Intriguing.

Scary maybe.

And a motherfucking vault.

But *nice* wasn't in her list of attributes.

We'd barely spoken, and when she looked at me I wasn't sure if she was suspicious or displeased. And some sick part of me was attracted to that. Like one of those sick perverts who get off on getting hot wax dripped on their balls. But I wasn't about to admit that out loud, or confess to Googling her during my limited screen time. Especially the part about the hot wax, which, I'll admit, I also Googled.

"Yep," chimed in Johnny, agreeing with Nico. And let me be clear, hardly anyone *ever* agreed with Nico. "I was expecting some no-name secretary to call me, but it was her."

Intellectually I knew they—Domination—needed to get everyone on board for it to work. Hard for White Trash Circus to play a show if we were missing band members. But like Johnny had said, I'd assumed that conversation would be delegated to some low-level A-hole further down the chain. Just dangle the cash, get them to agree and wrap it up. Gillian didn't fit the brief.

"She called you?" I tried to be casual, lounging my arm across the back of the chair like it was no big deal. "Did she talk about our meeting?"

Jesus. I sounded like I was in eighth grade asking if the hot girl had asked about me.

"She mentioned you'd agreed." Johnny pulled out his phone and shook his head. "Man, I keep getting messages. It's like every asshole I've known since middle school wants to reconnect."

I waved my hands, not interested in Johnny's growing friend list. "Screw your messages, what else did she say?"

"Nothing." Johnny lowered his phone, giving me attention I didn't want. "Why, was she supposed to say something?"

"What about you?" I turned to Nico, hoping he had more intel.

He shrugged, not giving me hope as he opened his mouth. "Not really. We just talked about other stuff."

Considering the last thing I did was ask her out for a drink, I wasn't sure what I was hoping for, but the lack of mention ate at me a little. And what the hell else was there to talk about? How did they get "nice" from a phone conversation and all I'd gotten was a frosty reception.

"What other stuff?" It begged to be asked and no matter how casual I tried to throw it into the ring, it still made me sound needy. "Band stuff?"

They took turns filling me in on the topics of conversation, which for the most part sounded boring. I'd been unnecessarily worried, the discussion that happened between the "offer" and the "agreement" being nothing more than sanitized chitchat. Not sure why I hadn't received the same treatment, but I assumed it was because she needed to get them onside and I'd already agreed. I didn't even want to think about what she said to Connor. Not that it mattered.

"So it seems we sit and wait. They give us a date, promote the show and then we play. Our last hurrah!" Nico didn't tell me anything I didn't already know.

"And lay low until then," Johnny added. "They don't want us doing interviews or making comments online. Complete radio silence until we're announced and the gig is played."

Made sense. For some reason, we'd struck a chord and people were interested. And since I'd been so generous in washing my dirty laundry, they wanted to get their fix of drama—whatever that meant. But Domination had eighty thousand reasons to keep the mystery alive and foster that curiosity. We each had NDAs and stern warnings, and big New York money wasn't something I wanted to go up against. Which is why we were keeping tight-lipped and low key.

"Just one show. Just one last time," I repeated more for myself than anyone else. "We do this and then who knows where it will take us."

No matter what happened on that stage, I was positive our lives were about to change.

Vaughan

L aying low sucked balls.

Firstly, I had never had so much attention from women in my life, and I'd been playing in bands since I was twelve. Blondes, brunettes, redheads and every single shape and size you could imagine.

And ALL ready, willing and able.

My inboxes across social media accounts were stuffed with so many messages I didn't have a hope getting through them, and in the three weeks since I wrote the post, the attention hadn't shifted.

A gig—our one-time-only show—had been set for Monday night at Barclays Center in Brooklyn. And to our surprise it had sold out—almost fifteen thousand—with people traveling from all over just to see us play. And other than confirming the date and reminding us of our contractual obligation to turn up and actually play, I'd barely heard from Warrick or Gillian. Instead we had some other dude, Chase, checking in with us every other day, making sure one of us hadn't gone AWOL or ended up OD'ing in a bathtub before the big event.

Not sure why, but I was disappointed I hadn't seen or at least heard from Gillian again. She was totally not my type, way too straight laced and uptight, but there was something about her that I couldn't get off my mind. Not a lie, but she'd become my favorite jack off fantasy, just thinking about her with my dick in my hand got me where I needed to be quicker than any porn. Honestly it worried me a little, got me thinking I might need therapy for being some kind of deviant. Or maybe I'd been in a relationship with Lindsey so long I just didn't know the difference anymore.

Trying to get my mind off a woman who I wasn't even sure I would see again, I drew up the set list and sent it to the other guys. Both Nico and Johnny gave me shit, telling me playing without a rehearsal was a big mistake but I didn't care. We didn't need to rehearse, and as long as everyone did their part, we'd be fine.

It was one night.

One fucking Monday in Brooklyn and then I'd tuck away the memory and turn my attention to a new and improved—i.e. with band members who stuck around and didn't fuck my girlfriend—White Trash Circus.

The knock on my dressing room door was a surprise. I didn't have a lot of "friends" outside the band, well . . .not many inside either. I'd been so consumed with music and making it work that I'd let a lot of relationships slide. Didn't need them. And given that my folks were back home in PA—at my request—I wasn't sure who was knocking. Or if I wanted to see who was on the other side.

Fuck.

"Vaughan." Her shiny glossed lips had the nerve to freaking smile as they said my name, her eyes traveling up my body like they had no right to do.

"What the hell are you doing here, Lindsey?" My fist tightened by my side.

I'd never hit a woman, and sure as hell wasn't going to start, but punching a hole in the drywall wasn't out of the question.

She stepped inside, her body sliding through the space between the open door and the jamb. "Vaughan, baby. I wanted to tell you how sorry I am."

"You think sorry is going to fix it? You slept with my best fucking friend!" The words barely made their way out of my clamped jaw.

And I guess that was what hurt most about it. I wasn't even sure if I'd even been in love with her. I mean, I thought I had been at the time. Clearly I'd cared about her, why else would we have been together for years. But more than anything, it was that she chose Connor out of all the people in the freaking world. Never in a million years would I have guessed he'd have said yes.

"I was so lonely. You were always so fixated on the band, you never gave me that kind of attention." Her lip wobbled like she was going to cry as she took a step closer.

Without thinking, I moved back not wanting her anywhere close to me. "So you thought you'd punish me and take it from me? You could have just left me."

"I didn't want to punish you, I wanted you to love me more than you did this stupid fucking band." She hiccupped, her tears still not spilling from her eyes despite the elaborate performance.

My body was wound so tight I was positive I was going to explode, but I wasn't going to allow her to do any more damage than she'd already done. "This stupid fucking band? Are you kidding me? This was all I've wanted to do. And Connor was like a brother to me, so what? You figured you'd kill two birds with one stone. Fuck Connor, break up the band, and I'd somehow stay with you? Come on, Lindsey, I'm not that desperate."

Like I'd slapped her across the face, her cheeks got red and those fake tears dried up on a dime. "You bastard!"

"Yeah, maybe." I shook my head, wanting the conversation over. "You need to go, Lindsey. I need to get back to my *stupid fucking band.*" There was so much more I could have said to her, but she wasn't fucking worth it. Nope, we'd said enough and I didn't want the night ruined more than it already was.

She backed away from the door enough so I could slam it in her face without making contact. Guess it was too much to ask for to have the gig go off without a hitch.

Without thinking I grabbed a beer and twisted it open. I wasn't thinking about getting drunk but taking the edge off was definitely the plan. The cool pilsner traveled down my throat as I stewed a little more. Annoyed I'd once again let her shit on something awesome.

And because the start of the evening hadn't sucked enough, there was another knock at the door.

"Are you fucking kidding me?" I threw my eyes up to the ceiling, wondering how many other unexpected guests I needed to entertain before walking on stage.

Deciding not to be a pussy, I opened the door, my new visitor bringing with her a different kind of feeling. The jolt of electricity hit me right in the pants, like an exposed electrical wire had been connected to my balls.

"Vaughan, ready to go on?" She waltzed into my dressing room without an invitation—not that I would have turned her down—and looked around with interest.

Layered in black, her jeans and jacket were far from seductive, but it didn't matter, my eyes traveling over her with a greed I didn't understand or want to contain.

It was crazy, two seconds ago I had been ready to put my fist through a wall. Angry, frustrated and who knew what else. But there was something about Gillian that made me snap into focus. And in some weird way, I wanted to fucking please her. Maybe it was 'cause she didn't want to hear my sob story. Or maybe I'd lied to Lindsey, and was desperate, just for someone different.

I coughed, my jeans getting tighter in the crotch as she gave me her attention. "Yep, all good."

"Good." She shifted her eyes back to the room, looking at the bottle of beer I had opened. "I expect you to be sober when you get on the stage."

"It's my first and last. Not an issue, I promise."

I promise? What the hell was I saying?

She nodded, giving me a last look over before heading toward the door. "I'm glad to hear it, have a good show." She turned to leave.

Damn it.

My skin itched as I watched her at the door, wanting to keep her around a little longer. Not in a creepy way like where I chained her to a chair and fed her frozen T.V. dinners, I hadn't turned into a total degenerate. But so I could see if I could crack her code and solve the fucking riddle.

"I hope you're going to stick around and watch."

I had no game. No game at all as I threw out the only thing I could think of, hoping she might stick around for a few seconds more.

Her brow arched just slightly, probably wondering if I was going to sit and beg, and to be honest, I wasn't sure that I wouldn't. "Of course. I'll see you later."

God, this woman.

She couldn't show me less interest without being rude and I was panting at her like a dog in heat. It had to be a thing, a condition they wrote about in medical journals, or some kind of kink because none of it made sense.

As she closed the door, I rubbed the back of my neck and cursed out a breath. I needed to get laid, go find a girl with big tits and no plans for a relationship and let off some steam. Because between my ex-girlfriend and the weird obsession I had with Gillian I was losing my mind.

There was no support band, just a juiced up DJ spinning records until we got on. Then the lights dimmed, and our names were called over the PA, everything snapped into focus.

"You ready, Vaughan?" It was Nico, his bass hung across his body and a big freaking grin on his face. "It's the biggest crowd we've ever played for."

Considering the usual crowd we pulled was thirty to fifty people, it was an understatement that didn't need articulating. "Yep, I'm ready." My head nodded as I looked out onto the smoke-covered stage.

On cue, Johnny entered from the other side. He was still in the shadows, getting behind his kit while the audience was oblivious. I had a hunch Connor was waiting in the wings, but I hadn't seen or heard from him since that last call. Smart. Less chance of him getting carried off the stage in a body bag that way.

Nico tapped his hands impatiently against his leg, his grin almost bursting off his face. In his world, there was no scenario where the show ended badly. And I had to admire his optimism. "See you out there," he called over his shoulder, strolling out onto the stage like he owned the place.

Not sure why I was hesitating, after all, it was what I had always wanted. To be in front of thousands of people, for them to hear music I'd created. And even though it was right there in front of me, ready for the taking, it felt tainted.

Dirty.

Cheap.

Fuck.

There was a reason I'd asked my parents to stay home, promising them there'd be another time. A time that didn't involve the drama it had taken to get on that stage. Because no matter how much I wanted them to be proud, and see their boy doing what he'd set out to do since he was ten, I'd knew it didn't count.

Not really.

I picked a hell of a time to get caught up in the mentality of it all. Couldn't I just go out there with a smile on my face, a hard-on in my pants, and rock the roof off the joint?

Out of the corner of my eye, I saw him. The asshole strode out like nothing had happened, sharing a quick fist bump with both Johnny and Nico, and somehow, that just made it worse.

Whatever feelings I'd had before were shoved down as anger bubbled to the surface. Screw him. And screw the situation. Tainted or not, I was taking my minute of fame and I was done sitting on the sidelines and being a pussy.

With my spine jacked up straight and a forced grin on my lips, I strolled—taking my sweet freaking time—out to the center. People in the front had spotted me, my arrival not as stealthy as the rest of the band and they'd started making noise. Then with a pop, the spotlight was on us—both literally and figuratively—as we were lit up, the crowd cheering as we came into view. The noise was so loud that I felt it right in my balls.

I wrapped my fingers around the mic and closed my eyes. The single spotlight followed me, the volume of the crowd rose to fever pitched and the vibration in the air hit me like a brick wall.

My eyes popped open as Connor strummed his guitar, the opening notes to our first song ringing out. Like it had been a signal, what seemed like a million lights all ignited at once, the brightness burning my retinas.

"Hello New York," I called out to the crowd, seeing thousands of arms raised in unison, ready to hear what we had to say. "This song is dedicated to all the lying, cheating assholes." The noise got even louder. "It's called *What Goes Around Comes Around.*"

It wasn't a coincidence that it had been the song I'd chosen for our opening number. Everyone pretended like they didn't like drama, but like a car crash, they couldn't stop looking at it. So I was just giving the people what they wanted, what they were no doubt hoping to see.

As I sang the first verse, I couldn't help but smile. Lines about justice eventually being served and karma catching up with you, couldn't have been more appropriate. Of course when I'd written the song, it was directed at the lack of respect we'd gotten in the music industry. The lack of time anyone seemed to have for a metal band from da 'Burg. But intention was a funny thing, and wasn't I just freaking ecstatic that the *fuck you* could be multi purposed.

By the time we got to the chorus, the crowd was singing it back to us, the sound of our lyrics being chanted by so many people so weird that I almost forgot the words. God, it was perfect, the moment hitting me as I took a minute to look around and absorb the greatness. Unfortunately, the feeling of perfection didn't last long as my eyes snagged on Connor, the cocky son of a bitch reaching into the crowd and high-fiving the front row while he rocked out.

The fucking balls on him.

Pretending like every word I spat out about the righteous being avenged was *not* about him.

I might have forgiven Lindsey if it had been anyone else. Hell, even if I hadn't, we might have still parted as friends. But I expected more from Connor.

He stabbed me in the back and the freaking heart, tossing aside our friendship, the band, and betrayed me like no one ever had. He should have known better, he should have had my back—Jesus, we'd known each other since forever, he was more my brother than my real one was. It wasn't just a matter of pride either, how could I ever trust someone like that again? How could I be fucking vulnerable around someone who'd use what they saw as weakness?

Maybe some other man—one who didn't have a pair of testicles—might have let it slide. Played the gig, taken the adulation and let fate catch up to the sentiment of the song.

But I wasn't another man.

And he and I had been primed for a showdown I didn't have a hope of prolonging.

Harnessing every single ounce of willpower I had, I got through the rest of the song. Kept my eyes front and center, ignoring the douchenozzle and all his posturing. Oh, I hadn't changed my mind and decided to play the rest of the set like it was no big fucking deal. Hell no. Nope, I was just biding my time, getting to the end of the last verse so I could give it the attention it deserved.

So, as the last note rang out, the cheering from the crowd reaching an ear-bleeding roar, I calmly smiled and looked over at Nico. Like the bastard had read my mind, he started shaking his head, his eyes peeling wide as he wisely took a step back.

Sticks clicked from behind me but I raised my hand, signaling for the crowd to hush. "Vaughan," Johnny hissed, noticing I'd gone off script. "What are you doing?"

But it was too late for that.

The course had been readjusted and I was on a different track.

"You know," I started, a grin spreading across my face, "there's been a question that keeps going through my mind."

Nico and Johnny traded what-the-fucks before their eyes came back to me while Connor wasn't looking as cocky as he'd been a few minutes before.

Ignoring my band, I kept my attention on the crowd. "And there's no point ignoring the elephant in the room because let's face it, that's why you're all here." I bowed to the crowd, giving them exactly what they paid good money to see.

I felt like the dude in the movie *Gladiator*, in the center of the arena while the audience waited to see if I lived or died—in my case metaphorically—screaming, "Are you not entertained?"

The frenzy inched up a few levels, waiting to see what was going to happen next. "So let's settle this once and for all because I'm sure everyone else is dying to know too." I turned to Connor, opening my arms wide. "You still with Lindsey? Or has the novelty worn off now you're no longer tasting my dick in her? Because that's what it was all about, right? You being obsessed with me. You wanted to be me so badly, you took it the only way you could. Pity that all you'll ever be is a second-rate cocksucker and a less-than-mediocre guitarist who can barely write music or sing. I wonder which is worse? Having zero talent? Or no game, considering the only chick you can manage to keep was already screwing someone else. And unlike me, you knew you were getting my sloppy seconds."

He came at me like a freight train, his face red with either anger or embarrassment while I laughed my ass off. And had I been that other guy we established I wasn't, the one who took the highroad and didn't take the cheap shot, it might have turned out differently. But let's face it, I no longer gave a shit, and calling him out for exactly what he was—a second-rate cocksucker—in front of a crowd of thousands felt a hell of a lot better. Chances were some asshole was streaming the whole thing too. So he could relive the moment later.

Just like diamonds, the internet was forever.

His fist connected with my jaw before I'd had a chance to react, his guitar ripped from his torso and tossed aside as he told me what a conceited bastard I was. I felt no pain, throwing the mic to the floor and raised my fists. It didn't matter we were on a stage, in front of people who had paid to see a show. Nope, I no longer cared about the record executives or the deal or anything else. What was happening instead was a fucking prizefight, round fucking one.

Ding.

Ding.

Fists, arms and legs connected as we threw everything we had at each other in an uncoordinated dance of MMA, boxing and street brawling. I didn't care how I made contact as long as I did damage. Connor landed a few hits of his own, clocking me in the nose so hard I wondered if he'd broken it. The punch across my cheek didn't help either, the heat spreading across my face while my nose started to bleed.

We didn't stop, pulling each other to the ground while people screamed from all angles. I wasn't sure if they were cheering us on or they had some other agenda but it meant little to me. With so much juice pumping through my veins, the noise and the scenery all faded out and I felt more alive than I'd felt in ages.

It was just getting good when I felt my body being pulled off Connor. One minute I was tossing punches and watching him wear down, and the next I was on my back with a dude the size of a Buick sitting on top of me. It happened so fast it took me a few seconds to realize what had happened, the big guy wearing a shirt that spelled out security.

Likewise Connor had his own beefed-up accessory, although his was more holding him up than holding him down. It was clear Connor was having issues either with gravity or consciousness, my ex best friend weaving so much on his feet he'd have easily been mistaken for a zombie. He didn't even need the special effects makeup, his face bloodied and red.

"Chill the fuck out, man," the man parked on top of me warned as I tried to shrug him off. "You're not going anywhere."

He wasn't kidding either, my arms and legs pinned as I threw out obscenities. "Let me go, shithead. This is between me and him." Adrenaline pumped through my body as I seesawed underneath him trying to find a grip.

No use.

There was a better chance of swimming against the current at Niagara Falls than throwing the guy off of me. And I was a decent swimmer. Still, too juiced up to be reasonable and accept the inevitable, I refused to give up. And by some holy Jesus miracle I got an arm loose and took a swing.

And then the world turned black.

Lights. Out.

Goodnight.

Vaughan

"**F**uck," I groaned.

Every single part of my body hurt and I wasn't sure if I hadn't opened my eyes yet because I didn't want to deal with reality or because I no longer could. The metallic taste of blood lingered in my mouth while my skin was tight and sore. Swollen, broken, or maybe both—I tried to take an internal audit of my body as it came back online, limbs and organs checking in as I assessed the damage. Funny how I didn't remember how I got to be asleep or where the hell I'd ended up, but if I had to take a guess I'd say the security guard hadn't appreciated my effort. I didn't even know if I'd managed to hit him, getting my arm loose being the last thing I remembered.

A bed.

I was on a bed.

I wasn't sure exactly whose mattress it was—the memory foam underneath me feeling like Wonder Bread and nothing like mine—but I'd made it to a bedroom at some point. Not good considering I hadn't been close to sleeping with anyone the last time I was conscious.

"Are you feeling better?" an angelic voice I didn't recognize asked from somewhere beside me. Definitely female and so sweet, smooth and melodic it had to be a dream. Plus she sounded strange, her Rs rolling a little longer than they should, the words relaxed like an old pair of jeans.

Daring to make an already shitty situation even worse, I cracked open my eyes. While my face probably wouldn't win any beauty contests, I still had my sight.

And Jesus Christ.

If I hadn't already been horizontal I'd have ended up on my ass for sure, because leaning over me was probably one of the most beautiful women I'd ever seen.

Her hair was so blonde it glowed while her eyes reminded me of the ocean at midnight, dark sapphire blue that I'd been happy to drown in. Everything about her was perfect, from her unblemished porcelain skin to her pouty pink lips. And when I managed to tear my gaze away from her face and check out the rest of her, I felt the wind being knocked out of me.

I'd vaguely remembered deciding to find someone gorgeous to screw sometime after the show. And as far as types went, the woman in front of me was my dream girl. Or as close to how I imagined it. It seemed whatever prayer I'd offered up had been answered.

"Did I die?" I croaked, wondering if the beautiful woman with the strange voice was going to be my guide in the afterlife. I wasn't kidding myself thinking I was going to heaven, but if I got to kick it in purgatory with her then I'd be happy to stay there for eternity.

She laughed, her face lighting with amusement. "Almost, probably shouldn't have punched Zeus. Gillian had to do some pretty fancy talking to get him to let go. You owe her big time."

"His name was Zeus?" Well didn't that make all kinds of sense. "Gillian?"

While my body still felt like I'd cozied up to a wood chipper, my brain still mostly worked. And the mention of her name got me hot in places that it shouldn't. Firstly, because there was a woman who was mind bendingly beautiful in front of me. And even if I had a less than average chance with her, it was still better odds than I had with Gillian. Secondly, my attraction to Gillian made no sense. None. In fact, it systematically proved what had gone wrong with me and Lindsey.

I liked to think of myself as a player, but that shit just wasn't true. Don't get me wrong; I loved sex. I could spend hours worshiping a female body with my hands and my mouth, and not get my dick involved until she was speaking in tongues. But for some reason, I had a habit of getting my heart involved. Fell in love too quickly.

And while I'd never admit it to another living soul, I absolutely believed in love at first sight. I'd been falling in love with girls since kindergarten believing I was better when I had a good woman beside me. Not very metal, I know, but the heart wants what the heart fucking wants.

"You mean Gillian Duzan?" I clarified, the possibility making me more excited than it should. I'd only known two Gillians, and it was more likely for it to be a member of the Domination crew and not the chick who gave me my first hand job. Ironically, the mention of the first was the more pleasant memory, got me harder too.

"Yes, the security guard's name is Zeus, and yes I mean Gillian Duzan. No, don't try and get up." Her hands held me gently down as I tried to lift myself from the mattress. "You've got a concussion, you need to lie there a little longer."

Her touch was as delicate as everything else on her, just firm enough for me to notice but still soft and gentle. She was the kind of girl I should be vying for, not some other chick who barely gave me the time of day. Trying to recalibrate my brain and my hormones, my lips edged into a grin as I relaxed back onto the bed. If going a round with Zeus got me a babe like her, I'd be volunteering for another. "Baby, I'll do anything you want. And while this mysterious thing is really working for me, I'd give my left nut to know your name and where you came from."

Some exotic island if I had to guess. Where you laid in the sun, ate from a never-ending platter of tropical fruit, and ugly people didn't exist.

She raised an eyebrow, but didn't seem shocked or embarrassed, her lips twitching in what I assumed was amusement. "Let's keep your testicles where they are, okay? You're probably going to need them. I'm Emily."

"Emily." I tested it out, liking the way it felt in my mouth. Given half a chance I'd have liked to savor a lot more than just her name, but considering the circumstances, that was going to have to wait. "Your voice . . . it sounds so . . ."

"Australian."

Okay, so a slightly bigger island than I had in mind.

"But I've lived in the states for a while so it's less Crocodile Hunter and more Nicole Kidman," she continued. "Plus, I grew up in a city and not the outback, so I don't sound like I'm talking with a mouth full of marbles."

She fought her grin, trying not to smile as she pulled out her phone and typed out a message.

"Tell me everything about you. I could listen to you talk for days." I tried not to sigh, hoping like hell she couldn't see what was becoming an erection underneath the covers. Hey, I wasn't trying to be a deviant but waking up with wood was pretty fucking common and that was without the bombshell island goddess sitting beside me.

"Easy there, Casanova." Another voice joined the party, my head turning enough to see Gillian Duzan coming into focus.

Unlike Emily, Gillian wasn't angel like. Her eyes didn't bleed out kindness, her hair didn't float around her shoulders like a cloud, and she seemed to be allergic to color or something.

And while Emily was knock-you-on-your-ass beautiful, there was something else about Gillian. She was understatedly attractive, like she didn't need the fanfare while something simmering just below the surface teased at freaking amazing.

Both times I'd seen her she'd been wearing black corporate gear that was either put together by a bunch of nuns or a high-level government agency. It screamed *practical* and *conservative* and had the ability to make a porn star look like a senator. It was the first time I was being cat-fished by a jacket and skirt, having zero clue on what was underneath. The curves of her body—assuming there were any—hidden by the shadows and fabric more efficient than Harry Potter's invisibility cloak. It made my head hurt.

But for every part of her that seemed plain or unremarkable, there was something else that hinted at more. There was nothing ordinary about her eyes, I'd seen expensive bottles of single malt whiskey that weren't as clear and golden. They were crazy beautiful, almost unreal like she was wearing contacts. And while her dirty blonde hair was pulled back like it had been the first time, I had to wonder what it would look like unrestrained.

Or what *she* was like unrestrained.

And damn if that didn't get me inappropriately interested in the woman I was supposed to be thanking for something. I couldn't remember what that was at the moment, but gratitude wasn't what I was feeling that was for sure.

Her eyes dropped, either noticing the hard-on or doing a visual assessment. Maybe those fancy eyes of hers came with X-ray vision.

"You've been out through most of the night and the morning and are still under concussion protocol. Luckily nothing is broken, but you're probably going to be sore and swollen for a few days. Although, if you're still feeling flirty, I can call Zeus. I'm sure he'd love to sit beside you and chat." She nodded to Emily, a wordless exchange passing between the two. The bombshell left me alone with the black widow, and the fact I had no idea if that was a good thing, just got me more excited.

"Thanks but I'll pass." I shook my head, the gray matter between my ears rattling more than it should. "Want to tell me where I am and how I got here?"

Flirting with Gillian wouldn't have worked, that was obvious. I'd have stood a better chance charming a wild bear. And while a sick, masochistic part of me wanted to try anyway I figured I'd give into my other need. The one that needed to know where the hell I was and what I was doing there.

"How much do you remember?" she asked, taking the seat beside me that had been vacated by Emily.

"The song, Connor, the fight," I responded, pretty clear on what had happened up to that point. "Zeus sitting on me like a parked car."

"Yeah, well you tried to fight the *parked car* and while trying to get loose, you slammed your head against the floor. Knocked yourself out." She pointed to the back of my head, the big goose egg still tender when I ran my fingers over it.

"Wait? I knocked *myself* out? He didn't hit me?" I mean, not that I'd wanted the asshole to have incapacitated me because that wasn't cool, but knocking myself out was kind of embarrassing. Couldn't he have at least choked me out?

"Nope, he didn't hit you. But he was rather reluctant to let me near you until he was sure you weren't going to lash out again. He's rather fond of getting a pay check and figured if I got hurt, it might end his employment."

"Well." I coughed, feeling a little weird about the whole situation. "Maybe he shouldn't have gotten involved. Let Connor and I work it out. Like men."

Her lips spread into a grin.

Like an actual smile.

With feeling.

Every interaction—however limited they'd been—she'd had such a handle on her emotions, I was beginning to wonder if she had any. Good or bad—she'd never given an inch.

Not a smile.

Not a frown.

Nada.

Her expression was always pathologically neutral, a wasteland of nothing. So seeing her smile was not only unexpected but a little unnerving too. Was it a good thing? Or was it where she told me they'd injected me with an experimental serum and that made my balls drop off. Emily had mentioned I was going to need both of them, made sense if that were true.

"Like *men*? Why is it when you have a problem to solve, you think the best way to do it is by beating each other up? What does it actually solve other than prove evolutionally you're stuck in the Paleolithic era?"

She might have been pissed, but I wasn't sure. She hadn't raised her voice, and her expression hadn't changed but it was too hard to read. She almost sounded curious and I'd decided that earlier smile was the exception not the rule. "But if you want to fight Connor, you need to do it on your own time. Not mine."

Okay, maybe she was mad.

"Is he around?" I tried to lift my head and get a bead on where I was. That part of my question hadn't been answered yet and I wasn't sure if she'd forgotten or was avoiding it.

"No, his girlfriend picked him up after the show and I believe they drove home."

His girlfriend. Please, if it didn't hurt so much I might have rolled my eyes. "Good for them."

Ironically, I meant that.

Well sort of.

I gave them three months, maybe six, but I didn't expect them to last longer than that. And that wasn't sour grapes, it was from knowing both of them so long. Connor didn't do girlfriends, preferring to screw around with a trail of one-night stands in his wake. I never really cared, and as long as he'd been happy, that was good enough for me. But Lindsey needed a man. Hell, if I hadn't paid enough attention to her, the guy who doesn't usually date someone twice wasn't going to. And didn't that suck for both of them. That they chose each other instead of me.

But either way, at some point between stepping on stage and knocking myself out, some of the anger had dissipated. The urge to give him a beat down had been dialed down, and her . . . well, she was going to find out very quickly what she'd given up.

I wasn't going to beg, not Connor and not Lindsey. And it would be a while before I'd forgive either of them but I wasn't going to let it take what was left of my fucking sanity. Fuck that and fuck them too.

If my lack of reaction had surprised her, she didn't show it, continuing with everyone's locations. "Johnny left, asking me to remind you of your agreement and that he would call you when things cooled off. And Nico has been waiting in the bar downstairs."

"Downstairs?" I winced, wondering if I'd missed the important reveal of where I'd been stashed. Obviously it was a hotel room of some description but it could have been a fancy shipping container on a cargo ship to Hong Kong. They sure as hell had the money and resources to make it happen, and she'd yet to say how pissed off Warrick had been.

"You're at a hotel in Midtown. We had the paramedics bring you here instead of a hospital, and have been managing your care with a private nurse. You were given a mild sedative to give your body a chance to rest."

Funny how I remembered none of that.

Not the ambulance.

Not being brought to the hotel.

Not even leaving the stage.

"Is Emily the private nurse?" I found myself grinning. Not gonna lie, I was hopeful especially since I'd been asleep for who knew how long and hadn't got to experience her bedside manner.

Gillian didn't respond, instead pressing a buzzer beside my bed. I hadn't even noticed it, or anything else that was hooked up to me. My finger had a probe on it and I was naked. There was some bruising but other than that, everything looked pretty intact.

"Ms. Duzan." A dude who was about six-four, two hundred pounds and had the speed and agility of a running back popped out a side door like a magic trick. "Hey Vaughan, how's the head? Any dizziness or nausea? What's your pain level?"

My eyes peeled wide as I checked out the dude's threads, scrubs to be precise, and the picture of what I was seeing came into focus. "You're the nurse?"

"Pete, and that would be an affirmative." His big noggin bounced a couple of times. "We did meet when you first came in but you've been in and out most of the night. Looks like you're still having some problems with your memory but that's normal, so don't worry. We're just going to observe you for a few more hours."

Pete wasn't the kind of person you'd forget, his black hair was salted with grays and his face was way too smiley. He had that Santa Clause vibe going for him but without the gut, beard or the red suit. But I was coming up empty, and while there'd been flashes of stuff rolling through my brain, I wasn't sure what had been a dream and what had been reality.

Guess those fantasies of Emily getting me naked were just that—fantasies. As for who'd had the honor of stripping me down, I preferred to leave that little gem alone. It really was a blessing I couldn't recall, some things were better left not seen or remembered. Thank you, Jesus.

Pete checked my vitals, shone a torch in my eyes and asked me a bunch of questions. It hadn't been our first rodeo but apparently the only one I'd remembered. And after I'd satisfied some invisible checklist and taken some more pain meds, he went back to wherever it was he'd been hiding and left me alone with Gillian.

"If you're up to it, you should give your parents a call. Your mother wanted to fly in last night but we assured her you're getting the best medical care available and their arrival would probably tip off the press." She handed me my phone, it was locked but fully charged, with a string of notifications, missed calls and messages I didn't have a hope of answering.

Shit.

They'd wanted to come to New York and see the show but it was better for everyone involved if they sat it out. Gut instinct, or whatever but after some arguing, they agreed.

My parents—God love them—were barely on social media so they had no idea what they were in for. They were still holding on to hope there would be a resurgence of My Space, not trusting that Justin Timberlake looking dude who owned *The Facebook*. As for Instagram, Twitter, and everything else that came after, they lived in joyful ignorance. But I had no doubt that even with their limited exposure to the World Wide Web, news of my little performance would have reached their ears.

"How bad is it?" I cringed, having no idea on exactly what I was dealing with. If a status had gone viral . . .yeah I was guessing at best, and none of it was positive.

Her eyes dropped to my phone. "Nothing I can't handle. Call your mother and stay off social media."

Oh, so it was *that* bad.

Unlike Pete getting me naked, there were some difficult realties that I needed to know.

I tried to shuffle myself up the bed, but only managed halfway before I reconsidered. Besides, it might be best to stay down until I knew what I was dealing with. "Look, I know I didn't—" *what was the right word,* "handle it the best way I could have, but what's done is done, right? Just give it to me straight."

"Vaughan, you're going to have to trust me and right now, what you need is to rest and get better. We'll deal with everything else later." She pointed to the phone. "Call your mother and stay off social media."

It was a big call asking me to trust her. The last time I trusted someone, it didn't work out so well for me. But considering I was naked in a hotel in Midtown, I didn't have a lot of choice. Besides, who else was there? Nico was downstairs, so until I was able to speak to him I was shit out of luck.

"Okay. I'll call." Figured my mother was probably going out of her mind anyway so at least I could solve that issue. "But I want my clothes. And I'm done sleeping. No more sedatives."

She hesitated, giving my offer serious thought before she agreed. I got the feeling she was a hard ass negotiator and didn't do anything on the whim. Which was the complete opposite to me. "I'll get Pete to get you some clean clothes and we'll lay off the sedatives if you promise to stay in bed. You're still a liability and until you've been cleared, you're staying right where you are."

Not a problem on my end. While my head hurt and I wanted answers, being holed-up in a hotel room with Gillian Duzan was far from a hardship. In fact, it was a gift. Giving me the time I needed to either work out what it was about her that made my balls tingle or confirm I had serious issues.

Nope.

I was in no hurry to go anywhere.

"Aren't you worried people will get the wrong idea? You socializing with the talent and all." I couldn't help but smile.

She rolled her eyes, answering without hesitation. "No. I don't."

It was more than an answer, it was a warning and I wasn't sure if it was meant for me or someone else. But one thing was for sure, Gillian Duzan wasn't the kind of woman you wanted to mess with.

Except.

I couldn't think of anything I wanted more.

7

Vaughan

It was probably afternoon, or maybe evening before Pete allowed me to go take a piss by myself. Apparently getting dressed and proving I could sit up without feeling dizzy wasn't sufficient. No amount of telling him I was fine was enough for him to let me do it any earlier, the big guy following me into the bathroom and watching me with surprising disinterest. Part of me was offended that the sight of my dick didn't at least get a nod of appreciation. I'd say I was larger than average and never had any complaints. But considering he wasn't my target market I'd clearly hit my head harder than I thought if I was giving it so much thought.

I'd finally gotten to speak to Nico too. He'd been a better friend than I'd given him credit for, sticking around even though he didn't have much reason to. Truth was, I'd given him a lot of shit over the years, and we'd never been super tight so he easily could have bailed. But he didn't, staying at the hotel in another room until I was cleared to leave with him. He didn't hover either, giving me space to "rest" like everyone said I needed. Ironic that the guy I hadn't really counted on was the only one who'd stuck around. And didn't that just prove what a dumbass I'd been.

Gillian had been in and out throughout the day, but Emily was MIA. No word as to whether she'd appear again, or what she'd been doing in my room in the first place. *She* would have definitely appreciated what Pete hadn't.

I was just about to celebrate my solo bathroom journey when the hotel door burst open and a very animated Warrick Duzan waltzed in.

"Where is he? Is there a chance he might die? What exactly are we looking at?" The look of disappointment was obvious when his eyes found me, and noticing I was very much alive.

"You, you." He pointed his finger at me like I'd given him a nasty case of gonorrhea. "Do you have any idea how much you cost me? One song doesn't constitute a show, Vaughan. Tickets needed to be refunded, any profit we might have made is gone, and every asshole with a smart phone has uploaded footage so we can't even capitalize on an exclusive."

He took a breath, his face getting redder by the second. "I'm not even mad about the fight, hell, it would have made the perfect encore. At least then we would have had their money."

"Look, I can't go back and change what happened." And to be honest, not sure I'd want to. For as bad as I was hurting, I would bet Connor felt worse. And even though I was no longer angry, it still made me smile. "So I guess we just take the shot on the chin and move on with our lives."

"We, we?" He was back finger pointing again. It was no wonder his daughter was so dialed down, her dad had taken the lion's share of overreactions and was running with it. "Oh no, there is no we. I'm not taking shit on the chin and I sure as hell am not taking a loss. You think I got to where I am today by letting little no-talent pissants like you take my cash and not deliver on my investment? Nope, you will not only pay back the advance but you're also going to earn out the loss."

"What are you talking about? Earn it out, how?" I'd heard record labels could be unreasonable, but you couldn't get blood

64

from a freaking stone. And it would take a lifetime for me to earn the kind of cash he was talking about. Short of prostituting myself like a high-end escort, there weren't a lot of options.

"You're a smart man, surely you'll figure it out. And until you do, everything you write or perform is mine."

"Huh? What are you talking about?" I had to do a quick check to make sure Warrick hadn't turned into Ursula the Sea Witch, wanting to steal my voice. Ariel had been hot, not sure why Eric had taken so long to close that deal—getting sidetracked, and I needed to focus.

Anyway, the point was we had an agreement. "The contract said one show and then I walked. And sure, that show didn't happen but if we all pay back the cash, our business is done."

"That's where you're wrong. Read the fine print. *In the event the concert didn't eventuate—with the blame falling on the artist—Domination has propriety rights to recoup losses.* That means you sing, you dance and you make it rain."

I was just about to get up and risk another concussion when the door opened a second time. The conversation stopped, both of us turning to see the new arrival as Gillian strolled in.

"Outside." Her voice was eerily calm and I wasn't sure if she was talking to me or her dad—neither of us making a move. She stepped closer, her eyes locked on Warrick as she pointed to the door. "I said, outside."

Okay, it was him.

I fought the grin, amused that one of the most powerful men in the music industry was being taken to task by his kid. And in front of me no less. I was positive he was beyond pissed off. Family gatherings were probably going to suck for a while.

His face was red, veins bulging, as his white-knuckled fists bobbed at this side. "We'll finish this later," he sneered, cursing under his breath as he walked to the door, Gillian following him out.

I was up off the couch the minute the door had closed, my ear pressed against it like a moron trying to hear exactly what was going down. Too curious to even care how pathetic it was.

Nothing.

No hushed voices, no heated dialogue—no talking at all. And either the door was some zombie apocalypse reinforced wood or the discussion was taking place elsewhere.

I waited a little longer, tempted to go out and investigate but decided I'd already embarrassed myself enough. It was a realization I wished I'd come to about a minute or two earlier, the door pulling open and my body pitching forward.

"Oh hey." I tried to recover, getting myself steady on my feet. "Just checking out the acoustics of the room." I knocked on the door, opening my mouth and hitting an A flat. "Interesting."

She smirked—just barely—as she walked inside and closed the door behind her. "Oh really. That's what you were doing?" She wasn't fooled, waiting to see how far I was going to take the lie.

"Well that, and trying to hear what you were saying." I grinned, folding my arms across my chest.

Honestly, I'd have been disappointed if she hadn't called me on it. She seemed too smart to be fooled and a sick part of me liked the push back.

"Understandable considering we were talking about you." She breezed past, taking a seat on the couch and I had to contain my excitement as I joined her.

"Do you do that often?" I couldn't have hid my grin if I tried. She'd thawed slightly and I couldn't help myself.

An eyebrow rose. "Leave the room to have a private conversation or talk to my father?"

"No, talk about me."

And what do you know, I was flirting. Hadn't been the intention, genuinely curious as to what they'd discussed. But I couldn't help myself, sliding into it before I could stop.

I braced, ready for her to roll her eyes or worse, tell me I was delusional. After all, she'd never given me any indication she was interested and told me on more than one occasion she didn't date the talent. But her beautiful golden eyes stayed focused, tilting her head slightly. "Do you honestly get many women with that approach?"

Ordinarily a burn like that would have been a very clear rejection, but her tone said otherwise. She wasn't mad, like she was genuinely curious and couldn't work out if what I was doing actually yielded results.

"Honestly, I've been a one-woman man for a while, so I'm kind of rusty. But I've been pretty spoilt. I don't have to work too hard to get noticed in a crowd so I haven't really had to try."

Not sure where that gem came from, my mouth sprouting words that were probably too personal to tell a woman I didn't know. But what I said was exactly true and either I was still concussed or just didn't care.

"Not what I was expecting you to say." Like my lack of bullshit had prompted a lowering of her guard, she continued. "So do women throw themselves at you everywhere you go? Or just when you're on stage?"

Again, could have been condescending, but it wasn't. Not sure if I was seriously misreading her cues or she just wanted to know. "Mostly on stage or at a show, but I could be in a store and some random woman will come play with my hair." I picked up a length, fingered through it. "They like to touch and it doesn't bother me most of the time."

"You always had it long?" She watched as I pulled it back and twisted it into a man bun.

I laughed, remembering how many arguments I'd had with my parents. "Nope, short back and sides for the first sixteen years until my mom got sick of the argument. Figured long hair wasn't the worst thing that could happen. I have an older brother and sister, both married with kids by the time I was in high school. I guess they'd worn her down ahead of me. Not a lot I can do to freak them out, they're pretty supportive." It was weird talking about my family; it was something most people didn't give a shit about. "Anyway, most of my idols had long hair and it looks good on stage. The girls liking it was just a bonus."

Not sure how we'd moved from a poor attempt at flirting by me to discussing my hair, but it kept her talking so I wasn't questioning. "So are you going to tell me? Am I now Warrick's bitch?"

He was right about me not reading the fine print. I barely read anything at all. It was supposed to be a one-time thing so what could they possibly get out of us. Besides, unless he tried to sue me for my used pick-up truck, he was going to be shit out of luck. It hadn't occurred to me he'd try to own my ass like I was his hooker. That only happened in mob movies or Netflix dramas.

She hesitated, and I could tell she was being careful about what she said. Despite what might have gone down in that hallway, she had the dude's blood coursing through her veins and worked for the company. If it came down to a choice, I knew where her loyalties lay.

"There was a stipulation in the contract, in case you pulled out or canceled or were incapacitated, and we had to refund tickets. There would be some liability there, and Domination has the right to use the brand White Trash Circus, their likeness and their music to recoup the loss."

Whatever fun and flirty vibe that had been going on between us chilled as she said words I didn't think were possible. Impressing her, making small talk or even hearing about the concert took a backseat.

"Are you fucking kidding me?" My feet hit the floor, my head spinning from the change in altitude. My ribs didn't feel so hot either. "But it's *my* band."

She shook her head. "Not anymore. Anything you guys do moving forward, belongs to Domination. White Trash Circus doesn't belong to you, or Nico, or either of the other guys."

"Like those other guys give a shit," I spat out, the heat rising up my neck. "Johnny is going to be doing backflips, and Connor never really cared. Nico will probably be disappointed but he'll find some other gig. But that music, those lyrics—they were mine. I wrote them. Poured my heart and soul into it. And now what? I have to play like a circus—pun fucking intended—monkey until I work off a debt."

It couldn't be happening. I didn't give a shit if we never played as a unit again. Hell, given our last show it was probably for the better. But those songs, they were as much a part of me as an arm or a leg, and they suddenly belonged to someone else? I wouldn't have done that. If I knew what had been on the line, I never would have agreed.

My body was hurting, still feeling delicate from the fight and my own stupidity but I couldn't keep still, pacing as I itched to punch a hole in the drywall.

Gillian watched but didn't try to stop me, her eyes following me around the room as I moved. "No, Vaughan you don't have to do anything. You can walk away."

What?

I stopped, dead still and looked at her. Because if there was a way out of it, I needed to know.

"What are you talking about?" I asked cautiously, because I had a hunch I already knew the answer.

She rose to her feet but kept her distance. She was no doubt being careful because I had anger management issues and had just been informed I no longer owned my band. Not that I would ever hit a woman, but the fact she thought it might be a possibility just proved how much we didn't know each other.

"Domination owns White Trash Circus. The brand. The songs. We don't own you. You walk away and don't sing or perform anymore; they can't touch you."

She had no idea what she was suggesting. Couldn't know that she might as well be asking me to cut out my own heart.

"You're asking me to walk away from my life."

I couldn't look at her anymore. Or the fucking shitty room. Or this shitty fucking city. All of it had been a mistake, and I wanted out.

I'd thought that I'd lost everything before, when I'd been drunk in that cabin. But I'd been wrong. Not even close. Because in addition to losing my girlfriend, best friend and my fucking band, which was old fucking news, I'd ante'd up and put my freaking soul onto the table as well.

All of it, gone.

"I'll pay him back the money. Every fucking cent. I'll take out a loan. I'll work two jobs. I'll buy it all back." My mouth started moving like a crazy person, desperate to find a solution.

My folks weren't wealthy but they owned their house and I knew I could move back if I needed to. I'd sell my truck and give Warrick every cent I had until the debt was squared.

"Vaughan, do you have any idea of the figure we're talking about? It would take you years if not your whole lifetime to pay it back. And my dad isn't the most patient of men. He isn't going to want to wait thirty or forty years." She had the decency to look sorry, but I wasn't sure she meant it. After all, she was one of them. Finding us had been her idea; she was the one who'd suggested her dad look at us in the first place.

"This is your fault," I spat out through clenched teeth, anger consuming me like an inferno. "You and your fucking matrix. Why did you come after us, Gillian? Were you hoping I was so desperate for money or I was too dumb to read the contract? Which was it? Or were you counting on my life being so far down the toilet I no longer gave a shit?"

My voice echoed off the walls but she didn't budge. Didn't flinch, standing her ground as she let me unleash.

"Fuck." I ran my hands through my hair, realizing how stupid I'd been. My dad had told me to get a lawyer, but I'd been so preoccupied with revenge and chasing her skirt that I'd tossed away the only thing left that mattered.

"Vaughan, I think you should sit down." Her voice came from behind me but I didn't turn. I didn't want to see her, or sit down.

Not giving me an easy out, she walked around so I had no choice but to look at her. She was ice cold, whatever sympathy I might have seen earlier was gone and in its place was control and determination.

"I can understand you're angry, but that contract was industry standard. It's a business agreement, and when an investor is extending a large investment, they will want some insurance. So no, I wasn't looking to exploit you or use you, or try and swindle you out of anything. It was an opportunity, like any other and it was your choice whether or not you took it. There wasn't a gun to your head. And this . . ." she waved her hand around calmly, "was definitely not my fault. I'll leave you with Pete to cool off. Let me know when you want to talk about it rationally and find a solution."

She didn't give me a chance to respond, grabbing her phone from the coffee table and walking out the door. She didn't even slam it, strolling casually out like it was no big deal. And maybe for her, it wasn't. But for me . . . well I didn't know what the hell I was going to do.

I paced, my feet covering every square inch of that plush carpet like it was my job. My body ached, my head still hurt and I wasn't sure if I wanted to scream, curse or trash the place. Too many emotions, all of them fighting for attention and there wasn't one I wanted to address.

And Jesus fucking Christ, I was desperate to get out of that room. I didn't care about observation or whatever protocol, I felt like a caged animal and I needed out. My eyes flicked to the door knowing Pete would be back soon to babysit. It was now or never, I wasn't even sure where the hell I could go but it had to be somewhere else.

Somewhere I could think.

Somewhere I could breathe.

Somewhere I didn't feel like I was going insane.

Without a real plan or idea, I grabbed my phone, my wallet and my shoes and left before anyone saw me. And then like a cheap hookup dealing with next-day regret, I got out of the room and got ghost.

Gillian

"**W**hat do you mean, he's not here? Where did he go?" My body was practically vibrating, angry and concerned all at the same time while I tried not to lose my cool. Pete shrugged as we looked around the empty room oblivious to my many internal expletives as I tried to stop pacing.

I wasn't in the habit of losing rock stars especially ones with head injuries, and I wasn't going to start now.

Vaughan Hale was like most of them.

Cocky.

Attractive.

Emotional.

And impulsive.

Artists—they were a different breed of human.

But they were usually predictable, which was why I was expecting Pete to walk in and find a table lamp jammed into a wall or the mattress on fire. Not that I condoned that kind of behavior, and god knows I got sick of talking to hotel managers and settling accounts, but I never expected him to walk out. Because that was what a rational person would do, and Vaughan—and every other rock star that came before and probably after him—wasn't rational. Or so I thought.

"Call the security manager and see if we can get a look at the surveillance tapes. Tell them he's a health risk," I barked at Pete, who thankfully didn't question.

I could tell just by looking at her, Emily was itching to say something. She had a terrible poker face and even less ability to not get involved. "What?" I asked, knowing she was bound to tell me sooner than later. And I was already playing Where's Waldo with Vaughan, I didn't have time for any other games.

"I was just thinking that it probably wasn't the best idea to leave him alone." She crossed her gorgeous long legs, her lips spreading into a smile. "But you have to admit, it is kind of funny."

"Funny, funny? None of this is funny." It was hard to keep an even temperament even though I wanted nothing more than to scream. But I'd had years of practice, and not reacting had been practically my entire childhood. I had literally been training for it my whole life.

Being Warrick Duzan's only child had not been a walk in the park. He was almost worse than most of the men and women he represented. But he did clothe me, feed me and educate me, so I guess I should be grateful. He just had a real problem with the love department, which was why my mother had left him, and me as it turned out. It was either that or the infidelity; I'd only been two so didn't have the opportunity to ask.

But as I grew up I stopped taking it personally when I saw it wasn't just me. He didn't really know how to love anyone, going from one failed marriage to another—every one of them ending up with a bitter divorce settlement and a younger replacement. His latest wife was only five years older than I was, and pretty soon I would have to start carding them at the door.

Emily didn't understand that of course, because her life had been totally different. And even though she'd lived with my dad and seen first hand what a cold-hearted bastard he could be, she lived in a fantasy world that he, like everyone, was good underneath. Her mom, Mara, had been exactly the same, which was why as my dad's third wife, she had also lasted the longest.

Mara had been the nicest of my mother's replacements, and came with a daughter of her own—Emily—who was only a year younger than me. And if not for Mara and her ability to love blindly—and almost ridiculously—I might never have known what a regular family looked like.

But like the women who came before—and after—Mara eventually left. Not even unconditional, pure unadulterated love could thaw my dad's heart. And not sure why she did it, but when she and Emily walked out the door, they kept me as part of their family. I spent more holidays, birthdays, and even vacations with two Australians who had no blood or legal obligation than I did with my own family. And truly, it had been for the best.

Now that we were both grown and Emily had moved back to New York, we were living together in my Brooklyn apartment. She had dreams of owning a bakery in Manhattan, but until that became a reality, she was doing some temp work for me. *She* probably wouldn't have lost the rock star, although not many men ran from Emily.

Blonde, beautiful and a body of a supermodel it would be easy to hate her. But without a bad bone in the whole stunning package there wasn't a chance I could.

"Okay, he can't have gotten too far." Ever the optimist, Emily gave me a reassuring shoulder squeeze. "I bet he's just gone out for some air."

While I didn't share the same sense of confidence, I did know the bass player, Nico, was still in the hotel. I'd gone to see him right after my meeting with Vaughan, hearing about him going AWOL from Pete shortly after.

"Vaughan isn't answering his cell so I'm going to go talk with Nico. I'm guessing he's our best bet at finding him." I nodded to

Emily as I grabbed my phone. "Get Pete to call me if he finds out anything from the security footage."

Cursing under my breath, I shoved my phone into the pocket of my jeans and buttoned up my jacket.

I didn't have the body of a supermodel like Emily. I had boobs and an ass, and didn't shop in the size zero section of the clothing store. And while I liked my shapely figure, it had been an issue one too many times at work.

I was tired of having men talk to my chest, checking me out like I was an item on the menu. In an industry where everything was for sale, I wanted to make it clear I wasn't, which was why I dressed like a member of the Knights Templar.

The minute my wardrobe changed, so did the interest. Gone! And while my body became invisible, my mind and my mouth weren't. The work I did finally started to get the recognition I deserved, and I was no longer leered at like a piece of meat.

It was sad I had to make the choice, that I couldn't just wear what I wanted and expect everyone to just be an adult. But life wasn't ideal like that, and I wasn't about to go cry in the corner and lament the unfairness of it all. Screw that. Besides, my father—who most of the time tolerated me at best—had no choice but to give me the respect I craved and recognize the work I'd achieved. He'd even earmarked me to be his successor, although something he was probably going to reconsider if I didn't find Vaughan and somehow rectify the situation soon.

As I exited the elevator in the lobby, I didn't have too much difficulty locating the other member of White Trash Circus still in New York. Nico was in the bar entertaining a steady stream of women, something that seemed to be new for him. He wasn't unattractive, but I could see how hard it would be to get noticed when you had to compete with Vaughan.

The singer was . . . beautiful. Not the kind of word that you commonly used for a guy but it was the one that sprung to mind nonetheless. He had the most amazing green eyes, flawless bone structure—the kind most women would die for—and a body so sexy it was a wonder his clothes didn't incinerate on contact. His long hair was a surprise, the light brown locks looked more at home on a shampoo commercial than on stage but he made it work.

But I'd seen a lot of those guys before, in every kind of incarnation. And I wasn't going to dissolve into a puddle of raging hormones just because he was good looking.

Besides, I had a job to do and thinking about him and my hormones wasn't on the agenda.

As I approached the posse, there were raised eyebrows of concern on some of the women. Even though I hadn't spoken yet, they could sense I was the enemy. That was me, the thief of fun, coming to take their play thing away. "Nico, can I have a word."

No question mark at the end, because it wasn't a request.

His eyes shot up, meeting mine and I could tell he'd been surprised. While his entourage had sensed me, poor Nico was too engrossed in the redhead he'd been chatting to. "Hey Gillian, sure. Of course."

I didn't bother waiting for his groupies to scatter, telling him to follow me back to the elevator. And like a dutiful puppy looking to please his master, he followed, giving the girls a quick goodbye. I liked them when they were still new and eager to please; it made my job so much easier.

"Is everything okay?" he asked, shifting nervously on his feet. "Is it Vaughan's head? He seemed fine when we last spoke."

Appearing calm was easy for me, I had it down to an art form. So even though part of me was freaking out—contemplating calling hospitals and police stations—I smiled as I turned to face him. "And when was the last time you spoke?"

I had every intention of telling him Vaughan was missing but I didn't want some misguided loyalty shit getting in the way of finding out where he might be.

Nico scratched his chin, deep in thought as the elevator doors opened on the floor I'd selected—Vaughan's floor—both of us stepping out as he answered. "Like an hour or so a go? Maybe a little longer. I told him we'd have dinner together, maybe go see some of the city if he was feeling okay."

"See what in the city exactly?" I gestured to the hall, waiting for Nico to follow me. "Was there something in particular he wanted to see?"

Nico laughed. "Not particularly, he hates New York. Why? Did you want to come with us?"

Lord.

Not only was Nico eager to please in that new puppy way, but he was as naïve as one as well. It worked for him, his cluelessness making him sort of adorable which women seemed to love. That and his new found fame. But as far as helping my cause, it didn't.

"No. I want to know where Vaughan would have gone if he was alone in the city." I was still being cagey as we walked to Vaughan's room. I wasn't stupid enough to think he'd be sitting on the bed safe and sound, crisis averted. But I didn't want Nico freaking out in the hall either. Puppies spooked easily and I didn't need the one I was currently in charge of to pee on the carpet.

"Ummm, not sure. Why don't we ask him?" He stepped into the room, immediately noticing Emily. His smile was automatic—as was my eye roll—forgetting all about his buddy and the question. "Hey Emily."

Emily naturally returned his smile, nodding her quick hello even though I could tell she was concerned. "Pete didn't need to see the security footage. The concierge saw him leave half an hour ago."

Shit.

That wasn't good.

"Who left?" Nico asked, still wanting to keep his attention on Emily but turned to me. "Where's Vaughan?"

Wasn't that the question of the minute? Where was Vaughan?

"We're trying to find him . . . he left." Emily tried to be diplomatic, and maybe if he didn't have a head injury and wasn't my responsibility I'd have been too. But alas, when it came to patience I was all out.

"So if you have any clues, now would be good."

After my father came in like a wrecking ball, I had persuaded—more like demanded—he hand over Vaughan's account to me. His approach hadn't worked and if we'd played it how I'd wanted to at the start, we might not have had the disaster that was the concert. Coulda, woulda, shoulda—none of it mattered at the moment. What was important was A. Vaughan was alive, and relatively whole and B. I somehow made it right. How I was going to do that, I still wasn't sure. But if he wasn't laying face down in a ditch somewhere it was going to be mighty tempting to kill him myself.

"Maybe . . . maybe a bar?" Nico added, not looking so sure.

Great, a bar. Not like the city wasn't full of those. Finding him wasn't going to be hard at all. Not.

Ignoring what seemed to be an impossible task, I grabbed my phone and called a driver. Usually I hated that pretentious bullshit, preferring to drive myself where I needed to be even though it drove my father insane. He was convinced I'd be kidnapped and held for ransom. I had to wonder if he was more worried about the possible money loss and inconvenience, than me actually getting abducted. But I needed all my faculties to look for Vaughan and I couldn't do that if I had to drive.

"Meet us in the lobby." I ended the call, my instructions to Tyler, our driver, clear. He'd be driving in the city with the three of us, and we weren't coming back until we'd become a foursome.

Without the need for discussion, Emily and Nico followed me down in the elevator. And while I might have been keeping my freak out on the down low, Nico wasn't doing so well.

"What if he does something stupid?" He shoved his hands into his pockets. "When I found him at the cabin, he'd been drinking pretty heavily. What if he's gotten drunk and got mugged, or stumbled into traffic, or gotten kidnapped or something."

Jesus, again with the kidnapping.

"He will be fine and we'll find him," I said reassuring anyone who had any doubts. There was no other option.

I'd come too far to see everything I'd done at Domination unraveled by one shitty decision. No, I would find him and I would somehow fix the whole situation. Because even though I knew that none of it had been directly my fault, I felt responsible. I *did* bring the social media post and the data to my dad and tell him it was a goldmine just waiting to be mined. And I *did* allow my father to take control of the idea, letting him run with reforming with the original members. The feeling that it was a mistake had gnawed in my gut, believing we should invest time and money into Vaughan and parlay the attention into a long term goal rather than short term cash. I hadn't fought for it, stupidly letting my father's recent approval go to my head and believing he'd look favorably on my support when it came to handing over the reins.

But I had been wrong. I'd gotten to where I was by being aggressive and not giving a shit what people thought—not by bending the fucking knee. Well that shit was over, and I had an idea that would make things right, both for Vaughan and for me.

I just had to find him.

9

Gillian

When Vaughan wanted to lick his wounds after he'd found out about Connor and his girlfriend, he'd gone to a cabin in the woods somewhere in Pennsylvania. Not a legitimate possibility when that option was over three hundred miles away. Not sure if that meant he wouldn't be hitting anywhere overly popular or crowded or if he'd buck the trend. Just to be sure, we checked out a few seedy bars in the area—I thanked God my tetanus shots were all up to date—hoping he was still on foot and hadn't slipped into an Uber.

"Central Park." Nico snapped his fingers, randomly mentioning the landmark as we stepped out of another questionable establishment. "He's at Central Park."

He seemed so sure, the revelation hitting him like the gospel on a Sunday. "Where's the car?"

"How do you know?" I asked, and more importantly if he'd been so convinced he'd known Vaughan's location why had we spent the last hour possibly contracting a communicable disease in some of the worst dive bars in Midtown.

"Because there's that place . . . the one with the good acoustics? You know, people YouTube themselves singing there or whatever, and he'd always joked that if he did it, he'd blow the roof off it."

"Place with good acoustics in Central Park?" I tried to think of where he meant. Belvedere's Castle? The Boathouse? Even the old carousel was a possibility. "Wait, do you mean the terrace near Bethesda Fountain?"

Street performers and tourists liked to congregate in the stunning tiled lower passage underneath the terrace and admire its beauty. And he was right; the acoustics were pretty good in there. It was beautiful and when not crowded, extremely peaceful. Even as a local, I liked to hang out at the park though I hadn't been in awhile.

"Yeah, that's it. The place near the fountain. I bet you anything that's where he is." Nico waved his hands animatedly. "That's where we'll find him."

With no time to lose, it was quicker to walk to Central Park than to try to navigate afternoon traffic. So, while I called Tyler, telling him to meet us at the park, the three of us walked with purpose to one of the most visited places in New York. God I hoped Nico was right, because if he wasn't I was probably going to have to put a team together and have them discreetly comb the city.

Late fall didn't give us a lot of daylight and once the sun set we'd have a whole other set of issues. So our brisk walk turned to an almost jog, not ideal considering I wasn't appropriately clothed. Not that I was going to let some heels and corporate wear stop me from achieving my objective, and if he was there, I wanted to find him ASAP.

Emily—who incidentally could run in heels like a badass, Nico, and I made it down the stairs to the fountain, ready to split up and search the surrounding area. It turns out, it was completely unnecessary with the sound that could only be described as angelic echoing through the air as we got closer to the underpass.

Clean, crisp and nothing like his usual style, Vaughan had his eyes closed singing *Hallelujah* by Leonard Cohen so emotionally charged and pitch perfect I looked around to make sure it wasn't a recording. Every note rung out, the air vibrating with the power of just his voice as goosebumps covered my skin.

It was beautiful, rocking me to my core as I closed my eyes and let the sound envelop me. I'd never heard a rock star sing like that—no screaming, no voice distortion, no tricks—just pure and unadulterated talent.

His long, light-brown hair had been shoved into a woolen beanie, his skin so much paler than what I remembered. The bruising was still fresh though, his face mottled with purple and blue, doing its best to ruin what was an otherwise perfect canvas.

He looked nothing like the guy who'd been on stage, which probably worked in our favor considering the crowd continued to gather. They had no idea who he was, either not recognizing him or completely oblivious, assuming he was just another street performer singing for his supper or a virtuoso bum.

Emily's wide-eyed expression matched mine, her mouth hanging open as she stared in disbelief. Like me, she'd heard Vaughan's commercial stuff. And while no one was denying the guy could sing, it was nothing like what was coming out of his mouth.

Nico didn't seem surprised, waiting to see if one of us was going to take the lead as he edged closer to his friend.

My hand reached out slowly, not wanting to spook him as I gently tapped him on the arm. "Hey, I'm so glad you're safe." The relief one hundred percent genuine as he slowly opened his eyes and focused on me.

God, he was beautiful.

Any pretense or cockiness completely gone as he looked at me with sad but trusting eyes.

"Hey." His lips spread into a lopsided smile. "What are you doing here?"

Nurturing wasn't natural for me, but I had an urge to keep him safe. "I'm here to make sure you're okay." My hands wrapped around his arm as I looked at him carefully. "You're going to be okay." Not sure if I was reassuring him or myself, but I knew I had to make it right.

He took a deep breath, his chest rising and falling, ignoring the crowd, Nico and Emily, as he focused solely on me. "Am I?" he whispered like a scared little boy who wasn't sure.

"Yes, I promise." I had no right to make those kinds of assurances, but I did anyway.

He smiled, entirely too trusting as he nodded and whispered, "I believe you. You're kind of hot, did I ever tell you that? I know you try and hide it, dressing like you're heading to a funeral every single day. But you can't fool me," he leaned in closer, "and I've been dying to kiss you."

Great.

If his declaration of craziness wasn't enough of a clue—him finding me attractive absolutely ridiculous—the smell of booze confirmed he was far from sober.

"Vaughan . . ." I wasn't sure exactly what I wanted to say, slightly annoyed at my own disappointment.

I knew he probably didn't mean it, and if he was unlucky enough to remember it, he'd have regrets too. Because I wasn't the kind of girl a man like him wanted to kiss.

He pulled back, taking my face in his hands and looking at me through his clouded green eyes. His calloused fingers swept over my jaw, tracing the edges like he was committing them to memory. His eyes only dropped once, lingering on my lips for a second before coming back to me, standing together in what seemed like suspended moments. "You're so beautiful."

My breath hitched, parts of myself that had been dormant stirred to life as he touched me and called me beautiful. My body unable to move as I stood there silently. I wasn't sure what I wanted, but stopping him wasn't it.

"Vaughan." His name was a plea on my lips, convincing myself it was to try to talk sense into him. But if I gave the irrational part of my brain any airtime, it would be for other reasons.

He moved in closer, his lips so close to mine that I could almost taste him. His breath was smoky, the lingering peat of the scotch he'd probably been drinking daring me to reach out and lick.

"Gillian, let me kiss you."

The sincerity in his voice threw me, as did the lack of sarcasm, and for a second I was almost going to let him. But the clearing throats behind us broke through what was clearly a stupid fantasy, taking me a minute to get my shit together. I was annoyed at myself for losing my composure and precious time, staring and entertaining the possibility instead of ignoring his mumblings and getting him to the car.

Linking my arm around his in an effort to keep him upright and hinder his escape if he got any bright ideas, I lowered my voice as I leaned in closer.

"Awesome, why don't we get back to the hotel and we can discuss it there."

Oh I knew I was being shady, possibly giving him the idea that there was a chance of something happening. But getting him back to the hotel was more important. Besides, he'd be lucky if in a few hours he'd even remember what he said, me doing us both a favor and forgetting it as well.

His arm snaked around my waist, bringing me in tight against his—very muscular—body, his grin widening. "I'd love to go back to the hotel with you, baby. Honestly, there isn't a place on you I wouldn't want to put my mouth. But I don't want to disappoint my audience."

The acknowledged crowd cheered, eliciting a chin tip and a raised hand from our inebriated Casanova. Impressive that recognized or not, he'd already won their approval.

"Well, I'm sure everyone will understand." I turned to the crowd, making it clear I was addressing them. "You can come back and sing again later."

There were groans of disappointment and I wondered how long he'd been entertaining them or what else he'd sung. A weird sense of regret spread through my chest, genuinely sad that I'd missed it.

Nico joined me, grabbing Vaughan from the other side, knocking over a bottle in a brown paper bag that had been sitting at his feet. Probably for the best too because there wasn't a chance I was going to let him finish it. Although part of me admired he was able to get a bottle and get drunk so quickly, especially in a strange city.

"Let's get you out of here, dude." Nico nodded to me as I took a step forward. Emily did what she did best, diplomatically dispersing the crowd with a smile and laugh and allowing us to walk/carry Vaughan to the car.

It wasn't easy.

All that muscle wasn't decorative and though he was lean, he weighed a ton. His heavy arm was draped across my shoulder as his head lolled to the side, his face falling into my hair.

"Mmmmm, you smell nice," he chuckled, taking a big sniff. "Are you taking me back to the hotel?"

"Sure am," I huffed, wishing there was an easier way to get him to the car. Calling for a stretcher was probably unreasonable, but gee it was tempting. The growing burn in my arms and legs reminded me that I should probably go to the gym, not that I'd need to if I was going to be carrying Vaughan Hale around for the indefinite future.

Despite smelling my hair and making drunken declarations of wanting to kiss me, Vaughan was surprisingly respectful. No grabbing at my tits or ass, no requests for me to blow him. He also hadn't been spotted which had also been good news. Not sure that our run of good luck was going to last though, which was why we were moving as quickly as was possible back to the car.

Emily had her phone to her ear as we reached the edge of the park, Tyler pulling up in our blacked-out Escalade about a minute later. He was efficient, I'd give him that, easing along side the curb and hitting the hazards before jumping out and helping us muscle Vaughan into the backseat.

"You can sit up front," I directed Nico, stopping him from getting into the backseat with us. "We'll drop you off at the hotel first, and I don't need the press or anyone else to see him passed out when we open the doors." My head tipped to a hunched over Vaughan who was having a tough time with his seatbelt.

Nico shook his head. "I'm not leaving him again. I'll sit up front if you want but wherever you're taking him, I'm coming too."

Great.

Because that was what I needed.

While I hadn't vocalized my intentions, my plan was pretty freaking clear. I was going to get Vaughan to my apartment and lock him in my guest room. Okay, so maybe locking him in was a touch aggressive and infringed on his personal liberties, but I couldn't risk him going MIA again. The hotel provided too many escape routes. Besides, if I was going to be able to talk some sense into him, I needed him around, conscious and sober. It was absolutely insane that we seemed to be struggling meeting all three of the criteria.

"Fine, but you don't call anyone, you don't post anything and no one finds out where we are, understood?" Slightly more cloak and dagger than I'd like to be but I didn't usually bring musicians to my home. In fact, I didn't normally bring anyone to my apartment, preferring to keep my space a sanctuary.

And I wasn't sure if it was a lapse in judgment or some bullshit ingrained need to not fail in front of my father, but my apartment was exactly our destination.

With everyone secured in the car, Tyler started the engine and drove us to what might be the biggest mistake of my life. Hopefully neither of them turned out to be serial killers, because I was going to be pissed if I was going to have to defend myself against possible death with my new set of Global knives. I hadn't even had a chance to cook with them yet, but those sharp, perfectly engineered pieces of Japanese steel were about the only weapons I had in the place.

We drove in silence. Me, obviously too busy contemplating if I'd lost touch with all reality to bother trying to make conversation. What I was doing was crazy, and I had to wonder if my need to prove a point hadn't made me bite off more than I could chew. I wasn't responsible for Vaughan's decline nor was I to blame for the band's implosion. *Perhaps* I had *some* responsibility, but it was just business, it wasn't personal.

So, why the hell did I feel so compelled to make it right? What I should have done was taken the loss and walked away, exactly what I'd asked Vaughan to do. But instead of taking good and reasonable advice, I set off on a fucking crusade to correct everyone's destiny.

It made no sense.

But right or wrong, I'd made my choice and I was going to see it through. I was stubborn like that, something I'd definitely been gifted by my father.

Tyler pulled into the undercover garage, hitting the code and getting us safely inside. There'd be no reporters, press or unwanted visitors, and there was an elevator ready to take us to my penthouse apartment. Yeah, it was slightly pretentious, but it was the one thing I accepted from my father and I liked the view.

"Need help getting him up?" Tyler asked, opening the doors of the Escalade and waiting for us to get out. I could tell he was less than pleased with my grand plan but was wise enough not to question me.

My footsteps echoed as I jumped out of the car into the garage, shaking my head. "No, we can take it from here. But it goes without saying that you weren't here and have no idea where Vaughan or Nico are."

I wasn't an idiot, but while Tyler might be *my* driver, his paychecks were paid by Domination. Last thing I needed was him running to my father and confessing how he'd spent his afternoon. I knew exactly where his loyalties would go if Warrick Duzan threatened his livelihood, but if we could avoid the drama, it would be preferable for everyone.

Tyler nodded, grunting under his breath that he wasn't telling anyone. And rather than deal with whether or not he was going to snitch, I decided to quit hanging out in the parking garage and get Vaughan, and the rest of our motley crew, up to my apartment.

Nico and Emily had already joined me out of the car, but Vaughan was still secured in his seat, his head resting against the window. I wasn't sure if he was asleep, or just hadn't realized the car had stopped moving, but the movement of his chest going up and down meant at least he hadn't died. I might not have gone to medical school but even I knew mixing medication, alcohol and a concussion was bad news. It would have really sucked for me to get him all the way to my place of residence just to have to call a coroner.

His weight pitched forward, held in place by his seatbelt as I opened the door. A groan escaped his lips, further proving he hadn't died. Nico, Emily and myself worked as an uncoordinated but successful collaboration, getting him out of the car and onto his feet. It was probably just as well I'd allowed Nico to tag along. Maneuvering a one-eighty pound—I was guessing—singer who was vertically challenged wouldn't have been easy.

Tyler watched as our "unit" walked to the elevator and got in, the doors closing behind us as I pressed the button for my floor.

"How long do you think we have?" Emily asked, the *before Warrick finds out they're missing and loses his mind*, left unspoken.

"An hour, maybe two." I shrugged, knowing my father would check in after dinner. That was if he didn't find out sooner.

Nico seemed to understand that he probably shouldn't ask questions, ignoring our conversation as we climbed to the top floor, the elevator door opening when it stopped.

We moved Vaughan inside and laid him down on the mattress in my third bedroom in the back. Emily had her own room in my apartment, and I didn't like to entertain visitors, which meant the guest room went largely unused. Thank God my father's realtor had been so extravagant and talked me into the bigger penthouse.

Vaughan slid open his eyes as his body relaxed into the mattress, looking around as if slightly confused. His gazed fix on Emily, a smile of recognition spreading across his lips. " 'Ello gov'nar."

Oh Lord.

He was still drunk.

Emily laughed, shooting me a raised eyebrow. "I'm Australian, not English."

"Australian, English . . . it's the same thing, isn't it?" He smirked, trying to shuffle himself back up the bed. "Not that any of that is important. I want to know where you've been hiding all this time." His smile more than just a little suggestive.

If I'd believed his passing fascination with me was in any way serious, I might have been hurt. But it was predictable—words of a drunken man who would have flirted with a table lamp if that had been all that was on offer. Still a small—almost non-existent—part was disappointed, and I hated it.

It was stupid, and I had no interest in him. And so what if he was good looking, not like there was ever a possibility where I'd date him. That was a whole truckload of complications I didn't want or need, so why the hell did I even care?

"She was busy." I stepped forward, trying to keep my expression neutral as his attention shifted to me. "How's the head?"

"Gillllllliiiiiiaaaaaaaaaannnn." My slurred name spilled from his beautiful lips. "I was hoping you hadn't left me. Come," he waved his hand beckoning me closer to the bed. "Why don't you and Emily tell me everything I've missed. Fuck . . ." He stopped, like a realization had hit him. "You two aren't together are you?"

Jesus.

Not only was he not interested in me but he'd also thought I was a lesbian. It wouldn't be the first time a man made the mistake, assuming my lack of interest in him was because I preferred vagina rather than dick.

"No. We're not *together*." I rolled my eyes, contemplating how much I was going to share. Not that it mattered, I could've confessed to group sex with a KPop band and he wouldn't remember it later. "She's my sister."

"You're related?" Nico coughed out, his surprise reminding me he was still in the room.

"Waaaaaaaaiiit a minute." Vaughan tried unsuccessfully to sit up. "How can you be sisters? You look nothing alike."

Like I needed the reminder. Tempted to screw with his mind a little, I debated asking him to clarify. See how deep a hole he would dig for himself as he described our differences.

"We're step sisters." Ever the kindhearted Emily, put them both out of their misery. "We're not blood related."

"Ah." Nico nodded, satisfied with the explanation. Vaughan not so much.

He eyed us both intently, the words taking a while to form in his mouth. "Wow, so freaking hot. You ever have a threesome?"

"No," I almost choked out, wondering how he'd turned our family connection into something sordid. First a lesbian, then sharing men with Emily—it took real talent that every avenue in his head ended up with me and a woman. "Did you not hear how she's my sister?"

"Yeah, but not blood related. So it's totally okay," he reasoned, like it somehow made it acceptable.

Talking about my sex life even in the hypothetical with him wasn't happening. Especially when it involved Emily. "Why don't you lay back down before you hurt yourself." Or I hurt him, it could go either way.

"Fine," he yawned, having trouble staying upright. "By the way, I had this crazy dream I was singing in the park and you found me." His recollection ironically identical to the version of actual events.

"Huh, crazy dream. Why don't you sleep it off and we'll talk about it in a hour or so?" Because no reasonable conversation would be happening in the foreseeable future.

Nodding and rolling over, he mumbled into the pillow. "Why don't you curl up with me, you sound like you could use a nap too."

Yeah, that was my problem. I needed a nap.

Shaking my head, I questioned my sanity and my intelligence as I watched him curl onto his side. His beanie slipped, wisps of light brown hair falling around his face as he snuggled into position. He looked so vulnerable, unlike the persona of the rough and raw rock god he no doubt believed himself to be.

He was such a contradiction, and one I just couldn't work out, my feet getting restless as I edged towards the door. "We should go out into the living room. There's only one exit, and he'll have to go past us to use it."

Nico nodded, heading out the way we came in while Emily lingered at the door. "You think he remembers?"

I shrugged knowing most of his shitty day would come floating back eventually. "I'd say he'll remember the important parts. The stipulation in the contract, losing his band, and then running off to sing at Bethesda."

Emily chuckled glancing at a sleeping Vaughan before looking back at me. "No, I meant how close he was to kissing you."

"He was drunk, he had no idea what he was doing. Besides, did you not hear him? A fucking threesome no less." I rolled my eyes, silently annoyed she'd seen it too. Not that I blamed her, he was hard to ignore.

"Yeah, maybe." She shrugged. "Funny thing though is you looked like you weren't going to stop him."

And suddenly I was more annoyed at the attention she'd paid *me*.

Gillian

When Emily volunteered to go get dinner, it came as no shock that Nico very helpfully decided to go with her. And why wouldn't he when the alternative was to sit in the living room with me while I worked silently.

I hadn't intended to ignore him, but social conversations with strangers weren't my favorite. Business meetings were one thing, and I could out talk anyone around a boardroom. But turn it into a personal chit-chat and I wanted nothing to do with it. I was too suspicious, not willing to give anyone anything they could possibly leverage. I wasn't sure how much the defective Duzan DNA was to blame and how much was just me. It took a lot to infiltrate the wall, my talent for maintaining friendships and even relationships from a safe distance, rather impressive.

"Hey." Vaughan yawned, scratching his mess of hair as he walked out into the living room and smiled. "I keep waking up in strange places."

It was inconceivable that anyone could look as good as he did given what he'd been through in the last forty-eight hours. And yet there he was, looking like an advert for edgy male cologne.

Oh, and somewhere between my spare bedroom and the living room, he'd also lost his shirt.

"Hey." I deliberately kept my eyes off the amazing contours of his chest, ignoring how incredible his abs were and trying to look bored. "You're in my apartment. I figured there was less chance of losing you here."

He smiled, because apparently he needed to ratchet up the hot meter a little more and try and melt the decorative wallpaper off their surface. "Losing me?"

I blinked, trying to hide my surprise that he was so calm. Sure there was the possibility that he didn't remember singing in the park, but I assumed the showdown at the hotel wouldn't be forgotten. "Vaughan. I think you need to sit down."

With an eyebrow cocked, he took a seat right beside me, folding his arms across his chest and flexing all kinds of muscles. It hadn't been a party telling him about the contract provisions the first time, the second round was bound to be so much worse. Hey at least we weren't talking about me sleeping with women, so that was a positive.

Quickly glancing around the room for breakable objects, I packed away my laptop and turned to face him. Keeping my voice level, I once again explained the consequences of his and Connor's fight and shutting down the show.

His fingers pinched the bridge of his nose, his chest expanding as he pushed out a heavy exhale. "I thought it was a dream."

"It wasn't," I continued, revealing had it not only been real, but it led to him leaving, being drunk and singing in Central Park. Our almost kiss—I surely would have stopped it anyway—was conveniently omitted in the retelling, finishing with my decision to take him home like a stray.

"Yeah, so drinking on the pain meds wasn't a good idea," he winced. The vague memory and erratic behavior probably more attributed to mixing the two than a high blood alcohol level. "So that's it? It's a done deal?" He asked with such hope in his eyes that it almost hurt to look.

"Yes and no." I tempered my argument, not sure if it was the right time to broach the subject. "White Trash Circus is done. But you don't have to be."

"What do you mean? You said I can't write or perform. And if I do, it's all Domination's anyway. So I either get used to Warrick pimping me out like a cheap whore, or I walk away. And I can tell you that neither of those scenarios feels like a win."

Emily and Nico hadn't come back yet, the two of us alone. So I took a breath, knowing there wasn't going to be a better time and hoped for the best. "No, you have another option. You could be reborn."

He coughed, his eyes opening wide as he shook his head. "Whoa, hold on a minute. If this is a religion thing, I'm not interested. Besides, I thought the rumors of Domination being a cult weren't true."

I tried not to laugh, biting my lip. "Not in the religious sense, Vaughan. Artistically. Like when Prince became a symbol. You need to be someone else."

The verbiage in the contract was deliberately murky, and going on to form a new band with another name wasn't going to cut it. He had to literally reinvent himself. New band, new sound, new image—a complete flip of what he'd been doing.

Keeping a respectable distance—I hadn't forgotten he was shirtless—I leaned forward. "You do that, and anything you produce is your own. Domination can't touch you." Well, at least not in the legal sense. Whether Warrick wanted to be vindictive was another story. "After that, you'll be in a position to negotiate. Either for a new contract that negates the old one, or buy it out yourself."

It wasn't as easy as it sounded, and lord was it going to be a lot of work. But it gave him an out.

"Why are you telling me this? Aren't you on their side?" He scratched his chin, probably wondering if it was some kind of test. It wouldn't be the first time someone with my last name got creative with the truth, and I didn't blame him for being skeptical.

Getting antsy while sitting but not wanting to add to his suspicion, I stayed seated, locking my gaze with his. It was hard to be honest, to tell him that I had as much to prove as he did, so in the end I went with the alternative. "Because I don't like losing. I know I can make you a success, and this way we both get something out of it."

"Assuming I trust you."

Well there was that. "Yes, assuming you trust me. Although, what is your alternative? You want to do this and I know how to get you there. What else do you have to lose?"

It was probably harsher than I'd meant to be but I was being honest. If it all ended in flames, he could still walk away. It wasn't like I was going to chain him to a sink and make him wash dishes until he paid his debt. "If you really think about it, I'm taking the bigger gamble."

The door opened before he had a chance to answer. Nico and Emily laughing as they burst through carrying what I'd hoped was dinner.

"You're up." Emily set the plastic bag on the coffee table. "You hungry?"

Vaughan's eyes shifted between Nico and Emily. "You guys are here too?"

Nico laughed. "Well yeah, someone has to save you from yourself. Hopefully you didn't get into too much trouble while I was gone. No more mention of threesomes?"

While I had successfully ignored Vaughan and his inebriated musings, Nico hadn't been so generous. So instead of forgetting it—and most of the other stuff he'd said—there we were, reliving the horror for a second time.

"What threesome?" Vaughan asked, honestly perplexed at the mention.

Again Nico didn't take the hint, elaborating. "When you found out Emily and Gillian were step sisters you asked if they'd had a threesome. Not your finest moment."

"Okay, let's eat dinner and worry about everything else later, shall we." I stood up and inspected the bags of food. "Mmmm smells good. Did you guys go to the new Italian place down the road? I've heard good things."

Vaughan didn't look like he was going to let it go, but didn't get much of a choice when I started dishing out food. Besides, I had bigger problems than dealing with Vaughan's runaway mouth.

"I'll get some drinks," Emily offered, disappearing into my kitchen. I really hoped for everyone's sake she didn't come back with booze, surely we were done with the drama that came with it.

"Great, I'll be back in a minute." Using the excuse of needing to put my laptop away, I gathered it up and carried it to the office I rarely used. I'd had two missed calls from my father I'd conveniently ignored, but knew there was only a certain amount of time I could avoid him.

It wasn't going to be pretty; Warrick Duzan didn't like being disappointed, so better I just got it over with. As I picked up the phone to call him, I heard laughing coming from my living room. Maybe Nico and Emily were telling Vaughan exactly what he'd said, or maybe they were just enjoying dinner. Part of me was jealous, the ease of which they were able to go through life. It wasn't that way for me and I sometimes wondered what it would've been like.

"Gillian." My father's curt voice was able to convey his displeasure with an efficiency you couldn't help but marvel at. Not many people could say so much with so little.

"Before you start, we agreed that this was my deal now. And because it's my deal, I'll play it how I want it." There was no room for hesitation or weakness, those weren't traits he understood or respected. And I wasn't going to ask for permission either.

"And which way are you going to *play* it? Word on the street is that you smuggled the singer out of the hotel. I've settled the bill by the way so if that wasn't your intention, you're going to have to fund their accommodation yourself."

He was just so warm and fuzzy, I had no idea why people thought he was heartless. I rolled my eyes, ignoring his attempt to control the tempo. "Well then, your information is incorrect. I didn't smuggle anyone out of anywhere. And you'll know about my plans when I'm ready to share them. But you will get your money back so I expect you not to interfere and let me do my job."

"Listen, Gillian, I'm giving you a long leash but don't think that I'll roll over and take the loss. I don't care who is fucking who, or how they make it right in their heads. I want every last penny I spent on those clowns."

"Really?" I deadpanned, my sarcasm unable to be maintained. "Here I thought it was about the music."

He laughed, amused no less. "Fine. I'll wait. Within reason."

It was as big of a concession as I was going to get and more than I expected to be honest. I'd been ready for a fight, almost disappointed it hadn't come. "Noted, I'll take it under advisement."

"Gillian, you haven't listened to me since you were twelve. And I'm not delusional enough to think you're going to start now. Just get it done."

I assumed it was his version of goodbye since all the important parts of the conversation were over. We didn't do sentimental well wishes or bother with idle promises to catch up. As far as telling each other I love you, well mark that down as never. So when he paused, not ending the call like I'd expected, there was no way to predict what would happen next.

"Dad?" The prompt surprising us both as I broke the silence.

"Sorry, I was distracted. Emily still staying with you?"

Two things. I could count on one hand the times I'd heard my father apologize, which was only slightly less than the times he engaged in personal chatter. So the fact both had happened in the same sentence was shocking beyond belief. Maybe he had an aneurism or something? Or momentarily possessed by a human spirit.

"Yes, you know she is." I'd mentioned it when she moved in a few weeks ago, confirming it when I'd put her on the payroll. He hadn't even blinked, accepting my judgment that I needed yet another assistant.

He cleared his throat. "Good. Tell her I said hi. I still miss her mother, she was a good woman."

I didn't bother reminding him that he'd cheated repeatedly on that *good woman*. Or that he should probably go spend time with his new thirty-year-old wife. That would have been fruitless and not something he wanted to hear. So instead I ignored it, pretending the last few minutes hadn't happened and ended the call with a quick goodbye.

So freaking weird.

I'd have to check with his secretary and see if he'd had his physical recently. Maybe the old man was finally losing his mind?

The knock at the door was not unexpected. Our nightly ritual of Emily nagging me at least three times to come eat was due to start and I was positive she was going to be more insistent since we had company.

"I'm coming." I opened the door, ready to go pretend I wasn't uncomfortable with the amount of people currently in my apartment. I wasn't a good host, my leaving them to start dinner without me spelling that out loud and clear. But I stopped short

VIRAL

when instead of Emily, it was Vaughan standing on the other side.

I was really starting to hate how good-looking he was, especially when he stood so close.

"You looking for the bathroom? It's down the hall on the left." I tried to remain detached, ignoring that he still hadn't located a shirt. It didn't seem to bother anyone else so I wasn't going to make a big deal about it.

"No." He shook his head, rolling his eyes up and down my body. "I remember what happened in the park."

Vaughan

Flashes of memories sparked in my melon as Nico and Emily talked. Random, and probably out of order, but coming together like pieces of a puzzle as we started our dinner without the woman who's house we were in. And while my time on stage after the fight had been sketchy, I remembered being in that park, singing to a bunch of strangers and seeing Gillian appear like an angel. Granted she didn't follow the dress code and was probably more pissed off than most heavenly creatures, but there was something about her that set her apart. And my God did I want to know more.

Even half out of my mind—booze and pills, not a good mix—I'd wanted to kiss her. And the urge hadn't left yet. That she had a hand in the mess I was in—indirectly or not—didn't enter into the equation. Not as far as my balls were concerned anyway. Hey, I never said I exercised good judgment.

Sure there was lingering bad feelings because of Connor and Lindsey, but for no good reason at all, I trusted her. She wasn't like them. Not sure she was like anyone really—certainly not someone I'd met before—but if she were to screw someone over, she would do it right to their face. I knew nothing about her, but I fucking knew that.

"I remember singing in that underpass. And you finding me there." I moved through the doorway, wondering if she was prickly to everyone or just to me. "And I need to know more about your idea."

As far as bullshit went, that right there was at the top of my list. Oh, I was curious to hear her ideas on how I was going to cocoon myself in shit and turn into a butterfly, but that wasn't what had been on my mind. Nope, I had been thinking about other things, namely what made her tick.

See I was a huge believer in fate. Not that we were necessarily puppets on a string being controlled by some invisible dude up in the sky, but that energy moved us in a particular way for a particular reason. So why had she showed up when my life was in the toilet? Why was she at that park? Why was I in her apartment? And why the hell was she so invested? Maybe it was to do even more damage, to take what was left of my soul. But I remember that look when she found me, that softness in her eyes that she liked to keep hidden. And fuck me if I didn't believe her. Maybe I'd been premature in thinking my head was right, and maybe I was digging myself an even bigger hole, damn if I wasn't going to find out.

"What? Now?" Couldn't work out if it was surprise at the topic or the timing and I'll be honest, neither bothered me all that much. I just wanted her to keep talking, the analytical silent version of herself not one I was in a hurry to get back to.

"Weren't we about to discuss it before dinner arrived? Thought it might be something you didn't want to talk about in front of them, which is why I came to find you."

Something else I remembered was the unmistakable urge to kiss her. Stupid when I thought about it, because it made no sense. But as we'd stood inches apart in that park, I'd sensed something else in her. A crackling ember of warmth, and I'd wanted to put my mouth on hers, wondering if she'd kiss me back.

"You seemed concerned. Was that because of the money? Or something else?"

Her back jacked up straight and I could tell I'd hit a nerve. Whatever she'd told me—which hadn't been much—there was a hell of a lot more to it.

"It's in both our interest for this to work out."

She'd given me nothing.

"And how exactly do you see it working out?"

Make no mistake, I wasn't attempting to seduce her. There had been no grand plans to back her into a corner and see just how much she could unravel. Not saying I wouldn't have enjoyed peeling back each one of those black layers—literally and figuratively—and see how loudly she could say my name, but that was going to have to stay on ice. Besides, part of me was worried she'd cleaver my dick clean off with her death stare alone and I wasn't ready to lose him.

"Why don't we go have dinner with the others and we can talk about it later." She not so subtly gestured toward the door.

And had I been a gentleman, I might have taken the hint and gone and sat my ass down like a good little boy. But I wasn't in the mood, and regardless if I was attracted to her or not, I'd already been dicked around more than I'd liked.

"You do that a lot I've noticed. Phrase a question as a statement. You're not really asking anything are you, more just saying how it's going to be." She might have thought that shit had slid by me because I hadn't brought it up, but I saw exactly what she was doing. Cool, calculated—her conversations ran like Swiss time pieces.

"Asking for permission is a slippery slope, and I'm not in the habit of leaving my choices in the hands of other people."

There was a bite to her tone and it amused me a little. She didn't like people figuring her out or maybe it was she didn't like being called on it. Either way, I was in too deep to back down.

"Well, it seems like we have something in common. Imagine that." I smirked, knowing I was being an asshole. "So why don't you tell me what you had in mind and then we'll go eat."

"Vaughan, I know musicians like to live in their own reality, but let me remind you, you are currently in mine." Her eyebrow arched, a hint of a smile edging across her lips. "So why don't you relax, enjoy dinner and then when I'm ready, we can discuss it."

I had a hunch that when she told people to jump, they responded with how high. Maybe it was because her father was a heavyweight and she'd grown up with the keys to the kingdom in her pocket. Or maybe it was the impassive attitude that seemed like an impenetrable barrier. Either way, I could see how it might be intimidating, how her icy exterior could chill you to the bone. But unlike those assholes, I had nothing to lose. I mean, really, what else could she or her father take? So while others might scatter like roaches, bending over to please her, I didn't share the same sentiment. And wasn't I just curious as hell on how she'd react.

"No." Just one word, left hanging like a flag in defiance.

"No?" Her brow arched higher, her surprise juicing me up even more.

Not sure what it was about her that got under my skin, but there it was gnawing at me like a virus. It wasn't just a physical attraction—because on paper she was nothing like my "regular" type—it was something else, some chemical reaction in my brain that got me interested. She fascinated me, the curiosity more compulsive than a bad habit, and for whatever reason, I wasn't letting it go.

"I've lost my girlfriend, my best friend, my band and pretty much everything else in the last few days. I've been drunk, unconscious and felt sorry for myself. And while it's probably easy for me to sit in the misery, I'm going to do something else instead." I took a breath and prayed I wasn't making the biggest mistake of my life. "I'm not ready to go silently into the night, Gillian. I'm not ready to hand over everything I've done and everything I am. So if you have a plan, an idea on how I can climb out of this hole, then I want to hear it. Please," I added at the end, not intentionally trying to be a rude piece of shit but making it clear I was done being a victim too.

Not sure if it was my impassioned plea or the fact she could guess I wasn't kidding. But the two of us could've stood in that room for hours, eyeballing each other and I wouldn't have backed down. I'd been a dumbass and I'd made some really stupid decisions but standing there with her wasn't one of them.

"Okay." She nodded, her hands tightening at her side. "I have ideas, and you're going to have to trust me."

Neither of us had any reason to go down that road, but it was where we both found each other. And unless she was looking to stick it to her father, I wasn't sure what her motivations were. But for better or worse, I did trust her. Gut instinct, stupidity, or maybe it was just those golden eyes of hers and the promise of what was sitting just behind them. But I would trust her until she gave me a reason not to.

"Fine, I'll trust you. But you're going to have to give me something in return."

Her lips pressed together and I had no doubt she was trying to stop her mouth from saying something. Probably to tell me to go fuck myself but she didn't. Instead she kicked up her chin and looked me dead in the eye. "And what would that be?"

"Tell me why you're doing this."

If I was going to trust her, she was going to have to trust me. And part of that was giving me an inch. Sure, she could lie and how would I know any different? It wasn't like I hadn't been lied to in the past. But something inside me believed she wouldn't. That while she might not always be on the level, being deceptive wasn't in her roadmap.

Her gaze didn't shift, her tone as even as a lake on a clear day. "I told you, I don't like losing."

"Not buying it." I shook my head. Surely she didn't think I was going to let her off that easily. "If there is some ulterior motive, or some family drama, then I want to know up front. I don't even care what your reason is, as long as I know where I stand. Couldn't care less if this is about money, or bragging rights. But I expect honesty. I won't be blindsided again, Gillian. Not like Connor and Lindsey, and not like your fucking dad. You give me that, and I'll do almost anything you say."

"*Almost* anything?" The prospect seemed to excite her.

"Yep, I still have my limits and becoming a boy band is a hard pass." I grinned. "And I write my own music, I'm not becoming a mouthpiece of someone else's agenda."

She took a minute, like she was giving it consideration. And I honestly had no idea what she was going to say. "I'm not responsible for what happened to you but I'm not completely heartless either. The concert, original line up—none of that was my idea. And while it's true, I was using your viral popularity for our agenda, I wanted to see what *you* could do, not White Trash Circus." She took a breath, pausing but not quite done.

"But seeing you succeed isn't the only reason. And if I'm going to prove to my father and the rest of the company I've got what it takes to run Domination then I can't play it safe. I refuse to sit on the sidelines and listen to other people's ideas." Her eyes blazed with intent, not once bowing her head in apology as she stiffened her shoulders. "I'm more than Warrick Duzan's daughter, in or out of the company. This business is all I've known, the only thing I am good at, and I know it better than anyone out there. And if Domination is to not only survive but thrive in a culture where any asshole can upload something onto YouTube and become a superstar, we need to adapt. And trying to get a bunch of old white men, when you're under forty and have a vagina, to listen to reason is an uphill battle. I can accept not being liked, they can think whatever they want about me and my methods. I'm not here to make friends. But they will respect me. And not because of my last name, but because I've earned it."

My mouth opened and then closed again, completely shocked. When I'd suggested she had other motives, I thought she wanted to piss off her dad. Like dating the bad boy from high school. But the whole proving herself thing—well that just took me by surprise. I couldn't imagine anyone not respecting her. Hell she walked into a room and you had no choice but to pay attention. I had no idea when I'd asked her to be honest it would be so personal.

She watched as I continued gold-fishing like an idiot, not really sure of how to respond. "Not what you expected?"

"No." I swallowed, her silver-spoon lifestyle clearly different from what I'd imagined. "So, I guess we're in this together."

"I guess so."

The bravado she wore like her blacker than black wardrobe slipped as she held out her hand and offered it to me. It was obvious she'd said more than she'd meant to but she wasn't backtracking either.

My hand went out and met with hers, my fingers wrapping around her soft skin. I had a feeling both of us were in unchartered territory, and wrong as it probably was to even think it, I was glad we both had something to lose.

"I won't screw you over if you pay me the same courtesy," I promised, meaning every word of it as I held onto her hand longer than I should.

She didn't release either, a fire burning in her eyes and a determination that would've had most men pissing down their leg. "I have no intention of doing that."

Not sure if she meant in the business sense or the literal, but a tingle traveled down to my balls as she all but agreed to be on the same team. And I assumed that since there'd be dollars and cents involved, I'd have to sideline whatever other involvement I wanted to have with her. Wasn't entirely pleased with that scenario because she was more intriguing than I could ignore.

Yeah, that part of the plan was going to suck.

"Should we go eat dinner now, or are you going to stare at me a little longer?" The edges of her mouth curved, the makings of a smile threatened to come out and play.

My chest puffed out, a sense of pride filling me as I returned the grin. It might not be a huge breakthrough, but I'd cracked her armor and who knew where that might take us. "Look at you actually asking a question instead of barking a demand. Careful Gillian, I might think you're not as much of a hard ass as everyone else does."

"Don't get used to it. I *am* a hard ass, but you should be concerned with your own ass instead of mine." Her lips edged wider.

"Whoa, was that a joke?" I clutched my chest in surprise. "Easy there, you're going to give me a heart attack before we even get out the gate. Can't pay your dad back and seek greatness if I'm six feet under."

She laughed.

Like actually opened her mouth and chuckled, the sound so surprisingly sweet it was at odds with the tough exterior.

And fuck did I like the sound of it.

"Okay, rock star, dinner and then strategy. I have some ideas about new band members."

I turned motioning toward the door. "I can't wait to hear all about them."

Gillian

It had never been the plan to spill my guts, and show him my vulnerability. Hell, I'd prided myself on keeping an even keel and not wearing my heart on my sleeve. Emotions were bad. And if I couldn't keep them at bay, then at the very least I needed to keep them private.

Damn him.

And damn me too.

Because having a heart to heart and confessing my *feelings* had not been the plan. But it was too late for any of that now, and whether I liked it or not, he and I were partners, at least until we both achieved our objectives.

Dinner hadn't been completely bad. Vaughan had found a shirt, sparing us from looking at his ridiculously toned chest for which I was thankful. And while I didn't necessarily like having so many people in my personal space, it wasn't the worst thing in the world either.

It was weird, watching Emily laugh with Vaughan and Nico, I felt like more an observer than a participant. The conversation between them was so easy and relaxed, and it was obvious both of them were totally smitten. Not that I blamed them, she was stunning and smart, the heart of gold was a bit much but I guess everyone had their flaws.

Vaughan did his best to draw me into their little group, making a pointed effort to ask me questions or turn the attention my way. But he kept it light, and non-confrontational, and didn't push me for more than I was ready to give.

It was a strange balance and one I hadn't juggled before. Keeping the relationship professional—I still had a job to do—but having him in my private bubble. I liked neat lines on either one side or the other, blurring the boundary was a first for me. It made me uncomfortable, but I didn't outright hate it either.

"We should go to bed." I gathered up the dishes from the coffee table, our makeshift floor picnic Emily's idea. "We have a lot to discuss in the morning and I'd like to get moving on it right away."

While the plan had been to tell Vaughan my ideas, it had fallen to the wayside once we started eating. Every time I tried to talk business, Emily steered the conversation elsewhere. It wasn't an accident either, her effort obvious at least to me.

"Sure, we need to organize our flights back too." Vaughan stood, helping me clear plates.

My hands stopped cleaning, the dishes no longer important. "Flights? What flights?"

We'd gotten lucky tracking him down in New York and I didn't like my chances if he decided to get airborne.

"To Pittsburgh, you know, the city where I live," he tossed casually, ignoring my statue routine in my living room as he smirked.

Not sure if he was just looking to work a nerve—we'd had a pleasant dinner so I guess it was past due—but he had zero chance of flying home. "Vaughan, you do realize that you can't go to Pittsburgh. We have a band to put together, a game plan."

I shook my head, my to-do list so out of control he probably wouldn't be flying home for a month or two at least. "Not to mention recording the new material when you finally get there."

"Why?" He shrugged, my listed reasons obviously not as self-explanatory as I'd thought. "Why stay here? I can do all of that and not have to be in New York. Not like I can't travel if you desperately need me to. So give me one good reason why I need to hang around here any longer than I already have."

Emily bit her lip suppressing the grin; amused he was acting like a five-year-old and not being reasonable. At least she was enjoying it, even if I wasn't. "Because it makes more sense for you to stay here. We have a studio, resources—everything you need, right in the city. It makes better business and financial sense to stay put."

Not sure why I even bothered to argue, I thought we'd already established we were doing it my way. He didn't get to renege on our agreement.

"Really? Because wouldn't it make more sense for me to be at home, not living on your dime and getting myself deeper in the hole?" He tilted his head, daring me to argue. "Not to mention the extra attention we'd attract here, I go back and I can slide in under the radar. I can go out to the cabin; no one will ever find me. Then when you need to parade me out or record or whatever, I can either drive or fly up. I'll even agree to call you every twenty-four hours just to check in."

Great, I was a parole officer.

"No, not good enough." I shook my head, not prepared to enter into a debate. "No offense, Vaughan but you don't have the best track record. I need to keep an eye on you, I don't want to wake up some day and read about you being drunk and naked down at The Point because something wasn't going right."

"Ouch." He laughed, not as offended as he was pretending to be. "That's a bit harsh. I got drunk twice, and both times were justified."

"Maybe we compromise? We find a small place out of the city? Upstate?" Nico tried to play mediator, joining us on his feet. Little did he know I didn't need his help because there was zero chance I was letting Vaughan get on a plane.

Wasn't happening.

"Or." It was Emily's turn. "We can have a schedule. Plan a few weeks and then you can go for a while and then fly back? It's not forever, besides New York is so much fun, I love it here. We can go on a foodie tour."

Her offer to play tour guide was a good one, especially since they both had been looking at her like she was dessert. But I would never—not ever—consider pimping out my sister to close a deal. There were other ways to deal with it, like stuffing crystal meth in his luggage and call in an anonymous tip to the TSA. I mean, that would be the last resort, but I'd do it if I had to.

"We're staying here." The conversation ended as I took the plates I'd been holding during the entire conversation and went into the kitchen. Pfft, he wanted to fly to Pittsburgh, like that was going to happen.

"Or I could go and you could come with me." His voice startled me, coming from behind as he placed what he'd collected into the sink.

"What?" I spun around confused as to why he didn't get the memo. It had already been decided out there in the living room, wasn't even sure what we were still talking about.

He folded his arms across his chest, accentuating the perfectly sculptured torso underneath as he rested against the granite counter. "You can come with me, keep an eye on me out there. Make sure I don't end up drunk and naked." His brow rose in suggestion.

I laughed.

It was the second time of the night and becoming a habit when he was around. "Vaughan, I don't know if you've noticed but I have a business to run. I can't go out to the woods and babysit you. Besides, I don't camp."

While I wasn't a princess, I didn't do the great outdoors. I wasn't fond of nature, or dirt, or being in places where you weren't the top of the food chain. And yes, my upbringing had definitely been a factor. My dad's idea of slumming was staying at a three-star hotel. And while I wasn't as pretentious as all of that, the idea of being out in the woods when you hadn't been taken hostage by a serial killer wasn't in my wheelhouse.

"Have you ever done it?" he asked, pushing the point. "Camping I mean."

I sighed loudly, wondering why on earth of all the social media explosions to stumble on I had to pick literally the biggest pain in the ass. "No, don't need to. I also know I wouldn't like licking the floor of a truck stop bathroom and haven't done that either. When you know, you know."

"Feisty, I like this side of you. You know when we first met you barely said three words to me and here we are, in your apartment." He gestured around the room. "You cracking jokes and being all kinds of sarcastic."

As much as I hated to admit it, he was right. I had been incredibly measured when we'd first met. And if someone had told me then that I'd be having a heated discussion in my kitchen after seeing him half naked I'd have called them crazy. But that didn't change the fact that was exactly where we were, or that I had lowered my defenses a little when it came to him.

"Is your usual strategy just to drive people crazy and wear them down into submission?" I turned to glare at him, a little annoyed he'd gotten under my skin as much as he had. I usually had a better handle on myself, but for some unknown reason, he had worked his way in—completely uninvited.

He moved closer, his tall muscular body inches from mine, and he dazzled me with a blinding smile. "Nope, usually I try charm but that won't work on you. So I have to use whatever I have."

Knowing he wasn't going to try to charm me should have pleased me. After all, I was a strong, independent woman and thought with my brain, not my hormones. No cheeky grin and no amount of walking around shirtless would reduce me to a quivering mess, and it was encouraging he saw that. But damn me if I wasn't slightly disappointed he wasn't going to try. Because as much as I was everything I'd just mentioned, I was also a woman.

And I liked men.

And sex.

And being pleased.

I just hated that in most cases I'd had to choose one or the other.

The bitch or the doormat—you couldn't have it both ways.

"Assuming you were trying to charm me? What would you do?" my mouth asked before I'd had a chance to sensor the thought.

It was completely wrong for me to ask, inappropriate on so many levels and sending all kinds of mixed messages. But I didn't take it back, curious to see what he would do if he thought I was able to be plied by his manhood.

He raised a brow, his grin spreading as he dared me to stop him before he'd even started. "Is this a test? Because, while I dig this more relaxed side of you, I like my balls right where they are."

Mention of his balls shouldn't have made me hot, and not because I was embarrassed. My cheeks didn't pink when I dropped the word fuck or dick, and I didn't stammer like an old-timey southern debutant when someone talked about sex.

It wasn't balls that were the problem.

It was *his* balls.

"You're worried I'm going to castrate you?" It was a very blurred line, so close to flirting that I should have been ashamed of myself. It wasn't what I was supposed to do, and yet, there I was, doing it anyway.

He lowered his head, bringing it closer to my ear as he whispered, "Both terrified and turned on by it, but let's keep that between us."

There was the line.

And both of us had crossed it.

Knowing one of us was going to have to be responsible and not trusting it to be him, I tried to laugh it off like I wasn't burning alive inside. Oh, it was utterly ridiculous that the rumble of his sexy voice would get me hot and heavy, but there was no denying that was exactly what that mouth did. Dangerous, and worst of all, I'd been participating.

"Well, maybe it's for the best if you don't then, we are in the vicinity of knifes." My head angled to the knife block, the shiny metal handles glimmering in the light.

He coughed, his eyes widening. "Exactly, which is why I need to employ other methods. I do need to warn you though, I'm a persistent bastard."

"Noooooooooooo, really? I'd have never guessed," I mocked, the fake shock fooling no one.

He laughed. "Another joke. If you go back to being the ice queen tomorrow, I'm going to be really disappointed."

It was a nickname I was familiar with, and for the most part I didn't mind. Didn't care that people thought I was cold, because for better or worse, it protected me. But I didn't like hearing him say it, the conflict of wanting to maintain status quo and liking our banter too much to bear for one night.

I didn't have a lot of friends and as wrong as it was to consider, I would wager he'd make a really good one. As for what kind of lover he would be—I would tuck that thought away and reexamine it when I was alone. Safer that way.

Needing to change the mood, I instead directed the conversation to where it should be. Our location, both present and future.

"Assuming I went. To this cabin. In the middle of nowhere Pennsylvania. How would that even work? We need to find you a new band, and I need internet and cell service."

"Fair call." He nodded agreeing it would be difficult. "What if we compromised like Emily and Nico suggested."

"All jokes aside, Vaughan, I can't just let you get on a plane and leave." And it wasn't just because I didn't want him to go, as crazy as it sounded. He was an investment, and I couldn't and wouldn't abandon an investment.

"So come with me to Pittsburgh. No cabin in the woods." He raised his hands in surrender, cutting off the protest that was ready in my mouth. "My place."

"How is that a compromise? It's just you getting your way," I argued back, more tempted than I would have liked.

He put his hands out to the side. "Well, you let me hide out at your place, it seems fair I extend the same hospitality. Besides, think of how much easier it will be to work without your dad looking over your shoulder." His smile edged wider.

Not wanting to admit he had a point, I shelved the discussion for tomorrow. "If I agree to consider this in the morning, can we all just go to bed? It's already been a long day and I'm not making critical decisions without a clear mind."

His wicked grin could only mean bad things as mischief shone in his eyes. "All of us go to bed? Together? I thought you said you weren't into threesome with your sister?"

"I thought you didn't remember that." Cue my lack of surprise his momentary amnesia had passed.

"Parts are coming back to me, that's one of the highlights." He tapped his head, looking fairly pleased with himself.

"No one is sleeping together," I warned, not wanting to encourage him anymore than I had. "Unless you want to share the bed with Nico. I hadn't anticipated him spending the night, maybe the two of you can spoon so he doesn't have to sleep on the couch."

"Couch surfing it is for poor Nico."

"Well then let's go back out there and give him that bad news."

Regardless of where everyone was sleeping, it was going to be a long night.

Vaughan

It had been the worst sleep ever.

Wasn't the bed's fault, the sheets felt amazing and probably had a billion thread count, woven together by praying monks. But for all that Bed, Bath and Beyond luxury, the knowledge that a few doors away there was a possibly naked—at least in my mind she was—knockout, kept me up.

And I didn't mean Emily.

While the Aussie cheerleader was five different shades of hot, she wasn't the reason my dick had been hard all night. Nope, that honor had gone to her sister—step sister, whatever—making me lose circulation from the waist down.

Fuck, she was an enigma. Clearly less than impressed by me, not that there was any reasoning with my libido. And if I thought the dark, mysterious bullshit turned me on, I didn't stand a chance with the sarcastic playful side. She was still keeping mostly under wraps, but she'd cracked open a door and I wouldn't be letting her close it any time soon.

So rather than doze off into dreamland, switch off my brain and enjoy the bed that wasn't mine, I laid awake, staring at the ceiling and trying to fight off a hard-on.

It wasn't easy.

When morning finally came, I almost cried with relief. No shit, a tear formed in the corner of my eye and I whispered a thank you to the man upstairs. That thanks wasn't because I was going home either—yeah, nothing had been decided, but I was confident I was going to get my way. But because the thought of seeing her early in the morning, sleepy eyed with messed up hair almost had me shooting my load I was so excited.

Determined to not miss any of the good stuff, I snuck out of bed, doing my best to keep the noise down despite my big ass feet. The hall was still dark, Emily and Gillian's bedroom doors closed as I skulked my way through to the main part of the apartment.

Victorious, no one was awake. I fought the urge to fist pump as I peered over at Nico sleeping on the couch. He hadn't even complained, taking the blanket and pillow Emily had given him and thanked her with a smile. He'd have slept on the balcony if she had asked, so being inside on a sofa that probably cost more than his car wasn't a hardship.

Maybe I should have felt shady for creeping around her apartment, but I had a hard time working up the sentiment. Instead I was fucking giddy, excited about the day and the prospects, desperate to see her again.

And yeah, part of that was feeding the sick infatuation I'd seemed to develop. But there was also the promise of a fresh start that came with her too. So no, it wasn't just about fucking her, it was about opening the next chapter after White Trash Circus and getting back on that fucking stage.

Man, I wanted it. Wanted to sing in front of a crowd and have them sing my words back to me more than I could ever describe. I wanted my music to mean something, to have some dude I'd never met hear the lyrics I'd written and feel it in his soul. I wouldn't accept fading away, I couldn't just go off and do something else, music was all I knew.

"You're up early." A bright feminine voice tore me from my rock daydream, her eyes locked on me. I probably should have pulled on some pants and a shirt, but in my hurry to get out of my room, I'd left them where they'd been dropped the night before. My boxer shorts saved me from being totally naked.

"Emily," I coughed, ignoring her cute pajamas. "Couldn't sleep, was hoping if I got the coffee started I might earn favor with the queen."

She bit her lip trying not to smile. "Oh really? Was that what you were trying to do? Huh. And was being half starkers supposed to help you on your quest?"

"Starkers?" The word not one I was familiar with, wondering if it was code for something I should know.

Her hand waved in the general direction of my chest. "Your state of undress, sometimes I forget which words aren't universally understood."

"Well if being *skarkers* is going to help me out, I can lose the boxer shorts as well." Oddly enough I wasn't flirting with her.

Whatever attraction I might have had to Emily was superficial and very much in the past. But her sister was another story.

"It's STARKERS," she laughed. "And I don't think Gillian wants to find you naked in her kitchen."

"So what would she like?" Again, shady to ask but I did anyway. I had a wealth of information directly in front of me and I wasn't looking a gift horse in the mouth.

Emily hesitated, and I expected the none-of-your-business that would surely follow. But when she looked around to make sure we were alone, I was both encouraged and excited about what my early morning meeting might unveil. "Don't try and play her, okay? She isn't someone you want to be on the wrong side of. And I know you probably think she's a challenge or something, but she isn't some game. Just be real with her, she's a good person."

The warning was a mixed bag and I couldn't tell if she was warning me off out of concern for her or for me. Too many unanswered questions and not enough answers. "I'm the last person who wants to play anyone." I gave her the truth because it was legit how I felt. "But it seems like we're going to be spending a lot of time together, so we might as well be friends, right?"

Friends.

Sure, that's what I wanted to be.

Fuck, even to my own ears it sounded lame.

"Well, okay then." Emily nodded to the cabinets behind me. "There are pods beside the coffee machine. She takes her coffee black, no milk, no sugar."

"Black, there's a surprise." I couldn't help but laugh as I spun around and set to work making a cup. It was more complicated than the drip pot I had at home, but I wasn't ready to YouTube the instructions just yet.

The black hot liquid had just started to flow into the cup when I heard another voice, this one making me smile. "I didn't picture you as a morning type, figured it would be noon before we saw you."

I waited a beat, taking a moment to ready myself before turning around. Emily had been wearing a cute top and pants that had lambs and pink clouds and I was praying to whoever was willing to hear my prayer they'd gotten a two-for-one sale.

"What the fuuu—" My mouth dropped open. Gillian was already dressed, wearing her black uniform, and the only reason I knew she hadn't slept in it was because the skirt and jacket combo was different from last night.

"Something wrong?" she asked, walking to the coffee machine, taking the full cup and replacing the pod. She didn't skip a beat, getting another cup and starting the process over while she continued to eyeball me.

It wasn't just the clothes, the idea that she might have been self conscious about walking around half—what was that word again? Steakers?—nakey, something I understood. Some women were like that, and while it didn't bother me, I wasn't about to question it. But she was dressed, showered, hair and make up fixed like she'd stumbled out of an eleven a.m. meeting and we were just catching up.

"Did you fall asleep in a boardroom?" I pointed to her ensemble, wondering if she even owned casual clothes.

She shrugged, taking a sip from the steaming cup in her hand. "I've been up since five. I went for a run, then had a phone conference with the brand manager. This is my second cup."

It was perplexing to me that not only had she been up for hours—last time I'd checked the time on my phone it had been eight o'clock—but she'd managed to get up, leave the house, go for a run, come back, shower and have a phone conference all without me hearing a sound. Like a freaking ninja. And it wasn't like I hadn't been awake, looking at the cornices and wondering what kind of joints they'd used trying to stave off my morning wood either. How in the hell had I missed it?

Her eyes stayed on me as she continued to drink, moving up and down my body with nothing more than passing interest. And while I was disappointed I'd missed her fresh from the mattress, the idea of her being hot and sweaty and possibly wearing some active gear was a loss I couldn't stand.

"You should have woken me, I could have used a run."

She shook her head, shooting down my idea of suiting up and hitting the streets. "Brain swelling, no strenuous exercise for a while. Doctor's orders."

Her concern was heartwarming but I could assure her it wasn't my brain swelling that was the problem. Just watching her mouth say "strenuous exercise" was enough to create a situation in my boxers that didn't belong in the kitchen. And while I knew sex was off the table, if I didn't at least go jerk off soon, I was going to explode.

"Mind if I use your shower?" I dropped my hands discreetly to the front of my groin, camouflaging the growing bulge.

If she'd noticed, she wasn't showing it, nodding to Emily who was looking on with clinical interest. "Emily got your luggage from your hotel room, everything is in the closet. And you know where the bathroom is, towels are in the linen closet along the back wall."

"Thanks, enjoy your coffee. We'll chat locations after I'm done." I tipped my head in farewell and left the two women in the kitchen, retracing my steps back to the bedroom, without the need to be silent.

Grabbing what I needed from my suitcase, I moved to the bathroom and locked the door. While I gave zero shits about Gillian seeing me naked—the thought actually exciting me—I didn't want Emily accidentally walking in and catching me having a stroke. Because that was exactly the plan; the need to relieve the pressure in my balls more important than washing my hair.

With the water cranked up to *almost going to burn your skin off*, I dropped my boxers and hopped under the spray. My skin was still tender, the bruising from Connor and my fight still making its presence felt as the water hit me. It didn't bother me though, in fact I welcomed the distraction. I washed my body, soaping myself up with some vanilla lavender body wash that smelled too much like her. My hands moved over my arms and then down my legs, the suds spilling down the drain as I reached down and cupped my balls, giving them a firm tug.

"Fuck," I hissed out through my clenched jaw, the feeling so good I was concerned I might pass out.

Giving it a minute and letting the sensation settle a bit, my hand moved to my shaft.

Mmmmm, that felt good.

The tight squeeze of my fingers slid up and down my length, the glide smooth thanks to the body wash. My eyes closed shut, letting my brain take a little road trip as I breathed in her scent, imagining her hand wrapped around my dick while she was planted on her knees in front of me.

I had no idea what she would look like naked, no clue as to how her curves would feel under my hands but I knew they'd be fucking fantastic. She was fantastic, an undiscovered treasure trying to hide how beautiful she was and had almost succeeded. Just not from me.

Fuck.

My balls were heavy and I got even harder in my hand as I pictured her intense golden eyes locked with mine while her mouth was around my dick.

"That's it, Gillian. Taste me," I whispered, the thundering water drowning out my hoarse voice as I stayed with my fantasy.

She didn't blink, taking as much as she could down her throat before pulling me out of her mouth and sliding back up my body. Her tits pressed against my chest as she demanded, "Now, you taste me."

It was that thought alone, of her being naked touching me and allowing me to touch her that had me coming faster than I'd wanted. My load shot out, hitting the tile as I blew out a sigh of relief. It hadn't lasted long enough, the juiced up feeling still lingering in my bones as I pressed my head against the tile and let the force of the water beat the skin on my back.

It was only after taking a few deep breaths that I was able to finish what I'd started and clean up the mess I'd made, ignoring the urge to do it again.

Not happening.

Instead, I washed my hair, the strands sticking to my back, rinsed off and got myself acquainted with the fluffy white towels that were so soft I almost moaned.

"What the hell are you doing?" I whispered to my reflection, wiping off the condensation with my hand and giving myself a good hard look. "Even if she was into it—which she isn't—she's off limits, literally holds your career in her hands."

If hearing it out loud was supposed to convince me, it hadn't done the trick, my body no less interested than before our little heart to heart.

I swear, the minute I got home, I was getting laid. I was fucking every single woman who'd let me and getting whatever it was out of my system.

I needed to get my head in the game, and currently it was shoved way up my ass.

"Vaughan." Gillian's voice came from beyond the door, my silent curse hoping she hadn't heard any of that shit. "When you're ready I need you to meet me in your room. You don't have to be dressed. Boxer shorts are fine."

Jesus Christ.

I had no idea what the hell she had planned, but those pearls of wisdom I just sprouted, telling myself to keep my hands off went completely out the window.

I had no idea if it was going to all end up in flames—me, my career, my life—but my god was I desperate to find out.

14

Gillian

My day had started early like it always did. I ran because, unlike my genetically blessed step sister, if I didn't work out, my ass became huge. It wasn't anything hardcore, but running helped me think and got me outside. And while I was running—keeping my ass in check and my mind moving—I came up with a brilliant solution. I called in a favor, and before I knew it, the idea was more of a plan.

Of course, I still hadn't told Vaughan about it and was expecting he wouldn't be pleased. But if he wanted to go back to Pittsburgh then he would have to agree. Besides, it was good for both him and his career, market testing and research proving it would elevate him to a new level.

I'd waited, working in my office until I heard soft mummers in the kitchen. And since when I strolled passed Nico thirty minutes before to get my coffee, he'd been sleeping like a corpse, I'd assumed it hadn't been him.

But all my excitement in telling Vaughan my grand scheme evaporated when I saw him in the kitchen, wearing nothing but boxer shorts. And if all that toned skin on display wasn't enough to make me pause and lose my train of thought, the very obvious bulge in his pants was. Lord, even covered it was obscene, the thin cotton between us doing an outstanding job in saving me from being poked. *Not that I would have hated that.* Might have enjoyed it actually. No. I wasn't supposed to be thinking about him like that. So all of the words I'd planned to say got shoved down for later, and I tried to not act like I wouldn't have tossed him across my granite countertops and screwed him right there. It was a challenge but I was proud of my effort.

Pity all my self-congratulation wasn't enough, the discussion that needed to be had still very much required. Which was why I told him to meet me in his room. The clothing option I'd tossed in at the end of the request had been a mistake, but clearly I liked playing with fire. So even though it served my purpose to have a blank canvas, I hoped and prayed—only half-heartedly if I was honest—that he followed trend and didn't listen to me.

I did not get so lucky.

Vaughan walked in, his spectacular chest still damp, a towel slung low on his hips and a smile that could cause orgasms. He'd taken my direction, and raised the bar so to speak. God, I couldn't help but wonder what he looked like under that towel.

"Gillian," his voice rumbled, dripping in so much erotic suggestion I wasn't sure if I wanted him to keep saying it or never speak my name again.

"Vaughan." I kept my eyes locked on his, refusing to let them wander like they were dying to do. Their fact-finding mission would not help my cause in keeping it professional, and unlike the kitchen, we didn't have an audience to keep me decent.

He closed the door behind him, taking the last shred of accountability with it, and shutting us in—alone. My traitorous eyes dipped, taking him in whole as his arms spread wide and gave me a better angle. The recon they collected nothing short of fantastic. "Here I am, just like you wanted."

How simultaneously right and wrong that statement was.

"Right, great. Thank you." I did my best to keep my words clear and concise and not mumble what I'd been really thinking. Namely if he was really interested in what I wanted, he could lose the towel.

"So, I'm agreeing to Pittsburgh. As long as we keep your profile low and you keep off social media. You'll probably get less attention there than you would in New York." I swallowed, taking a much-needed breath before I continued. "But I'm coming with you, and we're doing it my way."

The smile that had been simmering, taunting me with seduction, morphed into full-blown delight, his happiness fucking palpable. "Yes! Gillian, you have no idea how much this means to me. Thank you so much, you won't regret this." He stepped forward, the gap I had been so cautious to maintain between us completely eaten up as his very hot, very naked body crushed me in a hug. I wasn't sure which of my prayers had been answered, my feelings so conflicted I couldn't even enjoy it entirely.

"Well, before you get too excited," *or I did*, "there are conditions. This isn't a free pass," I coughed out, unwrapping myself from his hug and reinstating the safety zone between us.

"Anything, I'll do anything," he agreed without proper thought, the attraction ten times worse when he smiled at me like that.

He wasn't the only one who wasn't thinking, my feet moving me forward as I reached up to his damp, long hair. It was soft, its scent familiar yet completely arousing on him as I ran it through my fingers. "This has to be the first thing to go." It was low; my voice nowhere near as confident or commanding as I'd meant it to be. I shouldn't have touched him, my hand lingering even though I had no reason to.

"My hair?" His brow scrunched in confusion, ignoring our closeness and my raspy voice. "What do you mean it has to go?"

Catching myself and finding my sanity, I released his light brown locks and returned my attention to his eyes. They weren't completely safe—vivid green like rare gems twinkling with mystery and excitement—but it was a better option than the alternative. "Yes, we need to cut it." I coughed, clearing my throat attempting to be professional. "It will make you less recognizable until we're ready to re launch you, and will also help with the image change. You can't be Vaughan from White Trash Circus anymore, so instead you're going to be Vaughan Hale from yet to be named."

"You want me to cut my hair?" he echoed, all smoldering looks sidelined as his smile dropped. "Change my image?"

I assumed I'd get push back. He'd already told me how many woman liked it. But it was going to be the first thing that went. "Yes, it works for heavy metal but you can't play that anymore. You have to reinvent yourself—your looks as well as your sound. The hair goes."

There weren't many men who could carry the length and not look like a hair-band reject, but it worked for him. It was also currently a big definer of who he was and we needed to get as far as we could from that. Besides, it was a distraction, hiding his beautiful face.

"Trust me. It's just hair and if this doesn't work and you hate it, you can grow it back."

I wasn't in the habit of explaining to the *talent*, and sure didn't open it up to debate. But with him it was different, and whether I wanted to admit it or not, I wanted him to trust me. Yeah, trust me. I didn't want him to like me or anything, because that would be completely juvenile, unnecessary and ridiculous. Sadly, even knowing all those things, I wanted it all the same.

He moved from me, switching his focus to the mirror on the door of the open closet. "I've had my hair like this forever." His hand ran through it, mussing it a little before pulling it back. "But you're right, it's just hair."

"Thank you, you won't regret it." I had to stop myself from smiling as his attention swung back to me.

I hated how much I liked that attention and the sensation inside my chest that it gave me. He was just a man like all the others, and I didn't need his approval. But I wanted it all the same.

"Great, I have a hair stylist coming in an hour or two and the style consultant should be here any moment. He's bringing some clothes for you to try on. Just be open with the suggestions, okay?"

"Fine." He shrugged, not looking completely convinced but not fighting me either. "But I still need to be me, and I won't wear anything that makes me look like a dick."

"No one wants you to look like a dick." Not sure it would be possible anyway. He could pull on a pair of flannel pajamas and make it look sexy, something I tried not to think about as I edged toward the door.

"I'll be out in the living room. Marcus will be here soon." My fingers were wrapped around the knob ready to leave when I felt him behind me, inches away from my back.

"You should go pack." His hand pressed against the door stopping me from opening it. "I'll get my hair cut, wear the fancy clothes, but we're leaving here this afternoon."

I turned knowing he would be too close and too naked for my own good. "I said we would and we will. I'll have a jet ready to take us to Alleghany County. Commercial will attract too much attention. And I'll organize a car to take us where you live."

"Fancy," he grinned. "But lets keep the spending to a minimum. I'm already in the hole by a lot, I'll organize the car."

"Vaughan, you can't tell anyone. The idea is no one knows you're back." I shook my head, envisioning a carload of his closest friends—and the local media—greeting us at the airport.

"Relax, it will be my dad. He can keep a secret, and they'll want to see me anyway."

The idea of his father picking us up seemed completely foreign to me, making me feel uneasy. Not only had I never met the guy—our brief phone conversations not character revealing—but I didn't have huge expectations of fathers in general. I couldn't remember my father ever coming to the airport. Even when I was younger and traveled to visit Emily, it was always a driver. But there were some battles just not worth fighting, and if he would play nice then I could too.

"Okay, but please tell him not to tell anyone."

He moved closer, every part of him invading my personal space. "Guess we're just going to have to trust each other."

"Yeah, I guess so."

Marcus arrived promptly with a rolling rack of garment bags and a directive to keep his mouth shut. I'd made the call myself, reassigning Melanie to another executive until I got back. It wasn't that I didn't trust her or doubt her ability to do her job. She'd been loyal since the day she'd signed on with me. But if I wanted full autonomy, I needed to keep my circle small, at least for the time being.

Marcus freelanced for celebrities and was well-versed in confidentiality, but most importantly wasn't on my father's payroll. Guestimating Vaughan's size, they shut the door of the bedroom and instructed me to keep out. I pretended my annoyance was strictly from a professional standpoint. Considering it was my project, the excuse should justify me being in the room gawking at Vaughan in various stages of undress. I was such a perv.

With my protest lodged, and insisting I got veto privileges, he caved and walked out in various ensembles for my approval. From jeans to a tailored suit, he rocked every single look like he was a model. Seriously, he went from sexy to smoldering with so little adjustment it was hard to sit still. And even though I could tell he wasn't crazy about the more tailored looks, he kept the eye roll to minimal and encouraged Marcus to try some edgier alternatives.

Nico even had a turn, a separate rolling rack being brought in for his fittings when Vaughan was done. His fashion show had been easier on my hormones, the tall bass player more cute than hot.

May—the hair stylist—didn't have the same objections to me sitting with them in the bathroom and welcomed the audience. My fingers were white, knotted in my lap as I sat behind them, watching as waves of light-brown hair tumbled to the ground as she worked. He didn't flinch, complain or argue about how much came off, his eyes locked forward on the mirror impassively as May's scissors got busy.

With each snip of the scissors, more of his face was revealed, the hair no longer a distraction but framing a face a million dirty dreams were made of. The bruising was starting to fade, and it would only be a matter of time before it was back to its sexy, unadulterated perfection. I couldn't look away, staring as she kept it slightly longer in the front, her fingers messing it up to look like he'd just woken up.

"What do you think?" May fussed with the back, my hands wishing they were hers.

"It's perfect," I answered, ignoring the question hadn't been for me.

Vaughan checked himself out in the mirror, "It's fine I guess. As long as the boss is happy." His eyes went to mine.

What I couldn't say was that I loved it. Not because it was shorter or because I thought it was more commercially viable, but because he was no longer hidden behind a veil. That I could *really* see him, see those beautiful kind and sexy eyes, see the sharp angles of his amazing jaw—and how excited I was to see him stripped back with no noise.

But I couldn't say any of that.

"It will be a crowd pleaser," was what I went with, standing up and walking toward the door. "I'll see you both outside."

It was only when I'd left the bathroom that I allowed myself to take a full breath. My back sagged against the wall as I listened to May going through the products she was leaving, Vaughan laughing along with her.

"He looks that good, huh?" Emily smirked, coming up beside me, her eyes directed to the door.

"Stop it." I pushed her playfully while looking around for Nico. Last thing I needed was our chat to be misconstrued as something else. Like that I liked Vaughan.

"He's in the guestroom, playing with his new wardrobe. It's just me," Emily assured me, guessing exactly why I was being cautious. It wasn't her first rodeo, and while she had no problem showing her emotions, she didn't force me to show mine. Except when we were alone, and then I was at her mercy.

"Just admit you think he's gorgeous. Last time I checked you still had a pulse," she added, not willing to let it go.

"Of course he's gorgeous, I never said he wasn't. Not that it matters, he's a client and completely not my type." I had no problem speaking the truth—well not when it was just the two of us—but it didn't change facts.

Her eyes widened, her voice dropping dramatically as she laid on the sarcasm. "Yeah, he sure as hell is not your type. I mean, does he even listen to a thing you say? And the fact he isn't scared of you must be a real turn off. I bet he isn't even impressed with your bank account. How are you supposed to work with any of that?"

I knew exactly what she was doing, pointing out that when it came to boyfriends, I'd had a hard time finding one who challenged me and wasn't with me for my last name or my estimated wealth. All of them had come with some sort of strings, be it hang ups, expectations, or just the intention to use me. Ironically, none of it really hurt, it was something I'd been conditioned to expect. Which was why my relationships weren't long lasting or memorable, with most of those men citing me for being a cold-hearted bitch when they walked out the door. And when they did, I was not only not surprised, but pleased I'd protected myself.

"He's a client," I reminded her, not willing to remind her of all my inabilities when it came to men. "It's not going to happen."

"So I can date him?" she asked, looking smug.

I didn't think for a second she was serious, but if she were, she had every right. I didn't control either of their love lives and I didn't think a guy like Vaughan would stay single for long. From what I'd learned about him in the last few days, he seemed like a nice guy. Emily was nice. Maybe they belonged together.

"Sure, knock yourself out." The words felt thick in my throat but I said them anyway. "You might want to make your move soon though, I've got the jet booked for seven tonight and we'll be out of here. And on that note, I'm going to go pack."

My back lifted from the wall as I waved and left, not waiting to see if she followed through. It was none of my business what she did, or if he'd agree but I couldn't deny the nagging feeling in my gut that hoped she was just kidding.

At least I had something to distract me, my suitcase pulled onto my bed as I opened my closet. What the hell does a person pack when they're holing up in the 'burbs of Pennsylvania for an indefinite amount of time?

15

Vaughan

A blacked-out Suburban delivered Nico, Gillian, and I to Teterboro Airport, avoiding JFK and LaGuardia. Emily had stayed back in Manhattan and I spent the entire drive pretending I wasn't freaking ecstatic I was going to have Gillian all to myself. We didn't really speak on the drive, Nico and I discussing our new "looks" before we were welcomed by an airline crew, apparently ready to fly us back to the Burg.

Every single one of those fuckers bent over backward, trying to impress Gillian like she was their emperor. It was funny to watch, her response polite and polished but no one getting the extra nod like they'd hoped, their attention turning to us when they were left disappointed.

The jet was something else. I'd never even flown in the extra comfort seats let alone first class, so a private plane was on another level. The chairs were massive—soft leather, fully reclining for maximum comfort. I was almost tempted to tell Gillian we should head to L.A. just so we could enjoy it a little longer. Flying commercial was going to suck from here on out.

It took us a little over an hour to touch down at the regional airport. The sun had set, the landing smooth as we said goodbye to the enthusiastic airline staff and stepped off the plane right onto the tarmac. I'd already worded up my dad, told him that I was on the way back and to keep it on the down low. Mom was insisting I come back to the house, concerned she hadn't been able to see me since I'd been hurt and cussed out Gillian and the label for trying to keep her away. Mom wasn't her biggest fan, not that I told Gillian that, hoping I'd be able to smooth things over before they came face to face. Dad was more laid back though, waiting in the airport wearing a faded Steelers hoodie nodding at us as we approached.

His eyes widened as he took in my new look. All the fancy threads were packed in my bag, my jeans and t-shirt not much different to what I'd usually wore. What was different was the lack of hair hanging down around my shoulders, my new style feeling weird as the air hit the back of my neck.

"Yinz redt to go?" he asked, Gillian staring at him like a deer in headlights. "Ye got yer hair cut, your ma will be pleased."

It was tempting to let it play out a little longer, have my dad ask her something else. But being the nice guy I am, I put her out of her misery, anxious to get back to my place.

"Yeah, don't get too excited, might be growing it out again." My hand ran through it. "And we're all good, Pops, you do a drive by my apartment like I asked?" I chuckled, glad to see my old man.

He nodded. "Yeah, I even went dahn Dickson street n'at. The coast is clear."

"Hi, I'm Gillian. Pleased to meet you, Mr. Hale." She put her hand out, not waiting for the introduction. "Thank you for picking us up."

"Nice to meet ya, hun." He shook her hand. "But nuna dis Mr. Hale crap, call me Donny. And no problem, I like da drive."

"Okay." She nodded, refusing to give over her suitcase as she pulled it behind her. "Thanks, Donny."

Nico made small talk with my pops as we walked out to the parking lot, Dad's shiny new Ford Expedition parked right up front like he owned the place.

"Put yer stuff in da back, I just cleaned 'er." He pointed to the tailgate as he hit the keyless entry.

"You following along?" I chuckled, leading Gillian around the back of the car while my dad hopped in the driver's seat. "A little different from Manhattan, huh?"

"I'm fine." She shook her head, not convincing me she was. "Just put your bag in so we can get out of here."

While she insisted on hauling her suitcase all by herself, she allowed me to help her load it into the back. Nico dumped his in and then jumped into the car, sparking a conversation with my dad like he'd just picked us up from summer camp.

With our luggage secured, Gillian slid into the seat opposite Nico, leaving me to take the front. I tried to hide my disappointment, wishing I could be sitting with her as we drove to my place. It was dumb, especially considering we'd been sitting next to each other on the jet. Not to mention we would be spending a whole lot of quality time in the coming weeks. And unlike her penthouse in New York, my apartment was a shoebox with no guestroom. Probably something I should have told her about before she agreed to come.

Dad asked me about the gig, my head and whether I'd spoken to Connor, but for the most part kept the inquisition to a minimum. He dropped off Nico at his place in Glassport, looking across to me and asking where he was heading next.

It was subtle, the question of whether or not Gillian was going to a hotel answered when I told him to take us to my place. He kept his feelings on that to himself, but I assumed my mom wouldn't be so generous.

The crowds that had been camping in my apartment building the day Nico and I got back from the cabin were gone, with no more or less traffic than normal. My place was dark, which was a good sign, my dad pulling in and helping us get out our bags. And after assuring him we didn't need any help getting them into the apartment, he got back into his car and reminded me to call my mother in the morning.

"And this is me." I unlocked the door and threw on the light, Gillian standing on the threshold as I pulled in the bags. She'd tried to stop me from grabbing hers, but I'd been too quick.

"This is . . .nice." She looked around in the clinical way she always did, her true expression hidden under a carefully maintained mask.

"Nice is such a bullshit word, even for you," I laughed. "And I'm sure compared to what you're used to it's a shithole. But it's my own little pad, and in my budget so I'm happy."

While I loved the idea of getting something bigger, and eventually owning a house, I didn't have hang ups about what I had or didn't. I knew it wasn't a palace, but at least I wasn't living in my parents' basement playing video games all night and drinking Mountain Dew.

"I meant it was cozy, lived in. I didn't mean it as a criticism." The mask slipped, a small smile peeking through. "And how conceited do you think I am? I would never judge someone's house."

I neglected to remind her about her firm stance on camping, preferring to go through into the bedroom and dumping my bag. She followed close behind, her suitcase left in the living room even though I'd already decided she could take the bed.

"Unfortunately, there are no guestrooms here. Just the one bedroom—mine. But you can stay here and I'll sleep in the living room. The couch pulls out to a queen and it's fairly comfortable." I flicked on the light, letting her see where she was going to be spending her nights. I'll admit a small part of me got excited at the thought of her in my bed, even if I wasn't going to be between the sheets with her.

"Don't be silly." She shook her head. "I'm not taking your bed, I'm happy to have the couch."

"Yeah, that isn't going to happen. So take the room and the bed, and let me see what I have in my freezer. I know we ate dinner before we left, but I'm already hungry again."

Her hands reached up, resting on my chest and stopping me from leaving. "Vaughan, I'm not taking your bed. I will take the couch and I will be fine. Besides, how am I going to keep an eye on you if I'm in here and you're out there?" She gestured to the living room, the front door not far beyond it.

"And what do you think I'm going to do?" I didn't move, leaving her hands right where they were, and liking it. If the idea of me bailing got her touching me, I might have played on that earlier. I didn't even feel guilty about it, happy to take whatever bad karma it attracted.

Her head tilted up, meeting my eyes as we stood there in my room. It would have been easy to kiss her, no danger of interruptions.

"Just don't argue with me. It's your bed, you should be in it."

And on that, I totally agreed. I should be in my bed, wanting nothing more than to strip off and get between the sheets. But only if she was going to be in there with me; the idea of it giving me a hard-on.

"Since it's my bed, shouldn't I get a say?" Threatening to tempt fate, I moved closer, and to my utter delight, her hands didn't move. "What if I promise to be a good boy?"

Yeah, I knew what I was doing, and unfortunately so did she. Those words broke whatever moment we had going on as she took a step back, taking with her any of her body parts that had been making contact.

"I've got the couch." She made it clear it was a done deal and pushing the issue wouldn't do me any good. It was probably for the best I let it slide, putting it on the agenda to argue about it in the morning.

"Fine, I'll get you some blankets and a pillow."

Leaving me to gather those up and kick my own ass for pushing the issue, she went back into the living room and unpacked her laptop. She didn't waste time setting herself up on the end table, checking emails and tapping on the keys without bothering to ask for the Wi-Fi password. If she was feeling weird about what happened in the bedroom, she wasn't showing it.

"You want to split a frozen pizza with me?" The pillows and comforter placed on the edge of the couch she currently wasn't occupying.

"Not really hungry, but thank you." She didn't bother looking up, continuing on her online quest, whatever that was.

Figuring it would be better to give her space, I went into the kitchen and got busy heating up the pizza. Given that most of my apartment was open plan, I could still watch her while I pretended to be engrossed in my food, turning on the oven and cracking open a pop while I waited the obligatory fifteen-to-twenty until I could eat.

She didn't lift her head once, effectively ignoring me while I went about my business. Got all the way through my pizza, got myself another drink and dumped the dishes into the dishwasher. All of it without not so much as a peep from her. And maybe that was the way shit was done at her place, but it sure as hell wasn't how it was going to go down in mine.

"Okay, this isn't going to work." My hand went to the laptop, pushing it down and closing it.

She looked surprised, but not angry, blinking at me as I kept my hand on her computer. "What do you mean?"

"I mean, if this arrangement is going to work, we need to figure out a better way. I'm not going to pretend you're not here and unless you want to do a number on my ego, you can't do that either. Call me sensitive but I like to be acknowledged when I'm around. You don't have to make a big deal about it, but I won't be invisible either."

My voice probably had a little more edge than I would have liked but it wasn't anger. It was frustration. Stuck in some strange in between where we weren't really friends and I wanted to sleep with her. Oh, and I wasn't even going to pretend not to be excited about eventually seeing her out of those clothes. If I was going to have to set the alarm for every hour, on the hour, I was going to see her in pajamas at the very least.

"Vaughan." She shook her head, biting her lip like she was going to say something and then dropping it. "I was just trying to get ahead of the curve."

"Can you leave it just for a minute? I can promise you it will still be there if you have a conversation with me."

It was clear she didn't want to, and I wasn't sure if it was just me or if it was conversations in general. Anything other than talking business seemed to be like pulling teeth.

"Okay." She turned to face me. "So I have the new contract. I was going to leave it until the morning but since you want to discuss things now, we can. I think you should get a lawyer to look at it this time and then sign it. It will make sure that you understand your obligations and how you'll be compensated."

"No." I shook my head, not willing to make it so easy for her.

The shock was written on her face, clearly expecting me to just nod and lay down like most people did. But that hadn't been our way, and I wasn't about to start.

"No? Vaughan, you've already agreed. Just get a lawyer to look at it and if there is something you want to change we can negotiate."

She was trying to be polite, her jaw ticking with frustration while she kept her tone even and her words *nice*. And I suspected she wanted nothing more than to tell me exactly how she felt.

"I'm not reading or signing jack shit until we work through this. I've agreed to do it your way. I'm going to trust you, hand over what little I have left, and believe in my heart you will not fuck me over. But in order for me to believe that, you and I need to be friends. We don't have to be besties joined at the hip, but I expect conversation, interaction, to seem like you give a shit. Even if it's only for my benefit. And you need to stop acting like a robot."

Her eyes flared, that carefully curated façade cracking as she stood up. "I'm not a fucking robot," she hissed out through her clenched jaw. "Do you think that it's part of my job description to sit here and smile and feed your ego? Well newsflash, it isn't. And given your track record with your *friends* I'd say you're better off without them. So read the contract or don't, but I won't let you tell me how I should or shouldn't act."

Every single word dripped with venom, nothing controlled or calm about her. And I bet if I pushed her a little more, she'd unleash the seven gates of hell. It was exciting and terrifying, and so freaking hot I was concerned that I'd become some kind of deviant. Even her insult, tossed at me casually about my poor friendship choices in the past, got me hard. The fact she hadn't censored herself turned me on more than it should.

"Well, I guess you told me." I bit back my smile, holding out my hand. "So let me see the contract."

It was tempting to keep it going, argue a little more and see how far I could push it. But I didn't want to be too predictable. Besides, pissing her off to the point I had to worry about being smothered in my sleep wasn't a good plan. She had money and a private jet, getting rid of my corpse wouldn't be an issue for her.

Her mouth dropped open, that jaw she'd been grinding, relaxing as her eyes widened. Not what she'd expected, the fight in her simmering underneath. She turned, unzipped the front of her suitcase, which was sitting beside the couch, and pulled out a folder. She opened it, looked it over and tossed it at me, the pages hitting me in the chest.

"Here. Enjoy."

Laughing wouldn't be a good plan, so I pushed down the chuckle and returned to my kitchen table about four steps away. There I sat down—casually—and perused the pages like I was actually reading them. Truth be told, I wasn't reading shit, too pleased with myself to want to ruin it with legal jargon.

I could feel her eyes on me, keeping her distance while she watched. And didn't that make me ecstatic, relaxing into the chair as I enjoyed the attention.

"Well everything looks in order." I turned the contract back to the front page and left it on the table. My feet hit the ground, standing as I faced her. "Got a pen?"

She scoffed, all the previous pretense abandoned as I got to see glimpses of the real her. "You're just going to sign?"

"Sure, we're trusting each other, right? Might as well go all in." I shrugged, not even the slightest bit concerned.

"Are you crazy?" Her brow crinkled in confusion, her voice hissing out. "I mean, *really* crazy? You signed a contract last time without reading it properly and you saw exactly what you lost. Why in the hell would you do it again?"

She had a valid point, but I was busy making my own. And really, what did I care if the manufactured band—and I used that term loosely—she created didn't work out? Seemed like it was a bigger risk for her than me. Sure, they could try and sue me, and they could enjoy the whole bunch of nothing available for them to take.

"Didn't you want me to sign it?" I chuckled. "Wouldn't be good business sense on your part to prolong it. You've already invested how much? Seems to me the one who is crazy is you."

And if I was worried she was going to crawl back into her shell, she didn't disappoint me. "You are infuriating, I don't know why I even agreed to this. I should have left you to sort it out all by yourself."

"Nah, you like me. I can tell." I grinned.

It was a throwaway line, the expectation that she'd deny it. She'd tell me she didn't want to be friends or I was delusional or some other BS, and maybe we'd even laugh about it. But she didn't, her expression changing as her eyes warmed. And if I didn't know better maybe I'd hit a nerve.

"Is that what it is?" I moved closer, throwing whatever game plan I had out the window as I closed the distance between us. "You like me?"

She didn't move, staying exactly where she was as I raised my hand. My fingers tentative, seeking permission before they touched her. And fuck me, she didn't stop it, my hands cupping her face as her golden eyes looked up at me.

"I remember touching you exactly like this in the park," I whispered, running my thumb along her jaw. "I wanted to kiss you."

"Why?" she asked. Not annoyed or sarcastically, just seeming to be genuinely interested. It was like it hadn't occurred to her that someone would want to.

I brought my lips closer, positive at any minute she was going to put on the brakes. "Because you're beautiful and I want to know what your mouth feels like."

Her eyes stayed locked on mine, her hands reaching up and touching my fingers. "I won't sleep with you, I don't have sex with musicians."

It was an interesting choice of words, because unless I was mistaken, no one had mentioned sex. Not that I wasn't desperate to touch more of her skin, or curious how far she'd unravel when she came. But at that moment, my focus was her mouth and how damn sweet she'd taste in mine.

"But you'll let me kiss you?" I asked, not wanting there to be any misunderstanding on what I intended to do.

Her pink tongue slid across her bottom lip, making me groan. I wasn't sure if she was just trying to torture me or if that was the green light, her hands on mine getting tighter.

"Yes."

Her voice was reed thin, breathy and hot, and so damn tempting I had to stop myself from attacking her lips. Instead I held back, bringing my mouth in slow and gently pressing it against hers. A small moan traveled up her throat, her lips parting and letting me inside. It was all I could take, heat roaring in my ears as mine crushed down on hers, my tongue explored the inside of her mouth.

It was exactly how I expected it, her taking and giving in equal parts, refusing to be dominated as I tried to control the tempo. Not that I cared, letting her believe she was the one leading the dance as I took what I wanted. It was hot and heavy, her teeth playing with my bottom lip when I threatened to take it away. And I can tell you, I had no intention of stopping.

My hands that had been busy cupping her face, moved, one sliding down to her neck while the other tangled in her hair. She decided to do her own touch and feel, her fingers bunching up my T-shirt and exploring my chest.

I loved it, the tips of her fingernails scratched against my skin as our kiss deepened, my need to keep it going higher than my need to breathe.

"Vaughan," she moaned out my name between kisses and I almost came in my pants. She might have made it clear that it wasn't going to end with sex but my dick wasn't convinced, the rod in my jeans able to cut glass as it struggled against my fly.

"Fuck." My hand tightened in her hair. "You have me so juiced up right now I'm going to blow my load."

She laughed, kissing my neck and nipping against my throat. "Just from kissing? I thought rock stars had more stamina than that."

The taunt made me snap, reaching down to her ass and hauled her onto me, grinding against her with my hard-on. She stopped laughing, her mouth forming an O as she felt me between her legs, the proof I wasn't kidding getting up close and personal with the seam of her jeans. Her hips bucked, moving herself into position so I hit her just right, her breathing accelerating as her fingers slid up and down my chest.

"Vaughan." Her eyes flashed with so much need, I almost blacked out. "That feels so good."

"Feels good for me too." My mouth returned to hers, wanting more of a taste.

If it had been any other woman, I would have stripped us both and sunk so deep into her she'd forget her own name. But unless she'd had a change of heart, she'd said we weren't fucking. And that was fine by me, I was happy to do exactly what we were doing. My mouth and hands on her while she explored me, my skin on fire as she reached down and rubbed my crotch.

"I shouldn't be doing this." I wasn't sure who she was trying to convince, her fingers squeezing through the denim. "I should be stopping."

"You should be doing what you want, and if that is me, then so be it," I hissed out, my jaw tight while she jerked me off through my jeans.

Not one to be selfish, my own hands got busy, rubbing between her legs where my cock had been. She mewled in approval, throwing her head back as she popped open my top button and lowered my zipper.

I reciprocated, following her lead as I did the same to her, waiting to see what she was going to do next. She reached for my cock, stroking it through my boxer shorts, as I also kept my hands outside of her panties.

The thin cotton barrier did nothing to disguise how wet she was getting, my fingers sliding over the fabric as I worked her clit. She did the same, tightening her grip as her strokes increased in speed.

It was fucking insane, my balls drawn up so tight against me as I rocked into her hand. I wasn't going to last, the little noises she made as she bucked against me threatening to do me in.

"I'm going to make you come, Gillian. Not with my dick like I want, but I'm going to make you come anyway."

She murmured, nodding her head with a breathy, "Okay."

Whatever restraint I had left was gone, my finger sliding into her panties and making contact with her skin. She moaned against my neck, digging her hand into my boxers and gripped me tight.

I pushed her against the wall, taking her mouth as I teased her, her fist locked around me as she pumped against my shaft. It was the hottest sex I'd ever had while not having sex, every tug and pull she gave me felt down to my toes as my fingers got coated in her honey.

I swallowed her groan, feeling her excitement growing as I plunged in a finger. My thumb kept busy on the outside, circling her sensitive skin as I pumped into her.

Not to be outdone, she sunk her other hand into my boxers, cupping my balls while the one that was locked around my cock continued its tight, fast slide up and down my shaft.

It was madness, racing to see which one of us would crack first as neither backed off. I was losing sensation in my legs, staving off the urge to come as she kissed me, the moan morphing into a muted scream as I kissed her back and felt her explode on my hand.

"Vaughan."

"I'm right here with you, Gillian. Right here."

It was both a plea and promise, her pussy squeezed my fingers as she rode out the wave, my turn coming soon after as I shot my load into her hand.

The kissing slowed, my lips lingering on hers, not wanting to stop. I had no idea what was going to happen after, but with my fingers still buried in her and my mouth on hers all I cared about was that moment.

"This was such a bad idea," she mumbled against my lips, not showing any sign of stopping either. "It must have been yours."

I laughed, kissing her neck as I pulled back to look at her. With her glassy eyes, a swollen mouth and messed up hair, she was absolute perfection. I liked her like that, sagged against the wall so pliable and relaxed.

"I might have been the one to suggest it." I chuckled between kisses. "You didn't have to agree."

Sliding my hand out of her panties, I noticed she still had a hold of my cock. Not that I was going to bring attention to it, happy for her to hold him as long as she wanted. Hell, if she was patient and waited a few minutes he'd be hard and ready for another round if that's what she wanted.

"I liked it." Her eyes dropped down between us, milking whatever was left in my dick. "I liked this."

And fuck me, I liked it too.

"Is that you feeding my ego? I noticed you were smiling and everything." The grin spread across my mouth. "Or did we become friends?"

Not a question I usually asked, especially after making a woman come. But with Gillian I had no idea if she'd suffered temporary insanity and was going to reestablish the distance the minute she let go of my cock.

Like she'd read my mind, her grip loosened, leaning back against the wall and letting out a slow sigh. "You were right, I like you. But I'm not sure that makes us friends."

It was such a bizarre statement I could only blink back in response. It wasn't like a brush off, more like a riddle. She liked me but didn't know what to do with it, the idea of some kind of exchange with me foreign.

"Because we have to work together, or something else?" I asked, wondering if she was concerned about professional integrity or if it was personal.

She shrugged, retreating a little into herself. "For a lot of reasons, but working together is a good one."

Well that answered a whole lot of nothing.

"I better go get cleaned up." She pushed off from the wall. "Please get an attorney to look over that contract before you sign it."

And just like that, she was gone. Like a door sliding into place, the woman I'd just been inside of with my mouth and my hand disappeared. Done. Reverted to her former icy self.

But unfortunately for her, I'd seen what was behind the wall and I wasn't about to let it go. Not a chance. Not when I knew how amazing she was.

"Sure, I'll get it looked over tomorrow." I stepped back, ignoring my dick was still hanging out of my pants. "Might call it a night then, see you in the morning."

And without turning to see if she was glad or relieved, I went to my bedroom and shut the door.

I'd give her the battle, let her think whatever happened next was her idea—I was in no rush. Because there was no way I was losing the war.

16

Gillian

He'd left without a fight or a scene, saying goodnight and going to his room. It was unexpected and a relief, thankfully he didn't suggest we both head to his bed and pick up where we left off.

What we did was stupid, a lapse in judgment and a complete lack of self-control. He was gorgeous and turned me on, but I wasn't an animal in heat controlled by hormonal impulses. Although looking at the evidence—two mutual orgasms—I guess I was.

It not only set a bad precedent, but would ruin my reputation if it ever got out. It was hard enough for a woman to succeed in a corporate environment, just a hint there'd been something sexual and I'd be the punch line to every lunchtime joke.

So fucking stupid.

I gently banged my head against the wall of the shower, thankful I was able to find it and the linen closet without needing to ask Vaughan. Not that his apartment was very big, the mystery of where his bathroom was hidden behind a door opposite his room.

As tempting as it was to drain all his hot water and linger in the shower, I got out, dried off and dressed in a pair of yoga pants and a T-shirt. There was no way I was slipping into the sleep shorts and tank top I'd packed, not when I was sleeping on the couch.

Once I was back in the living room, I pulled out the bed from the sofa and threw down a few blankets and pillows. It wasn't ideal but surprisingly more comfortable than I'd thought it was going to be. And while I hated being exposed, secretly wishing I was back in my apartment in Manhattan, I forced myself to close my eyes and go to sleep. I'd deal with whatever fall out in the morning, because last time I checked I couldn't go back in time. Not sure I wanted to, my mind wandered as I snuggled deeper under the blankets. It had felt so good so I was having a hard time regretting it. I knew that I should and yet . . .it was just one time, how bad could it be.

I woke up to the smell of freshly brewed coffee and toast, slightly confused as I reached for my phone. I never slept in, conditioned to wake up early so that I barely set my alarm anymore. It was only four-forty-five a.m.

"Good morning." His voice thick from sleep and who knew what else, rumbled from the kitchen, leaning against his counter as he lifted a cup to his lips.

I rubbed my eyes, not quite orientated as I sat up. "What are you doing up so early?" I knew for a fact he hated mornings, which was typical with musicians.

"You liked to run. Figured you might want a tour guide since you don't know the area. And I can't run on an empty stomach." He turned, putting his cup in the sink before stepping out into the living room and revealing his running shorts and long sleeved tight running top.

Nothing was left to the imagination, the fabric curling around his torso like a second skin, the shorts exposing his toned long legs, and his ass—it was too spectacular for words.

"You want me to make you some breakfast?" He folded his arms across his chest, flexing more muscles than I knew what to do with in my half-asleep state.

"No, no I can't eat before I run. It's counter productive." I shook my head, pushing off the covers and standing up to stretch. His eyes followed me, watching in silence as I twisted my body, elongating each muscle before releasing.

"What?" I asked, noticing he was staring.

He grinned making no attempt to hide the fact. "I've never seen you in regular clothes or colors." He pointed to my yoga pants and T-shirt. "Your body is amazing, why the hell do you hide it under all those layers?"

It hadn't occurred to me that he hadn't seen me in what he called *regular clothes*. My preference for structured corporate wear consisted of black functional garments that didn't accentuate my figure. It was easy, looked good and made me feel powerful. Like putting on my battle armor when I went out to war. Was it weird that even though he'd had his fingers inside of me, he hadn't seen much of my body?

"Grey isn't a color, it's a shade," I corrected, ignoring the part where he said my body was amazing. I didn't even know what to do with that or whether he was just saying it because he wanted to annoy me.

I'd assumed the next morning would be awkward. We'd dance around it, debating whether or not to acknowledge what happened the night before, the inevitable chat something I was dreading.

But none of it was there. No questions, no looks, no hint of assumptions—and other than commenting on my body, nothing much had changed.

He ran a hand through his new shorter hair, the edges spiking in all different directions. "Thanks for the art lesson, are we going or not?"

It was tempting to tell him to forget it, because I ran alone. I didn't like an audience, enjoying the time just for me. But missing it made me feel off kilter, the time outside a vital part of my daily routine.

"Don't overthink it. Get dressed and let's go. Besides, I'm going anyway. Don't you want to come and watch me? Make sure I don't get into any trouble?"

I rolled my eyes, cursing under my breath as I got up. He knew exactly which buttons to press, not shy about pressing them all. "Give me ten minutes."

He watched as I pulled out my running gear from my suitcase and carried it all to the bathroom. I changed quickly, brushing my teeth and pulling my hair back, looking at my reflection in his full-length mirror.

My body was curvy but fit. No matter what weight was displayed on the scales I'd always had a pair of boobs, hips and an ass. And I wasn't ashamed of it despite keeping it mostly under wraps. But when I ran, all bets were off. My compression leggings and top were designed for comfort and support, forming to my body and hiding none of it. If he'd noticed it before, he was definitely going to get an eyeful when I stepped out.

Refusing to be self conscious about it, I strode out with my runners already laced and ready to go. His eyes widened, rolling restlessly up and down my body as I put my hands on my hips and raised my chin.

"I'm back in black. Sorry to disappoint you if you were waiting for *color*."

His Adam's apple bobbed, taking a breath as he grabbed his keys. "Definitely not disappointed. But I'm not sure I'm going to be able to run with a hard-on."

I hid my smile, slightly annoyed at how pleased his reaction made me. The objective wasn't to try to seduce him, so not sure why any of it mattered. But common sense hadn't ranked highly in the last few days, especially in the last twenty-four hours. So rather than analyze or fight it, I gave in and enjoyed the attention. It didn't have to mean anything, and there was nothing wrong with an ego boost.

"I hope you can keep up," I called over my shoulder heading toward the door.

He followed a half step behind me. "Let's go find out."

It was still dark outside, the air crisp as we walked to the parking lot. It was nothing like Manhattan, the noise of the busy morning commute missing as we started off slow down the mostly empty road.

There was no discussion, no questions as to what route we were taking or how far we were going. Instead we fell into a comfortable rhythm, Vaughan letting me set the pace and matching my strides. His legs were longer, and he could out sprint me in a heartbeat but he didn't even try. While speed was tempting, I preferred distance, settling into the run after a half a mile, my breathing evening out.

By mile three, I almost forgot he was there, my mind taking its usual vacation while my feet continued to pound against the pavement. The burn of my muscles energized me as we continued for two more miles in silence.

It wasn't until we rounded the corner, and I saw we were back at his apartment that I realized we'd ran the whole time without saying a word. It was as if he knew it was my solace, joining me on the journey while respecting its sanctity.

He grinned opening his front door. "You want the first shower? Or second?" Waiting for me to step through before following me in.

"You should go first, it's your bathroom." It seemed only fair, especially after how considerate he had been. I tried not to let it excite me, his sweetness so unexpected. It was just a run; it didn't mean anything. And for all I knew he didn't like talking while exercising either.

"Okay, I'll be quick. Not so much to do in there now I don't have so much hair." He tossed me a wave, striding in the direction of the shower.

It was a completely innocent statement, devoid of any innuendo. But all I could think about was him naked under the spray, and what that might look like. How his hands would glide over his skin as the suds snaked down his body, caressing those muscles before washing down the drain. I closed my eyes and let myself enjoy the fantasy, picturing myself in that steam-filled room as he touched himself.

My internal temperature rose, a flush spreading across my skin, and the run not responsible for any of it. And instead of changing my focus and banishing my dirty thoughts, I delved into them deeper, inserting myself into the fantasy with him.

I'd seen him wearing only a towel, and touched him all over. Unfortunately when giving him a hand job, he had still been wearing clothes, so I wasn't able to get a decent look. But I'd felt it, my imagination not having to stray too far to conjure up what he would look like. And even in my conservative estimate, I bet he was spectacular.

He was thick, my hand barely getting around his girth, the bulge it had created in his pants, impressive. And based on what he was able to do with his hands, I was positive his equipment wasn't decorative.

All those reasons for not sleeping with him started to seem invalid. Oh, I knew it would probably still be a mistake, and I might even regret it later. But as the water continued to run in the bathroom, I stopped myself from knocking on the door and dancing with trouble.

I was still deep in the debate when the water cut off, the decision made for me when he immerged from the steam-filled room with a towel around his waist. All that kindness and consideration he'd shown earlier was completely gone, my body tingling as I watched him stride with confidence toward me.

"All yours." He smirked, and I had to remind myself that his body wasn't what was on offer, the bathroom the only thing that was mine if I wanted it.

I pushed down the urge to kiss him, moving to the bathroom and closing the door before I had a chance to change my mind. It was only once I was inside that I realized I didn't bring in any clean clothes.

"Shit," I muttered under my breath, annoyed I'd been so distracted.

Either I walked back out there and at the very least grab the yoga pants and T-shirt I'd slept in, or put on my dirty, sweaty running stuff. Yeah that wasn't going to happen, the tight leggings and top hard enough to pull on when they weren't damp. There was a third option, something I normally wouldn't even consider. Of course I usually didn't let men I wasn't dating finger me to orgasm, so the point was probably moot.

Guess I was walking out there in a towel like he had, my mind made up as I stripped off. And all the justification in the world didn't convince me I wasn't thrilled at the prospect. I'd already established when it came to him I made bad choices, what were a few more? My grin widened as I stepped into the water, the fantasy I'd had a few moments before suddenly getting a reboot.

17

Vaughan

I'd been in the bathroom exactly a minute before I reached down to my cock, the need to release the pressure at an all-time high. It was either I took care of myself or chop my dick clean off. I went with the former given I was kind of fond of it.

Her running outfit was not the sweatpants and hoodie I was expecting, instead a tight combo of lycra that showed exactly what I was missing. And it was either run, keep my body moving and my mouth shut or pin her against a wall and do a repeat of the night before. Yeah, cause that had gone so well for us.

So we ran.

Ran five freaking miles and I didn't say one word, let her do her thing and if she wanted to pretend I was invisible, so be it. Not a hardship, especially when I got to spend time with her and got a peek behind the curtain. It was obvious she didn't share her runs with anyone, preferring to go it alone. But that wouldn't fly, so I played by her rules and was rewarded with greatness.

Not a kiss like I'd wanted, but with her smile and her time. Something told me she didn't give either of those things away easily, and I was just a sucker for the attention.

The shower had been great, the tug necessary, and it wasn't until she emerged from my bathroom that the full extent of my awesome morning was revealed. Gillian was not only pink and damp from her shower but showing all kinds of skin, barely covered by a towel.

Thank you, I whispered a silent prayer to the man upstairs. I didn't care what I'd done to deserve it but I was taking it as a win. The rewards just kept coming.

"I'm making eggs, you want in?" I waved the spatula, keeping the conversation polite but unable to pull my eyes away from her cleavage. The running shirt had done a stellar job showcasing her rack, but that towel she was wearing deserved some kind of award.

She nodded, strolling over to her suitcase like she wasn't half naked. "Thanks, that would be great."

Like some stupid game, neither of us willing to concede, we didn't acknowledge the elephant it the room. Namely what we did last night, and whether or not she'd let me do it again. And if she thought I'd be the first one to crack, she'd greatly underestimated my patience.

Grabbing what she needed, she went back to the bathroom to get dressed. If I was a halfway decent guy, I might have looked away. But I didn't, enjoying the view as she disappeared.

It wasn't just the eggs that were scrambled, my brain feeling the same as I grabbed the bacon out of the broiler and shoveled breakfast onto plates.

She remerged in her usual garb, black on black, with some extra black for good measure. Too bad the damage had already been done, the game of hide the hotness a complete waste of time when I knew what she was packing underneath. Still, if she wanted to go through the motions, she'd get no complaints from me. But I was definitely going running every morning, and buying a bunch of smaller towels.

We sat at my kitchen table, my grin unable to be contained as she looked at the signed contract sitting right beside her plate. I knew it would needle her, and call me crazy but I was sort of itching for a fight. It was the one sure-fire way to unveil the real her, and that was the Gillian I preferred.

"I thought I told you to get an attorney to look over it." She met my eyes, fire brewing in hers.

Game. On.

"And we've already established I don't do what you say. So there you go." I forked some of my eggs, bringing them to my mouth and chewing thoughtfully. Hey, I had manners, or at least I did when it came to eating.

"Fine." She shoved the contract aside and started on her own breakfast. The unspoken curse simmered inside her, the grip on her fork a little too tight.

If she thought quiet time was going to continue, she was going to be disappointed. I'd been respectful, keeping my mouth shut during the run, but breakfast was a different story and I wasn't going to sit there in silence.

"So, I was thinking about band members. Obviously Nico is still in." Lord knows the guy had more than earned his place, not to mention he'd been a better friend to me than I'd probably deserved. "And I have a few buddies who might be interested, maybe we should give them a call?" I glanced over, waiting for her reaction. Considering she hadn't even told me what kind of music I was supposed to be playing, I'd say my *suggestions* were a little premature.

"I assumed you wanted to keep Nico. But these other guys? They play a similar style to you?" She surprised me by entertaining the idea.

"Yep, hard hitting, and monstrous guitars. They're not the best in the biz but they make up for it in enthusiasm. Not heavy metal, because I know that's out. But hard rock for sure. BIG sound." It was almost like a regular conversation, who knew it was possible. The subject content making me more excited about playing than I had been the last few days.

"Well, it's a shame that isn't the direction we're going in. I've got Emily fielding some prospectives for me, we should know in a day or two." She shot it down so fast it was clear she'd been humoring me. No intention of meeting my friends or considering them for the band.

It should have annoyed me, but it got me curious. Where was she going to find these magical mythical band members, ready to play on her command? Not something you could pop down to the store to pick up, snatch up a decent guitarist while grabbing a quart of milk.

"Emily is fielding prospectives?" I raised a brow, wanting to know more. "She holding open auditions like they did for those boy bands back in the 90s?"

This earned me a smile, not a big one but one she didn't bother hiding. "No, she's scouting. Finding someone tailored to our needs."

"You realize this is a band and not a sports coat? All this talk of tailored to our needs makes me nervous." It wasn't a lie, it was still going to be my name on the docket. And if she recruited a bunch of clowns based on some invisible bullshit criteria, then we were going to have issues.

"Relax, I've got this," she said with surprising ease. "But while we're discussing it, now would be a good time to talk about your voice."

For all the calm I'd shown earlier—not even mentioning how amazing her tits were—talk of my voice put an end to it. I knew I was cocky, and got a fair amount of attention because of the way I looked, but my voice was solid and I sure as shit could sing.

"What about my voice?" I gave up eating, dropping the fork and trying to keep my cool. If she was going to turn it into some bullshit critique and pick me apart, we were going to have problems.

She noticed the chill, and possibly my death stare, because she immediately started talking. "No, not like that. Your voice is beautiful, so much light and shade, you have amazing tone."

Not what I was expecting, but still nice to hear. "But?"

"But no one can hear it when you're screaming. Your talent is completely wasted growling lyrics like it's a satanic ritual. In the park, where you *actually* sung—it was breathtaking. That is what you should be doing. That is how you should sound. You're done hiding behind the hair, so step out from mediocrity."

I was not mediocre.

"You really want to talk to me about hiding?" I pointed at her outfit, the threads responsible for disguising her form and where sexy went to die.

"This isn't about me." She screwed up her brow, unable to see the parallel. "And you've been wasting your talent. Vaughan, do you know how many artists I've seen? How many would *kill* for a voice like yours? You've been given a gift, don't waste it."

"Pot. Kettle." I stared right back at her. "I could almost repeat all of that back to you verbatim. Well, not about the singing part, but you're smart, gorgeous and driven. You're funny and honest. A lethal combination that both men and women would sell a kidney for. But most people wouldn't know, too afraid of you to notice. You're so fucking cold."

She pulled back—both literally and figuratively—as what I said hit her square in the chest. I hadn't meant it to be so harsh, the words clearly hurting her even though she'd schooled her expression. It wasn't a good thing; any strides we'd made moving forward decimated.

"Thanks for breakfast." She lifted her half-eaten plate and carried it to the sink. "I need to start working on proposals and you should get working on some songs. Keep them free of distortion, and let your voice feature." And with her final directive, she went back to her laptop, retreating behind her wall.

Deciding to give us both some space, I grabbed my keys and went over to see my parents. Gillian didn't ask where I was going, and I didn't volunteer the information. Instead, I went to the house where I'd gotten my first guitar, and I let my mother yell at me a little for causing her worry. I didn't even mind she was getting on my case, happy to be around someone who didn't think thirty-five times about what they were going to say before it came out of their mouth.

Then after I'd gotten an earful, a bunch of hugs and enough homemade cookies to negate the morning run, I got back into my truck and headed to Point State Park. The confluence of the Alleghany, Ohio and Monongahela rivers was the very place where White Trash Circus was formed. Wanting to prove that we could be just like the Mon—flowing south to north—going in the opposite direction of everyone else and still be a part of something great.

I was about to leave when I picked up my phone and dialed a number I didn't think I was ever going to call again.

"Vaughan?" He sounded surprised but no less surprised than I was, which was funny considering I was the one making the call.

"Why did you do it, Connor? Why her?"

I'd never thought I'd needed the answer, convinced both of them were just evil assholes and I was better without them in my life. But even though I'd talked a good game, the sting was still there, lingering just underneath the surface.

"Dude . . . honestly, it just happened. She was sad you were spending so much time with the band and thought you didn't love her anymore. I," he paused, probably evaluating whether or not to keep going. "I guess I told her that you'd never love anything as much as the music. Her, me . . .we were always going to be second place."

A strange sense of calm spread through me, the anger I'd previously felt ebbing as I looked out at the water. Ironic that the birthplace of White Trash Circus is where it finally died too. And maybe he was right in some ways, I'd cared about both of them but White Trash Circus had always come first.

"Look, man, I'm sorry," he continued, reading my silence like I needed to hear more. "If I could take it all back—"

"It doesn't matter anymore." And strangely, I meant that. The past couldn't be changed and to be honest, I didn't think I'd want to. Not that I was going to be hanging with either of them drinking beers and reminiscing, but I was done hating them. "Have a nice life, Connor. I hope it's everything you wanted."

I ended the call, the venom and malice I'd have thrown behind those words a week or so ago was MIA, and for the most part I was sincere. Okay, maybe I wasn't completely zen about it just yet, but I knew I would be. Lindsey, Connor—none of it was important anymore.

I didn't bother to linger, the trip down memory lane no longer needed. My phone buzzed as I got back in my car, the message from Nico letting me know he was stopping by later. I'd half expected it to be Gillian, demanding to know where I was. I wondered how pissed she'd be when I got home, my little excursion taking hours. I headed back to my apartment and found her exactly where I left her, she was deep in thought, tapping her lip as she stared at her computer screen.

"Going to write, let me know when Nico gets here." I waited to see if she had anything to add, or grill me on my disappearance.

"Vaughan." She looked up, no doubt she'd been concerned but held back like usual. "I'm really looking forward to hearing it."

I'd been such an asshole. Not only for what I'd said earlier but for not telling her where I'd been. I owed her more than that, not because she was staying with me and I'd kissed her, but because it was the decent thing to do.

"Thanks." I nodded, the gratitude for so much more than the compliment. And with not much left to say, I disappeared back into my room, determined to write something good.

Not something I screamed, filled with noise and head banging, but something from the heart, and that meant more than just pleasing a crowd.

18

Vaughan

Much to my disappointment, we didn't end the evening with a hot and heavy make out session. Chalked up as a one-time deal, I wasn't sure I'd get the chance again. And what a freaking shame that would be.

Proving she wasn't as predictable as I thought, she changed into jeans and a T-shirt, shocking the hell out of me when she sat down to dinner with Nico and me and made small talk.

I played nice, kept my dick in my pants and the conversation polite. And when Nico left, I went back to my room and slept alone. Of course I couldn't be held responsible for the three times I'd needed to jerk off. That was between me and my hand, both of us giving full consent.

The early morning alarm had been both a blessing and a curse. Waking up before noon wasn't my favorite thing to do but infinitely more enjoyable when I had a project. Spending time with Gillian better than most reasons.

And yeah, I had a bad track record. Getting infatuated with a woman was as easy for me as getting a cold. But I'd learned a lot in the last few days, and despite my tendency to fall hard and fast, it wasn't about some revenge fuck I needed to have because my girlfriend cheated. Or even just the urge to get laid. With Gillian, it was different. Something about her and the situation that was more than me just having a boo to tag on an Instagram post. Assuming I did that, which I sure as shit did not.

I didn't even curse as I pulled on my running shorts, fucking delighted about getting to watch her run another five miles. That outfit she wore was freaking amazing, and whoever designed it needed a Nobel Peace Prize. Her tits, a motherfucking Oscar.

Like she'd anticipated the repeat, she was already awake and dressed—thank you Lord, she had another one of those outfits—by the time I walked out to the living room. She'd even packed the bed away, the mattress folded up into the couch with the pillows and blankets neatly staked on the end. Almost as if she was trying to get out and get gone before I'd woken up—Ha! Not likely.

"You weren't trying to ditch me, were you?" I smirked, my hand hovering over my heart like I was wounded. "That wouldn't be very nice."

Her eyes flared in surprise, the time closer to four thirty than five and there I was, ready to go.

"No," she lied. "I was going to do some stretching before we went."

I waved my hand, folding my arms across my chest and pretending I wasn't going to enjoy it. "Well go ahead then, don't let me stop you. I can wait."

Her eyes narrowed, needing to decide whether to cut the bullshit and admit the lie or continue with the ruse. And much to my delight, she chose option two, lowering herself to the floor and giving me a show I would have paid good money for.

Who needed porn?

Seeing a woman with a knockout body limber up on your living room floor was better than anything on the internet.

When she was satisfied she'd played it out enough—or got tired of my obvious gawking—she jumped up, ready to get on the road. She wasn't the only one who had jumped, with me finding out first-hand if it was possible to run with an erection.

Happy to know that it was.

Not that I wasn't hating life as we finished those five miles, but I got through it and had even managed to keep my mouth shut. Not that I hadn't wanted to partake in conversation—especially with her—but it was obvious that while we were running, she needed the silence. It was the least I could do, keeping my thoughts to myself and hoping she wasn't plotting my death or anything like that. She'd touched my dick and let me make her come so she couldn't hate me all that much, but I wasn't dumb enough to think that put me in the safe zone.

After showers and breakfast—the first separately, while the second done together—she sat down ready to do whatever it was that she did during the day.

I was bored just looking at it, not understanding how someone could stare at a computer screen all day and not want to toss the thing out the window.

"Hey, want to go on an adventure?" I wiggled my eyebrows hoping to tempt her.

"Vaughan, we both have work to do." She let out a disappointed sigh. "We can't just blow off work."

Ha!

We most certainly could.

The reason I'd been fired so easily was my missed shift hadn't been an isolated incident. I *might* have had a tendency to not show up if I had a better offer, the idea of sitting behind a register making me want to hang myself. And yes, I knew it was irresponsible, save your freaking judgment.

"I'm here to tell you that we can and we will." I lowered her laptop, not willing to take no for an answer. I hadn't even decided what the adventure was going to be yet, but sitting around my apartment didn't qualify.

"We're trying to keep a low profile, the less attention you draw the better." Her rebuttal not something I hadn't already thought of.

"Nothing a ball cap and a pair of shades can't fix." I pulled both out from behind my back, my disguise chilling until required. "Assuming anyone suspects I'm back, they'll be looking for the long hair. I'll even change into something douchey, I think Marcus snuck in a pair of skinny jeans and button-down shirt." I'd told him it would be a cold day in hell before I'd pull on the threads but it wasn't my dime so whatever. But it looked like Satan had called a snow day because I was ready to hipster that shit like no other.

"You're going to go change into skinny jeans and a shirt?" she asked, like she couldn't quite believe it either. "And what about me?"

"Gillian, you getting into skinny jeans has my full support. You should skip the button-down though." I'd been good most of the morning, but a man could only do so much.

She rolled her eyes, not looking too overly annoyed. "Very funny."

"No seriously, we should go." I reaffirmed my stance. "But we both need to change. You go out like that," I pointed to her usual get up, the black shroud of depression. "And people are going to know you're a tourist."

If I didn't know better, I'd say I was wearing her down. She probably would've preferred to stay in her little bubble of predictability—snore town central. But she still had a pulse and knew I'd make good on the amazing time I promised. Hell, she'd seen what I'd done with just my hands, imagine what I could achieve with my whole body.

With my clothes on, perverts.

"Okay."

The one word came faster than I'd expected, shocking the shit out of me. The urge to do a victory lap around the room too great as I fist pumped around the coffee table.

"Jeans, don't worry about the top." I gave her my pointed instructions. "Take your hair down, it's pulled up so tight I can hear your scalp screaming."

Her eyebrow rose. "No top?"

"Relax, I'm going to give you something to wear, help you blend in." My intention hadn't been the least bit shady, but since she'd mentioned it, I was going to have a hard time wiping away the grin.

"Fine. Go change." She waved her hand, giving me the green light I needed.

I didn't waste a second, sprinting to my room and pulling out one of the garment bags and getting into my disguise.

It didn't take long, my excitement making the redress happen quick despite needing a crowbar to get into the denim. If I lost the ability to have children, Marcus and I were going to have some serious words. Before heading out to meet Gillian, I pulled the jersey from my closet, pleased beyond measure she'd be wearing something of mine.

She'd already changed, a plain black tee—much to my disappointment—topping her faded blue jeans. Her dirty blond hair hung loose around her shoulders just like I'd asked, curling rebelliously around her face. Man, I could never get sick of looking at that. If I wasn't sure it would have me ending up in a pine box, I'd have offered her "work" clothes up as a sacrifice and burned them all.

"Here." I handed her the addition, watching with interest as she took it from me to inspect.

"Polamalu? Who's that?" The old Steeler jersey in her hand proudly displaying the number forty-three.

"Only one of the greatest defensive players of all time. He was a warrior, completely fearless on the field. Thought it was appropriate." And that wasn't a line either, I honestly believed it. "Look, it's black and everything," I laughed.

She groaned, hiding her grin as she pulled it over her head. It was big, the jersey flopping down and hiding more than I would have liked but still sexier than anything I'd ever seen.

"Well, get your hat on and let's go. I'll give you a half day and then you need to write at least one more song," she bargained, not knowing I already had worked on something through the night.

"Deal." I grabbed her hand even though she hadn't offered it and led her to the door. My keys were already in my hand, not sure there was enough room in the jeans. I'd barely gotten my wallet in, needing to take it out when I sat down and I had real concerns for my phone screen too.

We got into my truck, the beast having sat dormant for a while, and fired up the engine. It spluttered, needing a decent run but I had no doubt it would get us where we needed to be. Our destination—downtown.

It was a twenty-minute drive, only longer if we hit traffic, but I was in no hurry. We cruised, the stereo left off as I warmed up my voice.

She turned in her seat, openly giving me her full attention as I started to sing *Queen's* "We Are the Champions" acapella.

Not only were the lyrics ironically appropriate, but it gave me a chance to show off, stepping into Freddie Mercury's shoes as I did my best to give the song justice. My ego usually didn't need the boost, but seeing her enthralled made me feel like the biggest rock star on the planet, my chest puffing out, sitting up straight as I belted out the classic.

Unfortunately, the song wasn't long enough, the last note vibrating inside the cabin before we'd even gotten half way. But I wasn't about to give up the limelight even if it was for an audience of one. Knowing she wasn't a metal fan, I left Dickinson and Dio in my back pocket, instead proving I wasn't a one-trick pony and breaking out some Bruno Mars.

And while she might have been able to resist joining me in the chorus of my last number, she had no choice but to join me on the "woo"s of "Uptown Funk." Honestly, it was a relief too because I didn't want to have to pull the truck over and demand it. I totally would have too.

Amazing how those little things made my freaking day. Seeing her having a good time, smiling and singing—albeit limited—and knowing I was responsible. I could have driven her to Cleveland and she wouldn't have noticed, tempting considering we were already on Forbes Avenue.

We managed to get to the end of the song, finding a parking spot on the street. It felt like the universe was giving me a nod, not having to circle the block like I usually did.

"Let me guess, Primanti Brothers." She chuckled, the Pittsburgh icon the obvious choice.

"Nope, too classy." I shook my head with a grin, my fingers killing the ignition. "We're slumming it today."

Not giving her any more clues, I opened my door, her following suit and meeting me on the sidewalk. Then just as I'd done at the house, I'd grabbed her hand and led her to my first destination, *The Original Hot Dog Shop* in all its dirty, greasy glory.

The place looked like a shithole, built in the shadow of Forbes Field. Older than dirt with a similar chemical makeup, it wasn't a place you went unless you were cool with having your dining experience with a side order of hand sanitizer. But for all its grunge and questionable bathrooms, the food didn't share the same danger of Ecoli; the fries some of the best I'd ever tasted.

"We're having hot dogs?" she asked, looking less than impressed.

I laughed, wondering if I should push my luck. Ah, screw it. I'd never been a safe kind of guy and being cautious didn't get you anywhere.

"We call this place the O, figured I'd give you one, one way or another."

Her hand ricocheted off my chest, her smirk proving she wasn't mad. And thank God for that.

It was the first time I'd even alluded to what we had done, able to bite my tongue for only so long. If she wanted it to be her rebellion, her almost one-night stand, then I'd have to deal with it. But pretending it didn't happen didn't sit well with me. Besides, I was working at chipping those walls she had around herself and making her laugh seemed like a good way to do it.

Refusing to be embarrassed—which just made me happier— she pulled open the door and walked inside. Like a puppy, I followed her in, ordering us two hot dogs, two pops and an order of fries.

We grabbed a table around the back, waiting while they cooked up the awesomeness, and glad she hadn't insisted we got our food to go. It was a possibility, and while I'd told her straight we were slumming, it was a universe away from the places she was probably used to.

Content to just sit there in silence while we waited, I couldn't help but look at her. She looked younger wearing my jersey with her hair down, looking like she hadn't made it her mission to solve all the world's problems. Of course I knew it wasn't world hunger and the economic crisis that kept her up at night and wearing an almost permanent scowl. But in her world, her problems were no less important. Even a guy like me got that, that with her privilege came responsibility. But at least at that moment we could put a pin in it, pretend she was just a girl I'd met and we were on a date.

"You come here a lot?" she asked, attempting to make conversation as she looked around.

Jesus, she made this shit too easy.

"Are you hitting on me, Gillian?" I smirked at her, knowing full well that hadn't been her intention.

She shook her head, unable to hide the smile. "Come on, Vaughan. I know I'd have to use a better pick-up line than that. Especially since you took me to such a fine establishment."

"Ha, now with the jokes. I have to say, if you're trying to impress me, you're doing an excellent job."

That wasn't sarcasm; I was genuinely impressed. But she was wrong about needing a better line, she could have given me any number of BS dripping with cheese and I would have eaten it up. The fact she had no idea was freaking bewildering.

Our order being called saved me from making an ass of myself and telling her my thoughts. Instead we ate, her eyes bulging to maximum at the massive basket of fries that we just called large.

"Have you spoken to your parents?" She nibbled on her dog, her second attempt at small talk more successful than the first. "I'm assuming they aren't pleased you're still working with me."

Yeah, that was an understatement.

"My parents just want what's best for me," I reasoned, their hearts in the right place and always supporting me. "But they haven't told me what to do in a very long time. Even if they see me making a mistake, it's mine to make."

"Is that what they see this as? A mistake?"

It was the first time I'd heard hesitation in her voice, the confidence she usually rocked, MIA. And I wasn't sure if she meant Domination or if it was her.

"Doesn't matter, I know it's not." I waved off the question, not giving a shit what anyone else thought. "What about you? Your dad is obviously a hard ass but what about your mom?"

There was a second of panic, her eyes locking with mine and I immediately regretted the question. After all, even though I knew Warrick liked to upgrade his wife more than a Microsoft operating system, I had no idea if the trend had started after burying the first.

"Look, Gillian, you don't need to tell—"

"I don't know." She cut off my apology, surprising me by answering the question. "I haven't seen her since I was two and my recollection before she left isn't great. I don't remember a lot."

Whoa.

What?

Of all the reasons I'd conjured up, her mother leaving wasn't even in my top twenty. The idea of her mother bailing and not even checking in once and a while not something I could wrap my head around.

"She just left?" I heard myself ask, wanting to beat my own ass for being such an insensitive prick.

"Yeah, one day she said she was going out and didn't come back. She packed a bag so it was obviously something she'd been planning. Not sure if that makes it better or worse." She let out a humorless laugh. "A few months later she filed for divorce, or at least that is the story my dad tells me. I don't really have another side to go on."

"I'm sorry."

What for I hadn't decided. For asking the question? For life dealing her a shitty hand when it came to parents? For growing up without a mother? All valid and all making me feel like a tool. I'd always assumed she'd had it easy—or at least easier—never thinking what she might have had to do without.

She shook off my apology, taking none of it as her gaze didn't waver. "Don't be. I got Mara and Emily, and they made the choice rather than sticking around out of obligation. Choosing to be in my life and care, that's a million times better than a biological parent who doesn't. It's hard, you know. Not feeling wanted, especially by someone who is supposed to love you. But I guess it was for the best, from what I've heard about my mother, she wasn't very maternal."

There was no sadness in her voice, all of it spoken so matter of fact that I had to wonder if expecting people to be assholes was her default. I sure as hell didn't need confirmation to know it wasn't the kind of thing she shared. Not Gillian Duzan, who believed lowering her defenses was letting someone see her in a pair of yoga pants. What she'd given me was a gift, a treasure that I wanted to hold close to my heart and give thanks for.

And fuck me, I wanted to kiss her.

Not because I felt sorry for her—because she didn't need my sympathy—but because she was ten thousand ways of special, and I was honored I got to see it.

"Don't look at me like that." Her finger pointed in accusation.

"Like I want to kiss you?" I answered honestly, respecting her too much to give her a lie.

If she leaned across the table even an inch, I would have made up the rest of the distance and done exactly that. Just a hint, that she wanted me to. But she didn't; her gaze looking clinical, my motives not clear enough.

And I'd wear that; she'd sure as hell earned it.

"Let's finish our food." She was diplomatic, while completely avoiding my offer. "I want to hear you sing some more."

I followed her lead, her mood shifting with subject change.

"Sure, whatever you want."

19

Vaughan

We didn't immediately go back to my apartment after The O.

She reminded me about her half-day concession, and I drove around the city telling her that if I was so agreeable she wouldn't know what to do with me.

It was partly true, but I wasn't in a hurry to go back to my four walls and whatever unknown happened next.

She agreed on my impromptu tour provided I continued to sing. Not even an issue, my voice stretching its legs as I sang everything from my older originals to the new stuff I'd been working on. I didn't have a lot, mostly melodies and a bunch of lyrics. I even threw in some covers, letting her pick the tunes like her own private shuffle play.

And when we got back to my place, she surprised me by changing things up. Instead of going back to her laptop, banishing conversation and any attempt at fun, she kept on my jersey and put all of it aside. Her attention on me as she sat, watching me tinker with my guitar as I fleshed out a song.

One of the hardest things I did that night was leave her alone in the living room. It wasn't about wanting to sleep with her—Okay, not *just* about wanting to sleep with her—I just hated the idea of her sleeping on the couch alone.

So the next day after we ran, and we'd sat down to eat breakfast, I told her she was taking my room. She argued, I refused to concede and we were left at a stalemate.

That night she slept on the couch while I set myself up on the armchair beside her. Refusing to go into my room when I'd already told her she could have it.

And in a way, we did *sleep* together. Both of us sleeping a couple of feet apart but in the same room, with a perfectly good bed going unused just down the hall.

Either way, I wasn't backing down.

I woke up with a pain in my neck, the armchair not designed for nocturnal activities. It sucked, my back not feeling so great either as I tried to straighten what was left of my spine.

"You should have gone to your bed." Gillian yawned rolling over before either of our alarms had gone off. "I told you I wasn't sleeping in it."

"Then I guess no one will." My neck flexed first left then right. Nope, still didn't feel any better.

Needing to take a piss and get suited up for our run, I left Gillian and her *suggestions*, and headed to the bathroom. It was tempting to blow off the run, get in the shower and let the hot water loosen up my muscles. But I wasn't a quitter, and the strides we were making were huge, feeling like I knew her better than most people.

Just as I was pulling on my running shorts, there was a knock at the door. I still had my shirt in my hand as I yanked it open.

"You need in here?"

She looked down at my chest before lifting her eyes back to mine. She was slick about it but I knew she checked me out, seemed only fair since I did the same to her.

"How's your back?" She didn't answer the question, her hair a mess from sleeping.

My hand rose and gave my neck a rub. "Fine, a little tight but I'll live."

"Let me see."

She walked me back toward the tub, pulling me down until I sat on the edge. It was a little early for her to be pushing me around but the change in position did perfectly align my line of sight with her tits. Figured it was a trade I was willing to make.

Once I was where she wanted me, her hands reached up and gently touched my neck, her fingers kneading the tightness.

"Mmmmmmmm, that feels good." I closed my eyes, not knowing how long it was going to last and wanting to absorb every second of it.

Not sure if it was a hidden talent or my neck was so messed up back there I couldn't tell, but her hands on me were magic. Firm but gentle, they moved across my back like she knew what she was doing.

Fuck, it was good.

So. Good.

She cleared her throat, prompting me to open an eye and catching her glancing down at my crotch. It seemed someone else thought they might be getting some hands-on action, my morning wood straining against my running shorts.

I made no excuses; her hands stopped moving the minute she caught me looking at her, *looking* at me.

Ignoring it wasn't an option, the attention he was getting making him even harder. Her not leaving was also encouraging, her eyes toggling between my hard-on and my face.

Your move, Gillian, I silently dared her, thanking Jesus for the crick in my neck that got us there.

And she didn't disappoint.

With the confidence I knew she possessed, she reached down between my legs and squeezed the head of my cock.

The groan out of my mouth—automatic.

Not sure what her plans were, if it was ending in a hand job or something else. But I would be damned if I wasn't seeing it through.

"Go ahead, Gillian. Touch me."

20

Gillian

I'd never expected to tell him about my mother, but he'd been so incredibly sweet. And while I knew maintaining a working relationship should have been the priority, I couldn't help that it became something else.

Friends.

The idea of it all more exciting than I was willing to admit.

So I was attempting to do something nice for him.

Hoping if I loosened his muscles a little, I could undo some of the damage from the armchair. And yes, it might have given me a very convenient excuse to touch him. The bare chest made it almost impossible for me to keep my hands off.

He moaned in approval, the noises making my nipples pebble as I tried to ignore the tug in my gut. It wasn't easy, Vaughan not cutting me any slack as he closed his eyes, surrendering to my hands. The erection—had been my final straw.

I wasn't even sure if it was for me, or a biological response to relaxing. But as he sat there watching me as I stared at him, my hands took over, making up my mind for me.

"Go ahead, Gillian. Touch me." His invitation a rumble as I gripped his cock. My hand releasing him only for a second before diving into his shorts.

My fingers touched skin, the contact making us both hiss, as I refamiliarized myself with his anatomy. And while I'd done it before, jerking him off with my hand down his pants wasn't going to cut it.

"I want to see you. Take them off." I yanked at the waistband of his shorts, encouraging him to lift his butt from the tub.

He stood, doing what I asked with very little encouragement, pulling down his shorts and boxers, allowing me to stare at him while he was gloriously naked. It was the first time I'd seen him completely bare, the overhead light showing me exactly what I'd missed the last time, as his cock jutted out from his hips.

"You're so unbelievably attractive." My fingers traced over the lines of his body, snaking their way down his chest, down his abs until I reached his hard-on. It jerked on contact, his jaw clenching as I stroked him.

It was all the encouragement he needed, leaning into me and kissing me hard. It was desperate, demanding and so hot I could barely breathe. My brain misfired as his hand slid under my top and palmed my breast. God it felt good, his fingers pinching my nipple as desire pooled at my core.

"I want you naked," he growled, yanking off my top with one hand while the other continued to play. He didn't even flinch, ignoring what I was doing to him as he gave me his full attention.

Next were my yoga pants, his fingers letting go of my breast long enough to push them down, my underwear going with them. They pooled at my ankles, my bare skin goosebumping as it hit the cool air.

Slowly he unwrapped my hand from his cock, confusing me as he took a step back. The distance forced him also to let go, his eyes roaming restlessly over my body.

"You're so fucking beautiful. I've imagined seeing you like this, touching you like this and my fantasy isn't even close to how perfect you are." His jaw clenched, closing the distance as he took my mouth again.

I'd heard similar words before, but they'd never meant much. But when he said them, when he looked at me like he did, they vibrated through every nerve in my body.

I was starving, desperate to be touched and kissed and he had no hesitation, taking what I was ready to give him as he gathered up my body and carried me out of the room.

He kicked open the door, striding into his bedroom like I weighed nothing and lowered me onto his mattress.

"Just fucking beautiful," pausing to look at me splayed out like a gift as he kissed my neck.

His lips moved down my body, his hands followed not far behind as he explored every inch of my skin. I tried to do the same, his body kept out of reach while he kissed and touched me, making me so wet I was going to come before we got to any of the good stuff.

And before I could register what he was doing, his mouth covered my heated core. His tongue lapping me, his fingers pinching my nipples as he watched from between my legs.

It was too much, my back bowing off the bed as he continued his assault, not stopping, and using the bucking of my hips to his advantage.

One finger then two entered me, his mouth kept busy on my clit. I wanted to watch, see what he was doing to me as I struggled to keep my eyes open.

The tension in me rose, my body both hot and cold at the same time as everything became sensitive. Tingles radiated from the inside out, every nerve feeling like it was on fire as I coated his mouth and hand.

"Come for me," he mumbled against my thigh, swirling this tongue around my clit as his fingers pumped. "I know you're close."

I wanted to, desperate to feel the release as he worshiped me, but stuck on the edge as my brain tried to remind me how bad of an idea it might be. Uninvited thoughts crept in, trying to rob me of my orgasm as he unknowingly fought the battle on my body's behalf.

"I want this," I said out loud, reassuring everyone concerned that bad idea or not, it was my decision. "I want you."

"Good, because I want you too." He moved further up my body, his rock hard erection grinding against me as he kissed me.

He reached over to his nightstand, pulling out a condom and tearing it open with his teeth. He didn't wait, sheathing himself in latex as I watched. It was erotic, his big hands curled around his cock as he slid it all the way down to the base. I wanted to touch him, to feel his heavy length between my fingers and watch him come undone.

I didn't get the chance.

Lining up the head of his cock against my opening, he circled it, teasing me and pushing in slightly. He'd just filled my entrance, not going any further as he held himself back watching me shift my hips to try to get more.

He pulled out, stroking himself with one hand while the other went to my clit. Drawing it out like he knew I wasn't quite ready to come, teasing me a little while he played.

"You said you want this?" he asked, hovering at my entrance dragging himself through my folds. "You sure, Gillian?"

A smirk spread across his lips, my body jerking each time he made contact as my hands went to my breast. I needed to be touched, desperate to feel something even if I had to be the one to give it to myself.

"Fuck me." I didn't bother trying to dress it fancy, not caring how it made me sound. I wanted him inside of me, needing more than he was giving me.

"If you say so," he chuckled, pushing in a little further. He leaned forward, his mouth sucking against a nipple as he held still. The promise of more hovering just out of reach.

Frustrated, my hands reached around, grabbing his firm ass and bringing him in closer. A throaty laugh bubbled up as I unsuccessfully tried to get him deeper. He waited just a beat, just enough to make eye contact before he sunk into me in one hard stroke.

"This what you wanted, sweetheart?" He pulled out before filling me again, faster and harder than the first time. "Am I fucking you enough now?"

"Yes," I panted, his length filling me as the sensation in me started to build. Whatever mental stumbling block had been there before had been pushed aside, my mind on him and what he was doing.

He grabbed my knees, lifting them as he sunk in deeper, his thrusts kept hard and controlled for maximum impact.

"Yes," I moaned again, the drive of his hips picking up speed as he watched me writhe underneath him.

"Touch yourself, Gillian. Play with your tits like you were doing before." He licked his lips, dropping one of my knees so his hand was free to circle my clit. "I want to see them in your hands, teasing yourself while my dick is buried deep inside of you."

The men I'd slept with before never spoke like that. They whispered sexy—but mostly sweet—things in my ear while we had missionary sex. Nothing fancy and most of the time I got off. But there was something about him asking—no, demanding—I touched my breasts while he fucked me that was kind of hot.

He was raw and powerful, his shoulders tensed as he continued to piston, my body giving up control as he entered me again as I exploded around his cock.

I hadn't even seen it coming, the pleasure blindsiding me as my muscles spasmed. "That's it, baby." He didn't stop, teasing every inch of pleasure from me with every single drag of his hips.

Waves washed over me, the tingling spreading through my extremities as he got even harder, his jaw tightening as he finally let himself go.

"Yes."

He said it again and again, pumping into me, both of us panting as we came hard together.

I wasn't sure I could move, my body twitching as he slowed, lowering his head to kiss me like he hadn't had enough.

"I still want you." His lips moved down to my neck, his hunger undeniable. "And I don't mean later."

His eyes blazed with intensity, his softening cock still buried inside of me.

Part of me assumed that once we'd actually done the deed, he check that off his list and move on. That I was a conquest, a challenge, or worse, a distraction. But his words and his actions proved different, reassuring me that the feelings that had been building between us were real.

They meant something.

That *I* meant something.

The change hadn't been intentional, and lord knows I'd tried to deny my interest, pretending that the attraction wasn't there. My decision to keep my distance and ignore that maybe he felt that way too seemed like a good one, but he was so goddamn stubborn. Infuriatingly so. Who knew that I apparently liked a man who was a thorn in my side and an extra beat in my heart.

He was someone I knew I'd no longer be able to ignore.

Overlooking my silence, he kissed me. So deep, passionate and consuming that it made my toes curl. It was new—the unbelievable feeling especially in my chest—and I wasn't tossing it away.

I didn't think I could even if I'd wanted to.

And I sure as hell didn't.

"I thought we were going for a run." My fingers ran down his chest, loving how his muscles rippled underneath. "You punking out on me after only a few days? It hasn't even been a week."

He lifted his body off mine, laying on the mattress beside me. But he wasn't done, settling before bringing me in close. "I'll give you all the cardio you need right here. There's no way I'm going to let you out of this bed now I've finally got you inside of it. I knew you'd eventually cave, even if I had to get creative."

"So how long have you been planning to have sex with me? Before or after what happened in the living room." I turned toward him, his hands wrapped around me, strangely not bothering me at all.

"Oh, sex with you was a side issue, baby, but that wasn't what I meant. I mean literally getting you inside this bed, to *sleep*. You're done with the couch."

I laughed, pushing against his chest as the chuckle spilled from my lips. I'd expected him to give me some point in time. A day, a date, an hour that he'd decided he wanted to sleep with me. It wasn't like I hadn't thought about him and sex a thousand times myself.

But apparently that wasn't what he meant, referring to my refusal to use his bed. The sex we'd just had, somehow forfeiting my position.

"Maybe we can share the bed," I suggested, liking how he made me feel.

It wasn't just about the sex, although that had been pretty amazing. But I loved the way he touched me, the way he was holding me at that moment—so tender and caring that I couldn't imagine willingly giving it up.

His head tilted to the side, rubbing his chin like he was giving it some thought. "I like this proposal. And I'll be honest, I can't spend another night on that chair. It's a wonder I can still walk."

"You didn't seem to have any problems with walking or any other physical activity a few minutes ago."

If what he'd just done was an example of him impaired then I couldn't wait to see what he could do at full capacity. Maybe I should still go for that run, needing to build my stamina just so I could keep up.

"What can I say, I was inspired." He smiled, giving me another kiss before sitting up. "Let me go get the shower ready. Let's wash off and then you can give me another *massage*." His eyebrows lifted suggestively.

I gently smacked his chest, rolling my eyes. "Stop it. I hadn't intended it to go that far."

"I didn't care what your intentions were, I'm just glad you changed your mind."

There was more relevance in that statement than he could possibly know. My intentions since I'd met him so different to where we were. First, because I'd *intended* to keep him at arm's length like I did most people, then when that didn't work, I *intended* to only let him in a little. But over the course of the last week, he'd challenged me at every step, taking my *intentions* and tossing them right out the door. Somewhere along the line, he'd cracked through.

I was powerless to stop it, showing him a side of me very few got to see. It made me vulnerable, nervous but also excited.

For better or worse, I trusted him.

BIG. CALL.

But I would own it, allowing myself to not only trust him but trust my gut.

It might not be permanent but I could enjoy it while it lasted.

I watched as he slid off the bed and took care of the condom. His toned body caught fragments of light from the living room, the parts in the shadows not any less impressive than the parts I could see. He was beautiful, built to launch a million fantasies and I was willing to test run every last one.

"Come shower with me." He held out his hand, waiting for me to take it. "The acoustics in the bathroom are fucking amazing. I'll even sing for you."

And that was all he needed to say, the chance to be serenaded by him sealing the deal as I got up and followed. I had no doubt that I'd be adding some acoustics of my own, and not because I would be joining in the chorus. But greedily I wanted him, and not just the parts that made me come.

21

Gillian

"I have a guitarist and drummer flying in at three." I looked up from my laptop. "Emily organized a rehearsal space in Squirrel Hill, she paid them extra to keep it quiet."

We never did go for that run, the shared shower turning into more sex and I had zero regrets.

He walked over, kissing me, reaching out with one arm and moving my laptop out of the way. It was strange that him protecting something important to me was hot, but it was nonetheless.

"Vaughan," I mumbled between kisses. "Did you hear what I said?"

I had expected when we left the bedroom eventually that we'd go back to the way things were before. Workwise, I meant. Me—in my impromptu office in his living room—and him—in his room or the kitchen table working on music. I knew it would be different, the line that had kept us separate being blurred, and I was honestly excited. Okay, maybe not *excited*, because I hated working with someone looking over my shoulder. But the excitement was in that I could touch him and kiss him whenever I wanted.

But I expected us to work, not turning into a pair of teenagers who'd touched each other's genitals for the first time.

Vaughan didn't see things the same way.

Doing what he always did—ignoring what he should and doing what he wanted instead. And boy, was he making it clear exactly what that was.

"You know when you boss me around it only turns me on more." He groaned into my neck, his hands all over me like he'd grown an extra pair.

"So this whole time, you've been walking around with a hard-on? Because I'm pretty sure I've been bossing you around since the day I met you."

He was being impossible, absolutely impossible and I didn't hate it.

"Umm. . . yeah. I thought it was pretty obvious." His lips spread into a grin, freaking delighted.

Oh Lord.

Getting him to focus was going to take a miracle.

I untangled his octopus arms, wriggling out and managing to stand up. It had been a challenge. "O-kay. Band members. New ones. That you need to meet." I made sure to annunciate each word clearly in the hopes something would stick.

"New people? Where did you find them?" And praise Jesus, he heard me, his head snapping to attention as his face turned serious. "Please tell me they aren't country."

God he was adorable.

Maybe he wasn't the only one who was going to need a miracle to focus.

"They aren't country, you're safe."

With the knowledge my *alternates* hadn't been singing about heartbreak and pickup trucks, he relaxed, the tension easing out of his body. "So what's their story?"

"They're brothers. Really talented, really great guys. I think you're really going to like them."

Finding musicians to play with Vaughan and Nico wasn't as simple as putting out an ad on Craig's List. They were walking into a situation where their input might not be huge, but we needed them to be competent and not have too big an ego. So basically we were looking for someone who didn't exist.

Or at least that was what I thought until Emily—I was secretly praying her dream of owning a bakery never came to fruition—reminded me about Declan and Austin.

He folded his arms across his chest. "Gillian, you said *really* three times, what's wrong with them?"

"There is nothing wrong with them, they are talented. And nice. And—"

"And you're avoiding something." He cut me off, not letting me finish. "What's the deal?"

Ugh.

It wasn't going to be pretty.

I'd been hoping to avoid delving into the particulars, assuming Vaughan wouldn't really care. He needed a guitarist and a drummer, I would find them and everyone would be happy. But all of that was wishful thinking, his interest not something that could be ignored.

"Keep an open mind," I warned, knowing that he had a tendency to fly off the handle.

His feet hit the ground, standing as his hands settled on my waist. "Now you're just fucking scaring me. What the hell is it?"

"They were signed to a competitor's label, Emily and I met them at an industry event. They'd just cut an album, their debut effort launched them straight into the charts and making them hugely successful. But the singer, the bass player and the keyboard player decided to go in a different direction and so the band broke up. Declan and Austin decided they'd had their brush with fame so went back to their day jobs."

His brow scrunched in confusion. "So they were famous? Who was the band? If I don't know them, surely I'd know the band."

"Famous in their category," I clarified, knowing the worst was yet to come.

He waved his hand, encouraging me to continue. "Which was?"

Deep breath.

And wait for it.

Three.

Two.

One.

"Christian Rock."

"Oh my fucking God." It shot out of his mouth like a bullet, his eyes opened to maximum capacity. Ironic that had been his chosen curse.

"They were homeschooled in Iowa and have been playing in churches since they were five and seven."

"Oh my God." He clutched his chest, the possibility of a panic—or heart attack—very real.

"They don't drink or smoke, and of course no premarital sex," I continued, figuring there was no point in holding any of it back.

"Jesus. Christ."

Just one little bit to add.

"And they don't swear or use the Lord's name in vain."

"Fuck, Gillian, you can't be serious? Tell me this is a joke? Tell me that they are really two metal heads from freaking Norway who fuck, curse and enjoy a decent beer." He paled, his skin ashy as he swayed on his feet.

It was a risk, sure, but there were never any guarantees in the music industry. And while they hadn't been signed to Domination, their whirlwind rise in the Christian charts championed by Lighthouse Records, I had heard them play.

They were good.

Better than good.

They were outstanding.

His reaction, while not completely unexpected was mildly amusing. His body was bent over, his hands braced against his knees trying not to hyperventilate. Of all the things that I thought would send Vaughan Hale over the edge, a couple of clean living Christians wouldn't have been my first guess.

Against my better judgment, and knowing it was probably a little cruel, I couldn't help but have a little fun with it.

"Well at least you won't have to worry about either of them sleeping with anyone."

"Oh. Fuck. Me." He coughed, not finding it amusing. "You're making jokes? How is this funny? This isn't fucking funny."

"You're right, I'm sorry." I tried not to laugh. "That was really insensitive of me. I'm sorry."

If there'd been any color left in his face it was gone, his features hard or possibly defeated.

He was right, it wasn't funny and I shouldn't have been laughing. Wasn't sure what had gotten into me and I felt terrible. "Vaughan, I didn't mean to make fun of the situation between you and Connor."

His brow knitted in confusion. "Seriously? That is what you're apologizing for? Gillian, not saying that it didn't hurt having my best friend stab me in the back, because it did. But, you know. I'm kind of over it."

"Over it?" Now I was confused.

"Well . . . over it isn't really what I mean." He reached out, his fingers tracing my jaw. "But like if there was an exchange and I had to go through all of that to meet you, then it was worth it."

God he was incredibly sweet, his words touching, the warmth spreading across my chest.

"So then why are you so mad?" My fingertips smoothed the worry lines in his forehead, even with them he still looked amazing.

"Because how am I supposed to play with people I have nothing in common with? Not sure I trust a man who doesn't say at least a random fuck every once in a while. They don't want booze and sex, well guess that's their choice. But it's a band, not fucking Sunday school."

"Sure, it's going to be different but they're really good at what they do. Technically, they're amazing. Declan is one of the best guitarists I've seen. And Austin doesn't miss a beat. And they are incredibly friendly. Zero ego. Humble. It will be an adjustment but I think it will be a good fit."

It wasn't just rhetoric, everything I said was a hundred percent true. They hadn't even negotiated for a bigger fee, agreeing on an ordinary pay-to-play contract with the stipulation that any songwriting would be credited, receiving any residual royalties. They didn't even care what style they played, up to the challenge of just about anything.

He eyed me cautiously, clearly not sold on my everything's-going-to-be-okay. "I still get a say, right? Get to veto if they come and don't gel with me and Nico?"

"Yes, within reason. It just can't be because their ideals are different," I warned, not wanting him to red card the brothers purely because *fuck* wasn't in their vocabulary.

"Fine. But if this goes up in flames and your plans to sell millions turns to shit, don't say I didn't warn you. *Christian virgins who don't swear or drink.*" He shuddered, issuing his own warnings, my lips pressing together as I tried to stifle the laugh.

"I promise, I will take full responsibility. Every single ounce of blame." It was an easy promise to make and not just because I believed it'd work. If it did end in disaster, there wouldn't be anyone else to blame. I'd found Vaughan, I'd convinced my father to sign them, then I convinced myself the situation could be rectified. I was either fighting a losing battle or had the greatest vision of everyone combined.

God—no pun intended—I was really hoping it was vision.

Pacified—at least for the moment—Vaughan wrapped his arms around me. "So, you want to go have sex?"

"Vaughan," I huffed in frustration, only half tempted to give in. My head was still in control, even if my hormones were making a solid argument on why we should. It sure would relieve some stress. Extra cardio. So many positives.

"We're not having sex. You," I pressed my hands to his chest, "are going to work on some more material and I'm going to go back to what I was doing."

His mood deflated. With puppy dog eyes and an exaggerated pout, he made it clear that he was displeased. "This is how it starts . . . they're not having sex so no one else can."

"This has nothing to do with them," I chuckled. "Now go back to work."

"Such a buzz kill." He brushed his lips against mine, kissing me gently before heading back to his acoustic guitar.

Ignoring my own directions, I watched as he settled into a chair, tinkering with chords as he hummed along. At random, he'd pick up a pen and scribble something in a notebook. There was no real structure to it—the playing, the humming, the scribbling—working like a mad scientist while I spectated.

"I can get naked," he grinned, not bothering to look up from his guitar as he continued to work. "I mean, if you're going to keep watching me, I might as well make it more interesting for you."

Right.

Because of all the adjectives to describe Vaughan naked, *interesting* was the best he could come up with.

Not likely.

"Keep your clothes on, rock star." I made a show of moving my laptop in front of me and opening it, pretending like my mind wasn't on him.

"Suit yourself," he chuckled. "Some of my best material was written completely bare."

I shook my head, cursing under my breath, slightly annoyed at how much he'd managed to whittle away at my self-discipline. In what seemed like no time at all, I'd gone from regimented, controlled, and dedicating most of my waking hours to my work, to thinking about blowing it off and watching Vaughan sing naked.

And we both knew it just wouldn't be me *watching* and him *singing*. Cite my current lack of control.

"If you still feel like a naked performance after you meet Declan and Austin, I won't stop you." It was a compromise, one for him as well as for me.

His hand froze on the strings, giving me such a sexy grin that I almost rethought my stance. "Babe, let me let you in on a secret. I will always feel like it."

Vaughan

ook, I didn't give a shit who you prayed to when you got down on your knees. It could be the big JC, Buddha, Mother Earth or some other invisible friend that made you feel good. It was none of my business and as long as you didn't ram your beliefs down my throat like an unwelcomed dildo, I was all about people going on their merry way. Dress in your Sunday/Saturday/Wednesday—or whenever it was you got together and chanted—best and have at it. No problems here. But I didn't want it on my front stoop, cloaked up and masquerading as good will and judging my life choices. It wasn't right.

So while I agreed to keep an open mind, nodding and telling Gillian I was going to give God Believer One and God Believer Two a chance, it was going to take an act of God—something that should be no problem for them—for me to fall in love with the idea.

And sure, I knew I needed a band. Needed someone who was decent and wasn't going to be all Beyoncé about it, but surely there was a middle ground.

Shit.

Fucking Christians.

Not just the everyday garden variety ones either. You know the ones, go to church, say their prayers but know the Good Book was really fairytales. Just be good most of the time and have a few cheat days like a diet. But the ones we'd imported were straight-up hardcore, like the special forces of faith or something. It was like some sick perverted joke.

Trying to keep my mind off it, and concentrate on what I could control, I picked up my six string to see what would come out. It wasn't easy, Gillian not more than a few feet away, wearing "civilian" clothes.

I liked her.

I liked her a lot.

Probably more than just a lot.

And yeah, I had a tendency to get in deep with women way quicker than most but that was just my cross to bear. There were worse afflictions, like not falling in love at all.

In addition to my beautiful distraction, I had another issue to contend with. Writing music that *wasn't* metal. It was tough, the tendency to drop everything into a minor key and add a shit ton of vibrato a habit that was hard to break. But we—as per Gillian's directive—were going for a brighter sound. No distortion. No shouting. And no extended guitar and drum solos. Like Jeff Buckley but more rock with a radio-friendly slant.

Major keys.

Stripped down sound.

Real but clean vocals.

Nothing like giving you a tall order.

Jesus.

Yeah, I was probably going to have to stop that. I called on the Lord, or some other variation, so many times it would be easy to be mistaken for a man of the cloth. But trust me, there was a greater chance of me strapping on a pair of heels and a pageant gown and calling myself Delilah than me taking that vow.

So I strummed, trying to feel out the notes and see where they took me. Sadly, we weren't getting very far. I was a competent guitar player in that I could make the right shapes on the fret board and possibly play rhythm if my life depended on it. But that's where my talent ended. I was a vocalist—a singer —and preferred to use the strings like a capital letter at the start of the sentence. Give me a point, an X, a start here kind of arrow and then let my voice take us on the journey. Connor was good at translating all of it and putting it into music so doing it all by myself was new. Not that there was another option, Nico was more a point him in the right direction and tell him what to play kind of guy so that avenue was a bust.

And Johnny? Well I was sure he was already hanging from the chandeliers of a big top.

Not sure if it was my need to prove to myself that I could do it, or worried about disappointing Gillian, but I managed to string a few things together. The lyrics were solid, poems yet to be put to music as I tried to find the right chords.

"Vaughan."

I'd never get sick of her calling my name, the smile automatic as I snapped my head up to look at her.

"We should get going. We need to get to Sound Bites and meet everyone else. I've already messaged Nico."

She'd changed, her layers of ninja assassin chic replacing what she'd been kicking around in while it was just the two of us. I got it. She didn't share easily, and I wasn't there to champion anyone else's cause. If they wanted in, reap the spoils of what it was like to be on the inner, that was their crusade.

"Okay, baby. Let's go do this."

I closed the notebook, rested the guitar against the wall, and readied my soul for the burning it would undoubtedly endure.

I changed as well, staying in the same jeans but sliding on my Judas Priest T-shirt especially for the occasion. Gillian didn't seem amused.

"Really?" she asked as I walked out of my bedroom, big-ass smile on my face.

"C'mon, surely I can have a little fun with it? It's not like I'm promoting Satan worshipping or something." I lifted her chin, catching her lips in a kiss.

"Fine, the shirt can stay but the PDAs—the kissing, the touching, the calling me *babe*—are for behind closed doors only. It can only be when it's just the two of us, okay?"

Normally when she told me to do something, it was done with zero leeway. Not so much a request as a directive, with no room for feedback. But telling me to cool it on the "us" stuff, she had softened around the edges. Wanting me to do what she was asking, but with added concern. I wasn't sure if the concern was for her or me—me taking it the wrong way or going rogue and exposing her—but she had no reason to worry.

"Read you loud and clear." I raised my hands to prove how hands off I could be. "Won't even hint that I know what you look like naked or how much I want your mouth."

She sighed, shaking her head. "Vaughan."

"Seriously Gillian, it goes without saying. I'll be good, I promise."

Taking my word and concerned about the ticking clock, she let any further discussions drop and followed me out to the car. We got in, starting the ignition and headed to Squirrel Hill.

Sound Bite was one of the more fancier rehearsal/recording places around Pittsburgh. It had legit soundproofing, not just foam mats nailed to the walls, and state-of-the-art equipment only rich kids could afford. There was a reception with a person, numerous vending machines for when you get the munchies, and bathrooms that weren't covered in graffiti. It was a world away from the places we used to rehearse, the freshly painted walls and polished floors looking more like an upmarket office space than somewhere you'd find musicians.

Not sure how much coin she dropped to get us in and keep it on the hush, but our room was right in back, close to the rear exit. Handy when you were trying to keep under the radar, slipping in without so much as a sideways glance tossed our way.

Nico was already there, set up with his bass and his rig, fingering the strings like he was trying to tease out an orgasm. He stopped as we stepped into the room, grinning like an idiot, pretty freaking pleased at our temporary digs.

"Gillian, this place is amazing." He went to hug her but pulled up short. She'd definitely become less prickly the last few days towards him, but hadn't gotten to hugging just yet. I tried to not look too smug as he adjusted his stance awkwardly. "Thanks, I mean. We really appreciate it, right Vaughan?"

"Sure do." I nodded, keeping the grin tempered while looking around. He wasn't wrong, the place was amazing. "Thanks so much, Gillian."

"You're both welcome." She gave us a genuine smile, the phone buzzing in her pocket stopping her from saying anything else.

"Good, come right through, we're already in the room. Great, we'll see you soon." She hung up the phone, her eyes looking expectantly at the door.

"So anything you can tell us about these two dudes? You said they were professionals, right? Session or stage?" Nico rubbed his hands together with the excitement of a child. Which told me that Gillian and I sleeping together wasn't the only bit of intel he didn't know.

Oh, this was going to be good.

I could have played it two ways.

Change the subject, pretending like we could go on some bullshit wonderful world of discovery when they arrived. Getting not only Gillian off the hook, but rewarding myself with the pleasure of Nico's face when Testaments x2 walked in the door.

Or, I could do what I would have done if I didn't have the insider information, which was add a little more heat on that fire.

Tough choice.

But since we were keeping up appearances and status quo needed to be maintained . . . "Yeah, Gillian, why don't you tell us a little bit more about these guys. I'm sure you've already given them the brief on us."

If I hadn't been looking directly at her, I might have missed the jaw clenching. It was subtle, more of a tick—a marvel of schooling her emotions the likes of which impressed the hell out of me. Because for all her non reaction, I knew she probably was pissed. And we'd sort all of that out, when we got home.

"Declan is twenty-five and Austin is twenty-three. They've been playing since childhood and have a lot of experience playing on stages in both small venues and large." She was good, not lying, just keeping it to the facts.

Nico nodded, accepting her sweetened truth and probing a little further. "Awesome, what sort of music did they play? You said they were in a band before and then they broke up?"

"They sure were, very successful in their rock subgenre. They're great technically and know how to please a crowd."

She'd have been a prosecutor's nightmare.

Curious to see how much further she'd take it, I sat back waiting for Nico to shoot off more questions. He was about to, mouth ready to say who knew what when the door opened, revealing Emily and our two new "friends."

"Jesus Christ."

I'd lasted exactly one second, maybe not even a whole one if you wanted to get technical, dropping the Lord's name the minute I set eyes on the two.

They were both tall, over six foot but not as big as Nico, looking like they took care of what their maker gave them. Fit, healthy—a poster in a prayer group's summer camp waiting to happen.

And it looked like J. Crew threw up all over them.

Freshly pressed, all American—chinos and printed shirts.

Holy. Freaking. Shit.

Nico looked confused, and I couldn't say that I blamed him. I had been prepared and was still reeling.

"Hey, pleased to meet you." One of them stepped forward, his neatly trimmed beard and shoulder-length hair too close for comfort to a holy picture I'd once seen. "I'm Austin."

"Vaughan." I held out my hand, hoping I didn't burst into flames or anything like that.

Oh, look at that, no burning on contact. That was a relief.

"And I'm Declan." The other took his turn tossing a greeting my way, Austin doing the hello-how-are-you with a bewildered Nico.

Both Emily and Gillian looked like mothers watching their four-year-olds make friends at the playground—grinning with hope and expectation.

"So you guys are musicians?" Nico scratched his neck trying to solve the mystery that was the new guys. The *you don't look like them* left unsaid.

It was tempting to see how long it was going to take for the penny to drop, if he shuffled around trying to be polite or just out and out asked. He was more patient than me so it could take a while. And since I didn't know how long we had the space and I didn't want the boys to miss their flight back to Kansas or whatever, we should probably get the show on the road. Lord knew what we were going to play together. Doubtful they could shred out some Metellica and the only thing religious I knew was "Kumbaya."

"Christian Rock," I interjected. "They played Christian Rock."

Nico's head jerked back to me, my explanation still not making sense. "Huh?"

Yeah, exactly.

"Look gentlemen, why don't we get Austin and Declan set up and see what happens." Gillian tried to mediate, her wait-and-see routine only lasting so long.

Emily—who we hadn't even said hello to yet—looped an arm around Nico's and pulled him toward the door. "Van's out this way, I need some strong muscles to help get all the stuff out."

She got no resistance from him, my bass player forgetting we were entertaining the God squad and followed her right out the door.

"Let's get you guys squared away, interested to hear you play." I nodded to the one without the beard—I couldn't remember if that was Declan or Austin—and got my feet moving. Nico was a big dude but he wasn't going to be able to haul that load all by himself.

"Sounds good," non-beard said, walking out with me back toward the rear exit. Beard tagged along too, not far behind.

Their equipment couldn't have been any more pro, the road cases stacked neatly with their flight stickers still attached. No beat-up guitar cases or drums packed in boxes for these guys, everything looked neat as a pin and as expensive as hell. And I hadn't even seen what was inside of them yet.

We lugged everything inside, laid them on the floor and then let Austin—beard guy and the drummer—set up his kit. He didn't screw around, his hands working efficiently as he got all the cymbals and drums where they needed to be while Declan—non beard, guitar player—pulled out a shiny sunburst Gibson.

Wow. Baller.

Not sure if their playing was any good but they definitely had the right tools.

Nico and I said hello to Emily who then dragged Gillian to the sofa in the corner. Like an experiment, they were going to observe and not intervene.

The mic was already plugged in and sitting on its stand because unlike the rest of the guys I had nothing to bring. I wasn't flashy enough to have my own, so I was happy to use the provided one and pray the asshole who'd put his mouth there before me didn't have the plague.

"Let's get started, you guys set?" I turned around, showing I was considerate and checking on our guests.

Austin nodded, raising his sticks while Declan meandered over, fingers hovering above his strings. "What do you want to play?"

"What do you know?" I asked, hoping they at least knew something mainstream. Hell, I didn't even care if it was a pop song at this point, just hoping to find some middle ground.

"Again, what did you want to play?" Declan grinned, just arrogant enough that it gave me some hope.

Well okay, buddy, two can play at that game.

"Metal, your choice. We'll come in," I offered, knowing there wasn't a popular metal band in the last twenty years we didn't know.

He nodded, a look passing between the two brothers that I didn't fully trust. If something was said, it was on a different frequency none of us could hear, the two them seeming to understand each other as Austin counted them in.

Nico and I watched as Declan led, only a few notes being played before we looked at each other in shock. In what could only be described as freaky fucking perfection, Austin came in on the drums, the musical lead in explicitly clear.

"Jesus." It slipped out, my intention to curtail the curses against the big guy being shelved as I looked on in awe.

"Not quiet." Declan laughed, his fingers busy as he grinned.

Gillian and Emily clearly had no idea what was being played or how complicated it was, the intro almost done as I grabbed the mic and joined them in possibly the most awesome rendition of *Dream Theatre's* "Pull me Under."

Nico took the hint, palming the neck of his bass as he did what he could to keep up. It was a challenge, the parts literally written out like a classical piece and intended for a six-string, but boy did he work his ass off, making sure he wasn't the weakest link.

Opening my mouth I left nothing on the table. Every rise and fall, every sustain, every note sung to the best of my ability. And it wasn't easy, the song freaking vocal gymnastics for my chords.

I closed my eyes, my heart beating in my chest with excitement as Declan, Nico and Austin all joined in with backing vocals. No gaps, everyone doing their freaking part like we'd been playing forever. And by the time we'd reached the end of the song, I'd completely forgotten it had only been maybe an hour since I'd met them.

Magic.

Fate.

Or the big guy upstairs shuffling the deck.

I wasn't sure who or what was responsible but those two guys from Iowa were meant to be in that room with Nico and I. Fuck White Trash Circus, nothing we'd ever done had felt that fun, and I had thought I'd been having a ball.

High-fives were tossed in the air, all of us talking over one another with compliments and mutual appreciation. The fact we had an audience completely forgotten as my attention didn't deviate from the men in front of me.

"Sounded good." Gillian was all smiles as she joined our crew. "What do you think, gentleman? This something we're going to continue?"

She was being smug, the I-told-you-so not spoken but heard loud and clear, just waiting for me to admit I had been wrong.

"Hells yeah! That was fucking amazing." Nico fist pumped, quickly turning to the guys and adding an "Sorry, I mean . . . gee yeah. That was really amazing." Both Declan and Austin laughing at his attempt to sanitize his enthusiasm.

"Just be however you are naturally," Austin reassured him. "Don't need to worry about us. And I'm on board."

"Me too, would love to be part of your band." Declan nodded lowering his Gibson.

Gillian's eyes locked in on mine. "So, what do you say, Vaughan? You're the only one who hasn't weighed in here."

Admitting I was wrong wasn't happening, but I would concede that what we had in that room was special. How long it would stay that way or how it would play out was still remaining to be seen. But it wasn't going to be stopped on my account.

"I think we've got ourselves something here." I addressed the room, checking out my new band and needing to get a few things off my chest before we locked it in. "We've got some differences. Clothes and attitude for one, but I think it can work. I got no problem with what you believe, how you unwind and where you do or don't put your cocks. As long as you guys feel the same way about us. I mean, I'm all for turning water into wine because that's a handy skill to have. But if either of you tries to Jesus me and sell me commandments we're going to have issues."

Declan's mouth spread into a slow but confident grin. "You know that was Moses, right? Not Jesus."

"You know what I mean." I couldn't help but laugh. "And you need to get Marcus out here because seriously guys, we need to do something about those freaking chinos. At least for when we're on stage."

"What have you got against chinos?" Austin laughed, checking out his attire.

"Nothing if you work at the Gap, but this is a rock band." I shrugged, thinking if I had to cut my hair and overhaul my wardrobe, everyone else should have to do the same.

"I'll get Marcus on the phone, see when he can fly out." Emily giggled, stepping out of the room.

"Yeah, I think we can meet you halfway. No drinking when we play though. Likewise, don't care what you do in your downtime but on stage we put in a hundred percent or nothing at all." Declan made some demands of his own.

"Yeah, I can agree to that." I threw out my hand wanting to shake on it. He clapped it with his own, sealing the deal.

"Can we stop talking and play some more?" Nico whined, not interested in handshaking or discussing. "You guys know any Tool?"

"Yeah, we do." Declan tossed over his shoulder as he wandered back to his ax. "Pick your tune."

Gillian's grin simmered as she got closer. "Now that everyone seems to be playing nice, I might leave you boys alone to get to know each other a little better. I'll be outside if you need me."

"Yeah, thanks." I hesitated and then thought fuck it as I gently touched her arm. It wasn't a PDA, my hand on her elbow hardly qualifying for anything other than friendly. "Thanks for everything."

There was so much more I wanted to say and had no idea where to even start. But she'd done more than I'd deserved, willing to put her ass on the line just to save mine. And sure, I knew she was getting something out of it too, her reasons articulated more than once. But I had a feeling she could have picked some other no-name band to make her statement, and the fact she'd picked us not accidental.

She nodded, getting the subtext and not making me say it out loud. "You're welcome. Have fun. You have the room until ten."

And before anyone else could notice, she disappeared out of the room. No idea how a woman as beautiful, smart and goddamn amazing could be so invisible to so many people, but my eyes were definitely open.

I'd *seen* her, and no matter what happened with the band that wasn't changing.

The warmth spread through my chest as I turned back around to the guys, the three of them deep in conversation as to what song we were going to play next.

"Okay, boys, let's see what else you've got. And while we're tossing shit into the ring, let's start thinking about what to call ourselves."

White Trash Circus was dead, never to be resurrected, RIP, and I didn't feel an ounce of sadness. Whatever this new incarnation was, was going to be insane. And I was ready for all of it.

23

Gillian

Vaughan and company barely even noticed when it was time to leave. The four of them were locked in the room like they were discussing invading a small country, with about as much passion and determination too.

They had played music from other bands for about an hour, and then started working on their own sound. When I dared to crack open the door and see how they were doing, no one even noticed. Too busy, working on music while Vaughan played with lyrics. It was hard not to get excited too, their chemistry more than I'd hoped for.

"You guys want to go get something to eat?" Declan asked, packing up the last of his gear into the van. "I'm starving but have some more ideas on that last song we were working on."

Dinner had been a short pizza break hours ago, the calories eaten more than truly consumed by their time in the rehearsal room.

"Sure, I'm game. Where you guys staying?" Nico asked, helping Austin load in the drum kit.

"Hotel downtown. We just need to get the gear back and then we'll meet you wherever you want." Austin tossed Declan the keys as he locked the back of the van.

"There's a place right near Nico's in Glassport. Quiet, locals—his sister, Maree, works the bar. We can go hang out there," Vaughan added before turning to me. "You and Emily joining us?"

Honestly, I wanted to say yes, to go hang out and interact. Not because I didn't trust Vaughan or felt the need to babysit him, but because I genuinely liked being around him. But I couldn't, because as far as everyone else was concerned there was no reason for me to be with him off the clock. Sure I was living with him, acting as his life coach or some other bullshit, but going beyond that would raise too many eyebrows.

I couldn't risk it, even though I really wanted to.

"No, you guys go along. Emily and I have our own plans."

Em turned to me, her lips pulling into a frown. "We do?"

"Yeah, we do." I gave her my best don't-ask-questions look as I forced the smile. "So enjoy, but don't stay out too late. I have the room booked for eleven tomorrow and I would love to get a teaser track recorded and start circulating it on the internet."

"Business as usual, hey Gillian," Nico laughed, ignoring the intense look Vaughan was giving me. "We'll just have to manage without you."

Details and directions were exchanged, with Declan and Austin getting into the van and driving off. Nico lingered for about a second longer asking if either Emily or I needed a ride before doing the same.

And then there were three, which was about one too many for a conversation I knew Vaughan was itching to have. "Hey Em, why don't you go ahead and I'll catch a cab to your hotel. Meet up with you soon."

"You sure? I can follow you guys back." She waved the keys to her rental, the red sedan not parked far.

"No, it's fine. I'll want to reinforce the ground rules to Vaughan without the audience." I followed the script, pretending my need for privacy was business related. "I won't be long."

Whether she bought it or not was still up for debate, her eyes flicking between us before she got in her car and drove away. Vaughan hadn't moved, standing beside his truck, as he watched her taillights disappear.

"You want to reinforce the rules?" He stalked closer, his eyes flicking left and right to check if the coast was clear. "Or did you want me to give you this?"

Without waiting for the answer he sealed my mouth with his own and kissed me, the contact electric as he consumed me. I'd needed that kiss for hours, feeling ridiculous at how much I wanted him and I loved that I hadn't been alone.

He eased his mouth away, kissing down the column of my throat as his hand grabbed my ass. "You could have joined us, I would have kept my hands to myself."

"It's better this way," I gasped between kisses, my mouth wanting to do other things than talk. "No danger of raising suspicions."

Hanging out with the talent wasn't something that I did, something I was sure I'd mentioned early on in the piece. To go along even under the guise of looking out for my investment was out of character, and would invite questions I didn't want to answer. Too much a risk, and not one I was willing to take.

"Go without me, and I'll be home by the time you get back." I tried unsuccessfully to stop kissing him, my hands moving across the ripples of his chest.

His mouth stopped, his journey back to my lips put on ice as he looked at me. "You're not coming back to the apartment now? I thought I'd have some time with you before I'd have to leave."

It was tempting, and not something I hadn't considered. The mental calculation of how quickly we could get to his place, satisfy us both before heading in different directions already having taken place. But it was late, and we both still had a job to do. Which wasn't each other, as much as that sucked.

"Vaughan, it's late. It's better if you go ahead without me. I'll just go back inside and get someone at the front desk to call me a cab." I pushed on his chest when he didn't look like he was convinced. "Go, I meant what I said about not staying out too late. Ready or not, I'll be waking you at ten tomorrow."

"And I'll be waking you the minute I get home. Don't you dare sleep on the couch. You have your rules and I have mine, and you need to be in my bed," he warned, brushing his lips against mine one last time.

"Fine, just go already." I laughed, having no intention of being anywhere else. "I'll see you later."

He hesitated for a minute then climbed into his truck, the engine roaring to life as the window rolled down. "Bed. Mine." He reinforced his last instruction in case there was any confusion before driving off, leaving me in the parking lot alone.

Not wanting to hang out and wait to be mugged or worse—I had no idea what the crime status was in that part of town—I pushed opened the door and went back to reception. There I waited until the Uber I ordered arrived, having an interesting conversation with the guy behind the desk who had no idea who I was. He had very strong opinions on the state of the music industry, and it was refreshing to hear unbiased views from someone not attempting to kiss your ass.

It was why I liked being with Vaughan so much, loving how much who I was didn't impress him.

The ride to Emily's hotel was uneventful, she was up on a higher floor, ordering wine and dessert before I'd even arrived. She didn't believe in staying in a hotel and not getting room service.

"So is he going to be good?" She handed me a glass as I perused the buffet of sweet offerings laid out on the table. "Or do you prefer him bad?"

There hadn't been a lot of time to talk to Emily since I'd left New York. And when we did chat, I avoided any mention of what I was doing with Vaughan. But Emily wasn't an idiot and knew me better than I probably knew myself. She could also sense when I was holding something back, my tryst with the singer I was supposed to be developing at the top of her list.

"You can't say anything. Not to anyone," I warned her, taking a sip of the wine, glad she'd ordered a bottle. I was never good at talking about my feelings but it was probably easier for both of us if I just admitted it.

She picked up a chocolate tart, forking a piece before seductively putting it in her mouth. "I so knew it. And you know what. I'm glad. It's about time you did something for yourself and had some fun. Bugger the consequences."

"It's not going to be the consequences that are going to be *buggered* if anyone finds out. This is such a bad decision but I literally couldn't stop myself. How did I become *that* girl?" I shook my head, grabbing the Key Lime pie and a fork. If the night was going to turn into a confessional, I might as well have something to enjoy it with.

She reached across the table, her fingers gently touching my arm. "Gillian, who's going to know? I doubt Vaughan is going to tell anyone."

"No, I don't think he'll tell anyone." I fed myself calories I didn't need, not fully enjoying the pie. "But it's still a bad decision."

It wasn't just the fallout, the rumors, and all the innuendo that I was worried about. Eventually whatever we were doing was going to end. Relationships always did. Besides, he just got out of a relationship and even though he'd never made me feel like the rebound, what we were doing probably wasn't smart. Because even if it wasn't just an intermitted distraction, I knew everything had an expiration date. And I just didn't want to think about that with him. I rationed it was because it might be awkward working together or because I was worried people might find out, but deep down there was another reason.

I didn't want to say goodbye.

"I'm worried," I almost whispered, scared to admit it to Emily as much as I was to myself. "I could really like him, Em. I know if I really gave it a chance, there would be feelings I couldn't easily turn off."

Emily stopped having oral sex with her chocolate tart, lowering her fork. "Gill, are you saying you could fall in love with him?"

It wasn't the word I used but probably what I'd meant. I mean, who knew if I was even capable of it. My plans for marriage had been to choose a decent guy who treated me well and didn't suck in the bedroom. That had literally been my previous criteria for a husband.

Later.

Like when I was forty.

So the idea that I could fall in love with someone wasn't something I'd even considered, even when I had planned for the future.

Vaughan, well he was the wild card I hadn't anticipated.

"I don't know." It was the only answer I could give, my heart and my mind scrambled. "It's ridiculous that I'm even talking about it, we've been together for like a day and we're not even really dating. I highly doubt he's thinking about what this all means. But I swear, when I'm with him, I just feel different. I told him about my mother for Christ's sake, why would I do that?"

I had no explanation. No reason to why I'd allowed Vaughan to go where most people's access was denied. And other than him being so persistent and it *feeling different*, I had nothing else to go on. And it wasn't that I was afraid to take risks, I could be fearless with my professional life. My personal life, not so much.

"Maybe you let him in because deep down you already know."

Her words of wisdom didn't give me comfort, the idea that I could have *feelings* for someone so fast wasn't what I'd call an endearing quality. Still it was bad enough it was already consuming my thoughts, and I didn't want to spend the rest of the evening dissecting my psyche.

"Or maybe he's just really attractive and I haven't had sex in a while," I reasoned, knowing that I hadn't become a nymphomaniac overnight.

Nope.

Wouldn't get so lucky.

"You know what, let's just ignore it and drink the rest of this wine." I topped up our glasses, not giving her a chance to answer. "I'm going to be a regular human for a change and ignore it like the rest of you."

"Pfft, girl you could never be a regular human. You just aren't wired that way." Emily waved her hand, dismissing the idea as she laughed.

And I wasn't sure if I wanted her to be right.

24

Vaughan

It was probably around two a.m. when I got back to my apartment. Not that I had intended to stay out so late, but once we'd gotten talking, none of us had realized the time.

Being drunk hadn't been a factor either. With Declan and Austin nursing pop all night, I'd had two beers and then stopped, the need to stay clear headed and talk, more important than feeling the buzz. Even Nico who loved nothing more than to chill with a Yuengling switched to Pepsi. The natural high both of us felt far outweighed anything that came out of a bottle. And the feel-good mood had lasted until I'd walked in the door and saw Gillian asleep on the couch.

It looked to be unintentional, the laptop open on the coffee table with the screen just as asleep as she was. Her clothes were still on, her head resting on her hands that were curled up underneath her. She looked peaceful, completely at ease as her dark lashes bounced off her cheeks. I had no idea if she was dreaming, but I hoped whatever was going through that beautiful mind was good. And if it was about me, even better.

Doing my best not to wake her, I gathered her into my arms and carried her to my bed. She stirred a little, mumbling in her sleep, but those gorgeous golden eyes stayed shut as I laid her on the mattress and started to undress her.

And no it wasn't shady, the motivation for taking off her clothes nothing more than wanting her to be comfortable. Sure, once I got her down to her bra and panties, my dick woke up looking for some attention. But like the beer I'd chosen not to drink, my erection was also ignored, behaving more like those two virgins than I probably would have thought.

Once she was situated, I turned the attention to myself, stripping off with less care than I'd shown her, dumping my clothes on the floor and crawling in beside her.

Her body was so warm, melding to mine as I got in close and wrapped my arms around her. She sighed as I kissed her shoulder, my attempt at being good allowing the small concession. She must have been dog tired, not having woken the entire time, the low rustling of air through her lips confirming she hadn't opened her eyes.

I'll admit, I was disappointed. Not because I wanted to have sex with her, although I wouldn't have said no. But because I wanted to tell her about my night, about chatting with the guys, and the ideas we'd had. I was excited, the energy making me feel like my heart was beating too fast, and of all the people I wanted to share it with, she was the first one I'd thought of.

She rolled over, her eyes still closed as she nestled closer to my chest. "Vaughan." My name ghosted on her lips as I pulled her closer, the need to hold her driving me crazy.

"Yeah, baby, right here. I'm sorry it's so late." I mumbled my apology on the off chance she was awake. With her face pressed against my skin I couldn't be sure unless I pulled away to look and that wasn't happening.

"Did you have a good night?" Her words were slow, sleepy and unintentionally sexy. The hard-on I'd ignored flipped me and my good intentions off as he made his presence known. And unless she was in a coma there was no chance she couldn't feel it pressed against her.

I tried to be a nice guy, all that *what-would-Jesus-do* floating through my head as I swallowed hard. "It was great. Had a good time. Lots of fun." I babbled like an idiot who didn't have a firm grasp on English.

Better she think I was a moron with shitty vocabulary than a pervert, not that she wasn't going to come to that conclusion pretty fast if I didn't get a handle on Mr. Happy.

Oh.

Fuck.

My body froze, not one muscle moving as her lips started to make a slow seductive descent down my chest. I had no freaking idea what she was doing and whether it was some kind of test, but if I could have stopped breathing and not died, I'd have signed up for it stat.

And because I obviously didn't have enough problems to deal with, her hands decided to get in on the action too, fingers tiptoeing across my torso like an army of drunken ants.

"Gillian, baby." I kept my hands safely in the platonic zone as she continued with her mission. "I know it's late so I'm happy to hold you and go to sleep." *No we're not, you big fat liar*, my dick argued, urging me to shut the fuck up. "But if you want something from me, I'm good with that."

It was the understatement of the century, the *I'm good with that* more like I'd chop off my own cock and hand it to her if that was the only way she'd touch it. It was messed up and I didn't care, her mouth and lips throwing gasoline on an already out of control inferno.

She chuckled against my skin, the vibration traveling to my balls as she tilted her head up to look at me. Man, she was beautiful. Her dark blonde hair framing her face as those knockout eyes slowly opened.

"You're *good* with that?" she repeated, because it hadn't sounded stupid enough coming from my own mouth. "I don't want you to be *good* with it." She undulated against my body. "I want you to want me."

Fuck.

Me.

If there was a way I could have said those words in thirty different languages I'd have given her the world tour. But as it stood I could barely handle the one I was born with and even that had been a challenge. So instead of opening my mouth and telling her bullshit that didn't convey my *need* nearly sufficient enough, I took those beautiful freaking lips and showed her exactly how much I wanted her.

Good didn't even come close, I was in so deep that I was rethinking the need of oxygen, loving my lips pressed against hers. She sighed in satisfaction, my tongue taking the opportunity and exploiting it. She didn't seem to mind, her tongue finding its way into my mouth as she grinded against me.

While our mouths tangoed, her hand stayed the course, unwilling to be distracted as she grabbed my cock. God, it was good, the bastard jerking in her hand the minute she'd wrapped her fingers around it.

Soooooo.

Freeeeeeeeaking.

Gooooooooood.

As I continued to enjoy her astounding talent— unintentionally fucking her fist—her lips peeled off mine and moved downtown.

And I didn't mean to freaking Market Square.

Oh.

Fuck.

The risk of my brain short-circuiting went up to probably-going-to-happen, her lips around the head of my cock before I could fully appreciate it. Not one to not accept a gift when given, I yanked down my boxers to give her better access and thanked my two newest band members for ensuring my sobriety. There wasn't a chance I wanted the beer haze to dull how amazing her mouth felt, her talent with her wrist nothing to what she could do with her mouth.

"That feels so good," I moaned, my hands raking through her long hair as she twisted her fingers up and down my shaft. It was a symphony, the perfect amount of lips and hand, all working together in the greatest blowjob of all time. No, seriously, I didn't know whether to clap her performance or pat myself on the back for not blowing my load just yet. It wasn't easy, that was for sure, her eyes looking up at me as she hollowed out her cheeks.

Not going to last.

That was exactly the thought that flashed in my head as I pulled my dick from her lips—the fucking injustice of it all just appalling—and pushed her back on the mattress. "Not yet," I warned, sliding my fingers into her panties while cursing they were still on. "I don't think I adequately showed you how much I wanted you yet."

And talk was cheap.

Proving how agile my fingers were, I got rid of the panties pretty damn quick. Next was her bra because her tits were perfect and it was a crying shame to have them all covered up. Probably should have waited though, my mind having trouble remembering my objective as my mouth moved to her nipples. My tongue swirled, teasing each peak till it stood at attention as my hand slipped between her legs. Even though I'd barely started, she was already wet, our earlier activities probably responsible.

"I need to go down on you," I announced for no other reason than to watch her eyes flare with my intention. I loved it when they did, flames licking at her whiskey-colored irises.

"Do it." She arched her back, rolling her hips into my hand. "Put your mouth on me."

And I didn't need to be told twice, parting her thighs with my hands as my tongue went straight to her core with zero apology. She moaned on contact, her body writhing against the sheets as I alternated between licking and sucking, two fingers inserted inside of her just to make it more interesting.

"Yes."

The word music to my ears as I circled her clit, her body clamping around my fingers while the tension inside of her built.

I felt each tremble, each hitch in her breath and each moan of pleasure. I took ownership of all of it, their presence for no other reason than because of what I was doing to her. I was selfish, and didn't give a shit, wanting—no NEEDING—more of it.

"I want to make you come, Gillian. I want you to come for me just like this and then again when I'm inside of you." My thumb took over so I could watch her come undone. "I'm greedy, and once isn't enough for me."

"I'm close." Her voice warbled, the sound of it almost setting me off.

But close wasn't good enough, my hands and mouth finding new motivation to worship her body until she screamed out my name.

It didn't take long.

The "yes, Vaughan, yes" tumbling from her lips in loud breathy groans as I continued to lap her. "That felt so good."

"I'm not done yet." I kissed her thigh, her body still trembling as the echoes of her orgasm continued to wash through her. I wanted her to still feel it, for the tiny pulses to still be ringing through her body when I pushed in, bringing her back on the wave.

I was quick, getting the condom out and on while she still had her eyes closed, pushing into her in a long, hard, stroke.

"Oh!" Her eyes flew open, my cock filling her while her body was still riding the high, her pussy clamping around my length as it invaded her.

"I missed you tonight." My head dropped down, kissing her as I thrust in deep, her body feeling freaking amazing.

Her hands grabbed onto me, wrapping around my back as she looked at me under those sexy lashes. "I missed you too."

Those words on their own would have rocked my world. To know that the woman I was into was right there with me. But with Gillian I knew those words were prized. Rationed out, and kept for special occasions. And I felt like I was king of the world that she'd given them to me. It was sexier than any dirty talk she could ever utter through those perky pink lips and I was a hundred percent gone.

My hips rocked into her, each drag in and out getting harder and faster. She didn't flinch, not asking me to slow down or hold back, taking each drive and matching it with one of her own.

"Vaughan, I'm so close." Her back bowed off the bed, pressing her tits against my chest. "I'm so ready to—"

I didn't let her finish the sentence, lifting her leg higher on my hip and hitting her right where I needed to be. Her body clamped around me tight, taking everything I had to give her as she relaxed on the mattress, giving me some room between us.

It took just one swipe, my thumb on her clit and she fell off the edge of that cliff a second time. Her body contracted around my dick, shattering apart underneath me, the roll of her hips unrelenting as my name rushed out of her lips.

There was nothing I wouldn't do to please her. Wanting to see her sated and happy and knowing I was the cause was fast becoming my life's mission. It made me feel invincible, able to take a bullet straight to the chest and brush it off like it was nothing.

My balls got tight, and every ounce of self-control got up and left as I went over the edge with her. Hot jets pulsed out of me like a tsunami, my body shaking as every muscle tightened and then simultaneously released like a wacked out rubber band.

"Fuck," I groaned, holding myself up so I didn't crush her under my weight. My body stayed fused to hers as we both rode the wave, not moving an inch until the last tremor left her.

She didn't move, her eyes focusing on me as our lips brushed, every part of her feeling like it was mine. And in that moment it couldn't get more perfect.

"I'm the luckiest guy in the world." My head lowered, kissing her shoulder. "And I want to hold you all night."

Her lips spread into a grin, amplifying my already good mood. "I'll allow it. But that wake-up alarm is coming pretty quick."

She was right, who knew what time it was anymore and how much longer I had to sleep, but I didn't care. Given the choice between an extra few hours of shut-eye or doing what we did, I'd forfeit sleep every single time.

"Yeah, well I have no regrets. A second with you would never be wasted."

I kissed her again, taking her mouth as desperately as I did before. Partly because I thought she might argue and I wasn't giving her the chance, but mostly because I wanted to.

And she didn't know it yet, but whatever we had wasn't just some fling. Or an itch either of us wanted to scratch. I was all in, and no matter what happened with the band or the label or anything else, I wasn't letting her walk away.

25

Gillian

Being a rock star wasn't glamorous.

The hours were long, often being stuffed into boxes where you're expected to turn notes and words into something magical. And I wasn't even on that side of the equation, the observer— or tyrant depending on who you asked—watching it all happen slower than anyone wanted.

But I wouldn't have traded places with anyone.

Days were spent with Vaughan, Nico, Declan and Austin at Sound Bites, refining their sound and writing music. It was incredible to watch, each of them putting in the effort and working their asses off to form a band out of essentially thin air.

For Vaughan and me it was business as usual, me doing my job while he did his. And no one was any the wiser on what was going on between us. There were no kisses, no dry humping in the corner and no sneaky quickies in the bathroom. The most I allowed were a few stolen glances, a moment or two when our eyes would connect and I would know that smile had been meant just for me.

I loved it, the simmering passion underneath, just waiting for the moment when we could close that door and unleash it all.

The nights were when all bets were off.

It didn't matter how or when we got there. If we'd leave together, or if he'd go out with the band and then return later—every night was the same. He'd wrap his arms around me, take me to his bed and make love to me like I was a goddess.

Sometimes he was slow, purposeful, wanting to tease me to an inch of my sanity. Other times he was desperate, fast and hard, not wanting to waste a second. He didn't always get to choose though, needing to yield to exactly what I wanted and needed that particular day. He was incredibly generous, gifted in so many ways I couldn't even begin to count and I didn't just mean the sex.

Those concerns I had about developing feelings were no longer an issue. Not because I had been mistaken, and was totally cool with having emotionless sex. But because I didn't have a choice anymore; those pesky bastards sneaking right in whether I wanted them or not.

His ex-girlfriend had clearly been crazy for not seeing how amazing he was. He was so incredibly sweet and caring, and I felt like my heart was literally too big for my chest. No man had ever made me feel like that, and when I finally found one that did, it was someone I'd have to eventually give up.

"What about Reborn?" Nico suggested, the topic of what to call themselves still unresolved as we broke for lunch.

It had been three weeks since I'd arrived in Pittsburgh, over a month since I first met Vaughan and the entire time had felt like I was on a roller coaster.

"But you really aren't though, are you?" Austin argued, tucking into his hoagie without offering an alternative.

"We could pick something that means something, like a word in another language or something?" Declan threw his suggestion into the ring, his earlier ideas of *The Four Horsemen* and *Oculus* shot down pretty quickly.

"Nope." Vaughan shook his head, not even considering it. "I don't care what it means to anyone else, it has to mean something to us. We're four guys from very different backgrounds and yet we've come together as one unit. It doesn't matter if we'd formed finding each other on the street or we were put together by Gillian." His eyes flicked to me and my heart skipped a beat. "We're here now, moving together with one common goal and not giving a shit what anyone else thinks."

"Like a family?" Austin offered.

"No, like an Army," Vaughan corrected, his chin kicking up proudly. "You don't get to choose to be in a family, you're born into it. We've each made a commitment to be here, right now to do what's right for the greater good of the group."

"Rock Army? Ugh, that sounds so fucking lame." Nico scrubbed his face, not needing to be told it sounded like a high school musical gone bad. "Yeah, I've got nothing."

It was moments like that where I felt like I couldn't breathe. Sitting there with them, eating sandwiches on the floor like I wasn't the one who didn't belong. It was dangerous how much I enjoyed it, maintaining my distance from Vaughan while thankful I got to be there with him, being a part of his dream.

But the sexy singer who could make me come on a dime was right about two things. They—the band—desperately needed a name, my marketing plan missing the vital part. And two, they were definitely an army.

There wasn't a doubt in my mind they would fight to the death for the success they deserved, to stay in the trenches until the job was done, and there wasn't a chance any of them would leave a fallen man behind.

Musically, they had each other's backs, but I had a hunch there was more to the band than just that.

"Army of None."

I hadn't even realized I said it out loud until the other noise stopped, the attention of the band on me.

Vaughan's smile was slow, spreading across his lips as the name marinated. "I like it, we're fighting for our own interests and fuck everyone else."

"It can work," nodded Declan, his own grin making an appearance. "It can mean anything, and we know what it means to us."

"What a fucking superstar." Nico shoulder bumped me, clearly approving.

Austin took another bite of his hoagie, lifting his hand in support.

"Looks like it's settled. I'll get Emily to call a designer and work on the branding. If we can get a song ready to go, I want to launch it tomorrow."

It hadn't been my intention to name the band, wanting them to find something that they identified with. But it was a happy accident, being pretty pleased with myself as I went out to call Emily.

I could hear Vaughan chatting and laughing in the break room as I left, the happy noise spilling into the hall. Emily hadn't joined us for lunch, wanting to go out and check out the city on a rare day I didn't need her. While she didn't complain, I knew she was bored being my assistant. But I needed someone I could trust, and she was the only person who fit the brief.

"Em." I was glad when she picked up on the second ring, concerned her day off might have translated to being at a day spa with her phone on silent. "I need someone in branding and—"

"Gillian," she stopped me before continuing. "I just had a call from your dad."

It was funny, but I knew it was coming. The impending doom on what would have otherwise been a fantastic day, just waiting to screw with my mood. And really, I shouldn't have been surprised, that he'd waited that long had been unexpected.

"What did he want?" I felt my jaw tightened and my nerves tensing. "And why did he call you?"

"Why do you think? He assumes I'm going to blab."

There was nothing simple about my father, and if he wanted information, he'd go to whatever lengths to get it. It wasn't so much as he didn't trust me, as he was tired of being out of the loop. He wanted results, wanted to see dividends, and figured it was easier to get Emily to talk. It wouldn't be the first time, and sure as hell wouldn't be the last, his little wellness checks with her always with an ulterior motive.

"And what did you tell him?" I asked, not needing to be concerned but curious what kind of bullshit she fed him.

"That you joined a commune of Pennsylvania Dutch, and I hadn't seen you since Tuesday." I could hear the smile in her voice.

"And he bought that?"

"Hell, no. But he did tell me to let you know that he expected you and the band back in New York by next week. And Gillian, I don't think he was mucking around."

No, I didn't think he was either.

"Are you far?" I asked, cursing I hadn't gone out and rented my car. Usually I loved my independence—cursing my father's insistence at using drivers—but I hadn't even thought about it since I'd arrived. Hadn't worried about it once, happy to ride with Vaughan or Emily if there was a need.

So weird it hadn't even crossed my mind until then.

Emily was already in the car and heading back, letting me know she wouldn't be long. And while we ended the call with a commitment to ignore my dad and his *demands*, I knew it wasn't something I could outrun.

The little bubble I'd been living in was about to burst.

Because as much as I could pretend things had changed, the reality hadn't.

We'd always had an expiration date, even if I'd chosen to ignore it.

And Vaughan and I were about to become history.

While I'd managed to keep our relationship under the radar in Pittsburgh, I wouldn't have the same luxury in New York. Too many eyes, too many ears and waaaaaay too many of my father's people for someone to not notice.

Fuck.

My heart started to beat faster in my chest, knowing the day would eventually come but still being unprepared. It hadn't been long enough, annoyed I was going to be forced to give away the one guy who'd made me happy.

"Hey, what are you doing out here?" Vaughan had left the others, coming out to find me. "Is everything okay?"

He looked around, making sure we were alone before touching my arm. Even though I'm sure he hated sneaking around, he'd done it willingly for me.

"We need to go back to New York." I mustered up all myself control, refusing to be emotional. "Next week at the latest."

He nodded, not sharing the same amount of concern. "Well, okay. I'd hoped to stay here longer but we can probably go back and work in the studio." He moved closer, lowering his voice. "Is that what you're worried about?"

Having someone concerned about me wasn't something I was used to. My skin tingled, lapping up his affection like a potted plant starved for sunlight. I needed to tell him, let him know that our fairytale was almost over.

But I couldn't.

Wanting whatever dying seconds were left in my fantasy before I had to go back to my old life and face reality.

A reality that didn't have him in it.

"No, I think I'm just tired." I rubbed my temples, the lie passing easily from my lips. "I'm looking forward to going back, regaining my home field advantage." More lies, but so much easier than telling him what I wanted to say.

"Baby," his voice rumbled, the gap between us almost non-existent. "You don't need to be in New York to take advantage of me. Anytime, any place." He chuckled, making my body heat.

We never tempted fate when people were around but the uncertainty of it all made me take risks I usually wouldn't. Flirting with Vaughan where anyone might hear or see, too tempting to give up.

"Go back to rehearsal, rock star. I want a useable track by the end of today. You haven't got time to play with me." My hands grabbed his arm, turning him around and gently shoving him in the direction of the studio.

He had enough on his plate, and worrying about me or the situation wouldn't do him or the band any good.

It wasn't his problem.

It was mine.

"Oh, you'll have a track, Gillian," he called over his shoulder, smoldering even as he walked away. "Be prepared to be wowed."

I didn't bother telling him it was too late, and that had happened weeks ago.

Emily knew me well enough not to mention my father or going back to New York when she returned. Instead, she brought her bubbly enthusiasm, insisting that we head to her penthouse suite that night and camp together like a bunch of five year olds. It was a dumb idea. Other than with Emily, sleepovers weren't something I did when I'd been an *actual* child, participating when I was an adult was ridiculous.

But my gorgeous stepsister wasn't easy to say no to, the band helping to champion her cause especially since she was bribing them with late night room service.

Five against one.

So I caved.

The truth was, I was secretly glad for the distraction, thankful I wouldn't be alone with Vaughan. Because as much as I craved his body and missed his touch—yearning for those hours when it was just the two of us—he would sense something was up.

I wasn't sure how he did it, his ability to read me like last week's news nothing short of remarkable. But having to lie to him again wasn't something I was looking forward to.

"I expected you to fight harder." We enjoyed our last few minutes of privacy as he pulled into the parking lot. "I was looking forward to our own little celebration tonight." He pulled his mouth into a pout.

I swear the man had no idea how adorable he was. If he ever found himself up on murder charges, all he had to do was look at the jury like that and tell them he was sorry. I would never condone the misappropriation of justice but I'd understand.

"Then why did you tell Emily what a good idea it was, insisting how *fun* it would be?" I mused, wondering how it had sounded so appealing.

"Because I assumed you would say no. I was keeping up appearances," he joked, grabbing my overnight bag as well as his own as we walked through the lobby and up to the elevator.

"Well, it's too late now."

We rode the elevator in an easy silence. I'd managed to keep whatever maelstrom brewing in my brain under wraps and he'd kept his hands to himself. It was a solid effort, and no doubt difficult for both of us. When the elevator opened we strolled to Emily's room, Vaughan knocking on the door before shooting me a cheeky last-minute wink.

With no idea that Emily knew about us, he was playing with fire, just itching to get caught.

"Hey!" Emily threw open the door, her bright smile only overshadowed by her radioactive pink onesie. I had to shield my eyes, my retinas burning on contact.

"What are you wearing?" I coughed out a laugh, positive the color she had on was illegal in at least six states.

She waved her hands, dismissing my concerns. "Pleeeeease, we're having a slumber party. What did you expect me to wear?"

Not sure how to answer that but if she had a matching one tucked away for me, we were going to have some serious words.

She threw her arms around us and hugged us both, welcoming us into her suite and telling us to sit down. She'd gone all out, buying an entire aisle of snack food and laying it out on a dining room table. I was happy to see there were a few bottles of wine in her haul, the idea of too much wholesome goodness driving me to drink.

Wow, I was starting to sound like Vaughan.

Declan and Austin were already inside, their wardrobe noticeably different than when we first met. The chinos and button-down shirts hadn't made an appearance in the last week, Marcus working his magic with the pair. As they sat in their dark denim, fitted T-shirts and heavy boots it was tempting to do a double take. Taking them on tour was going to be interesting, the trail of disappointed groupies stretching a mile long.

"Gentleman." I nodded, greeting them as I sat down and noticing they were both nursing sodas. "No onesies for you?"

Declan laughed, his eyes flicking over to Emily. "Sorry, not on Marcus's approved list. I'm trying to be a team player."

There was another knock, Emily running back to the door and flinging it open. I hoped for all our sakes it was just Nico and not some other surprise Emily had planned.

"Ummm, are we crashing a kiddie party?" Vaughan took a seat beside me while Nico was given the same hug and welcome we'd received. "There is way too much sugar on that table."

What he—or any one else—didn't know was that it was Emily's M.O. It was a tradition started by her mother, spoiling us rotten whenever I'd come to stay. I was thirteen before I'd realized it was for my benefit, their attempt to give me a regular childhood and make me feel welcome. It didn't matter how old I got, whenever I'd visit there would be a king's ransom in treats and candy, Emily taking over for her mother when she turned sixteen.

It should have been obvious to me—the whole idea, her insisting—but I'd been too preoccupied with Vaughan to notice. Emily was doing what she always did when she thought I was nervous or sad, showering me with her version of happy and hoping some of it stuck. I hated that she needed to worry, and that even after all these years, I still needed the help.

"So I was thinking." I deliberately shelved the mixed bag of feelings I had and decided to give everyone a few surprises of my own. "How would you feel if we went live tonight?"

"Live as in one of those videos?" Austin asked, his face clearly not liking the idea.

I pulled the thumb drive from my pocket, waving it in the air for everyone to see. What? I was trying to be dramatic, embracing Emily's tone. "No, not a live video. One of the sound engineers gave me Army of None's first song."

They had recorded a few, some more polished than others but "Rise Up" was the one I had chosen to be the band's first single.

It was punchy, while still being commercial, the powerful lyrics and driving beat giving everyone a little something to enjoy. And I didn't need a crystal ball to know it was going to be a bonafide hit.

"I'm uploading the song online and seeing if we get it to viral, this time intentionally." I grinned at Vaughan, genuinely proud of what he'd achieved.

"You think we're ready for that?" Vaughan's eyes brimmed with an excitement that had nothing to do with me, and everything to do with the music.

"Yeah, I think we've kept you hidden in the shadows enough. It's time for you to get back on the horse."

"Then hells yeah we're ready." Vaughan nodded before shooting Declan a pained look. "I'm sorry, dude, but *hell* needed to be added."

"Not going to say it with you, but am totally willing to overlook it." He laughed before turning to me. "Let's do this."

Wrestling my laptop out of my overnight bag, I set it up on the coffee table and inserted the drive. It would only take a few minutes before I would be kissing it goodbye and sending it off into cyber space to do its thing. And if everything went the way I'd planned, by the time we touched down in New York next week, Vaughan would be getting attention of a different kind. Not for some rant or tweet, or a disastrous concert of unmatched proportions. But seeing what I'd caught glimpses of that first day in the hotel room, confirmed when I saw him singing not far from that fountain.

He was a star, needing to be shared with the world and I'd had him all to myself for too long.

26

Vaughan

Putting a song out so soon was a dream I hadn't counted on. I expected to spend another month or two in the studio. Then for some old asshole with a receding hairline who hadn't seen his dick over his gut in the last ten years, to tell me how to do it better. But the digital age was a wonderful thing. And if we were going to launch a successful album and hopefully make money, we were going to have to get us some likes and hits, the need for the thumbs up a necessary evil.

Not sure what old man Duzan knew about what was going on but Gillian had said he'd called and summoned us back to New York. I wasn't sure if he was aware that our renewed contract superseded the old one, meaning his hard-on for keeping me and Nico chained to his front porch like a bunch of house pets wasn't going to happen. Whether he liked it or not, we were going to be making money, and the debt he had with White Trash Circus was a problem that belonged to the past.

I couldn't wait to see the look on his face, perplexed by the fucking contradiction. On one hand, pissed beyond measure he'd have to cut us a bunch of checks. On the other, ecstatic over the flow of green that I knew would follow. Either way, there was nothing he could do, the songs were ours and ours alone and we were controlling our own destiny.

Not sure how he was going to react, knowing that the effort had been at the hand of his daughter. Or that she'd been in my bed most nights. But for what it was worth, I didn't care, itching to stop sneaking around my neighborhood and pretending my chapter had faded to black.

"This is so exciting." Emily jumped around, the monstrosity she'd been wearing giving us all eyestrain as we huddled around Gillian.

The mood in the hotel suite was electric, eyes glued to the computer screen as a little blue bar raced to the finish. Only part that sucked was not being able to kiss my girl at the end of it. But I'd find a way, willing to pull her into the bathroom for a quick time out and kiss like I wanted to.

"It's done." Gillian sat back, watching the screen.

The recording of one of our songs was simultaneously tweeted, Insta'd and Facebooked through the Domination network. With an audience of literally millions at her fingertips, she dropped the track tagging our newly minted—albeit barren pages—adding a logo with our name on it as the only profile pic. She'd reasoned she wanted them curious, hungry and not given too much information just yet.

"Shouldn't we post a welcome message or something?" Declan asked, eyeing our page, a measly thirty or something random likes staring back at us. "Let people know who we are?"

Gillian shook her head. "They don't care who you are, not now at least. They want to be entertained. Then, when we have them on the hook and they're looking for a face to match the picture they have in their head, that's when we'll give it to them. Not a second before. So don't any of you start laying claim to it just yet. Austin, no telling your family."

"Gees Gillian, I did that one time and it was years ago." He smirked, a private joke shared between them.

Irrationally, I was jealous. No reason to be, because Austin's virgin status meant the chances of him sleeping with Gillian were remote. But while he had a dick, it was still a possibility. And I didn't exactly have the best track record with band members.

Another bone of contention—clearly I had a few—was their shared history. He'd said years ago. So while working together was new and sparkly, their relationship wasn't. The years since they first laid eyes on each other, shit all over the month or so I had. And I didn't like the competition.

"What happened years ago?" Nico asked, saving me from looking like a childish piece of shit who needed to know every single interaction she'd had with both of those brothers. Virginity was only penetration, right? Oral and fingering were still on the table.

"In our last band, Austin texted our family our unreleased tour schedule. And our good meaning Aunt decided to share it with her church. A bootlegged version of our dates—some yet to be confirmed—were online and circulating within a few hours," Declan chuckled. "Our manager was furious, and stopped CC'ing him in the group emails."

"How was I supposed to know she was going to share it? I was just trying to see who wanted to come and when." He shrugged, smile on his face.

"Well, all the good intentions in the world won't mean shit if you blow my strategy. So keep it to yourselves." Gillian's warning lacked the usual venom, Austin earning himself a smile that I didn't like.

Stopping myself from grabbing the kid by the neck and asking him to state his intentions, I left them to ohh and ahhh all over the computer and went and grabbed myself a beer. While Em had catered like she was putting on the best three-year-old's birthday of all time, there were more than just a few adult treats. The Rolling Rock in her refrigerator, a sight for sore eyes.

"Hey, you cool, man?"

I hadn't noticed Declan follow me out, his judgment thankfully not shared as I twisted off the cap.

"Yep, all good. Just not good on the waiting thing though." I tapped my fingers on the bottle, trying to sort through my head while I was acting like a jerk.

She'd been nothing but professional with everyone else except me, and I had no reason for behaving like I was. Other than the fact no one else knew we were together, free to express any feelings they might have.

"Look, I know we aren't super tight just yet, but I can tell there's something on your mind. Maybe share the load? I know what happened in your last band, and the first contract, so having some mixed feelings about all of this is perfectly natural."

Great, I was being psychoanalyzed by a Midwestern Dr. Phil.

He'd mistakenly assumed I was having cold feet, worried I was going to shit the bed again or suffering some weird PTSD. And granted, his concerns were valid, my last foray into rock stardom had blown some serious balls. But I wasn't worried about stepping on stage—the four of us solid—or what some douchebag blogger in California thought of our sound.

We were tight.

What was probably going to keep me up at night was the no-man's land I was currently in with Gillian. Not really a relationship in the true sense of the word, but not feeling any less real despite it. And maybe that's why I was feeling like a lion ready to pounce. Because Gillian was mine, but I couldn't say dick about it.

"So let me ask you something." I figured if he was up for therapy, I wasn't about to look a gift horse in the mouth. "You guys date?"

"Dude, I've heard about your weirdo sibling fantasies, but Austin and I share DNA and I'm not gay." He smirked, totally giving me shit, which was something new. I wasn't too pleased about the Emily/Gillian reference, information that had probably come at the hand of Nico, but I'd deal with that later.

"Not each other, asswipe. As in, women." I rolled my eyes, wondering if the whole situation hadn't fried my brain.

The fact I was even having the conversation should have been evidence enough. That it was with some dude I barely knew who'd never even had sex . . . well that was the rubber stamp.

"Vaughan, I'm a virgin not a saint." He laughed, proving what I'd suspected, that he wasn't so holy. "Of course I date. I love women, and love spending time with them. Do pretty much all the regular stuff you guys do but we stop before it gets to sex."

"Why? Because seriously, I can tell you that you're missing out. Aren't you even tempted?" The sidestep the conversation had taken made me think I'd caught a break. Maybe me having a deep and meaningful wasn't the way to go, instead finding out how committed they were to the cause.

"Yeah, but that's the point. Not doing something because it feels good, but because it's right. I'm not embarrassed about saving myself for my wife, it was a choice I made. And I'm happy to wear it as a badge of honor. I'm not going to pretend to be something I'm not, just because it makes people uncomfortable."

Fuck me, the virgin had more fucking balls than I did.

Not cool.

I didn't even know what to do with it, concerned about how much sense he was making and I'd barely had a swig of beer.

"Back to my original question. Say you're dating a woman, and you're really into her." My head moved closer, meeting the dude's eyes. "Not Sunday school into her, like *really* into her."

Declan laughed, waving his hand urging me to continue. "Got it. Really into her."

"And you've not made your commitment to keep your dick for a wife that may or may not happen in the future, so you're having sex. Not cheap one-night stand bullshit, or fucking just for sport. But sex because you dig this girl so much and have feelings."

I wasn't even going to pretend I'd littered the conversation with more swears than I'd intended. He was probably going to need to drink a bottle of holy water and pray ten Hail Marys just on my behalf so his head didn't explode. But I had enough trouble being cagey and keeping the identities classified, I didn't have enough brain energy to do both.

"Okay," he nodded.

"And you think maybe this one could be it. The *one*. But you can't say shit about it and maybe she's not on the same page. So because no one knows, there really isn't a reason why some other asshole can't show he's interested, and maybe try and date her too."

Concise and clear, it was not. A field of landmine babble, not saying anything accurately and making me sound like I still needed to color in crayon.

"How do you stop some other guy from taking what's yours?" I tried again, willing to look like a caveman beating his chest rather than an educated idiot.

"You can't. Same way she can't stop some woman taking what's hers. Works both ways."

He had a valid point and not something I'd considered. Maybe Gillian had similar thoughts, wondering if I wouldn't jump the minute some chick wiggled her ass in front of my face. Not that I'd been a crotch hound before, but she didn't know that. And I knew what everyone thought of musicians, assuming we screwed everything with a pulse. She'd probably seen more than her share.

"Dude, I'm not interested in any other women, just her. Trust me, there's a greater chance of you going down that road than me, and we already know where you stand on the issue." I laughed, wishing it was her I was sharing those sentiments with instead of him. Either way, she needed to know, and be clear I wasn't going to start screwing around like a jackass.

Declan stopped, moving in closer and dropping his voice to barely a whisper. "Is this about you and Gillian?"

What.

The.

Actual.

Fuck.

"What?" I tried to laugh, wondering how much the bastard knew. "What are you talking about? That's just. . . yeah, not sure what you mean." I was back to sprouting bullshit, wading through muddy waters without a flashlight.

"You mean you *aren't* together?" His brow rose, just waiting for me to lie to his face. Whatever intel he had, it was reliable. That or he was guessing and incredibly convincing.

I put down my beer, grabbing him by the neck and bringing him in close. "What do you know? Don't leave anything out."

"Knock it off, Vaughan." He shook off my hand and straightened his T-shirt. "It's obvious you're together. The looks, you guys spending so much time together. I get you guys are trying to keep it on the quiet and that's fine, but don't insult my intelligence."

Busted.

So maybe we hadn't been as discreet as I'd thought. And maybe it was for the best, my mind reasoned. "Austin know?" Because if he did then maybe I could relax a little. Not that it solved any other problems, just the one I had percolating at that moment. Then maybe we could go back to enjoying unleashing our song or whatever, and I could dial down the rage for later when it was actually valid.

"Yeah Austin knows. Seriously man, it's no big deal. Gillian is an amazing woman and has great business sense. She's smart, knows the industry and works harder than anyone I know. She's not going to drop the ball regardless of what's going on with you guys. Short of that, it's none of my business."

Never in a million years had I expected him to be so understanding or being so goddamn cool about it. Hell, White Trash Circus would have called a group meeting, weighing all the pros and cons on how great the potential to fuck us over was. Guess that's why Johnny never mentioned the acrobat thing, preferring to live the lie. But these guys didn't care, trusting me to handle my business and respecting me by keeping their mouths shut. And I don't think I'd ever been more thankful that Connor fucked Lindsey than I was at that moment.

Seriously, I'd won the fucking lottery. Pulled the handle and spun up all gold bars, and nothing about the situation sucked.

Not.

A.

Thing.

"Really appreciate that." I nodded, swallowing the lump in my throat. Who knew I'd get so emotional. "And thanks for everything you've done. Stepped in, taking on my shit. You wouldn't have been my first choice, but I bet a million dollars we weren't yours either."

Not sure how Gillian dressed it up and made it sound appealing, because Declan and Austin sure as hell didn't need us. Add in my reputation for being a hothead and our musical tastes that didn't match up and it would have been a solid pass from almost anyone else.

"I was curious when I heard your voice. Figured it was worth the shot."

"Hey, you guys having a secret band meeting I should know about?" Gillian strolled in, her face so lit up with excitement it took everything I had not to kiss her. "We have some extreme traffic happening online, likes, comments, shares—conservative estimate is you're viral by the morning. Why don't you come and share it with the rest of the band?"

"Sounds good." I glanced over at Declan who gave me a silent nod. "Let's go see the fireworks."

The urge to sleep on the floor on a mattress with a bunch of guys wouldn't normally have rated high on my to-do list. But as far as nights went, the one we'd had was pretty freaking spectacular.

As Gillian had predicted, "Rise Up" was getting all kinds of attention. Rumors began swirling as to who we were and what our story was, everyone worth their salt weighing in and tossing in a guess. And Gillian's phone hadn't stopped ringing.

Her dad had been the most persistent, wanting to know why she was launching another band when she was supposed to be concentrating on The Circus. And lord was he pissed when he found out what she'd done, annoyed beyond recognition that she'd switched out the contracts, our deal completely separate to the one before.

She hadn't even needed to tell us what his thoughts were on the matter, hearing his booming voice cursing up a storm as she shuffled to the bedroom to take the call in private. No doubt he'd calm down a little when he realized he was still going to be making a truckload of cash, but I imagined her little act of defiance was not going to go unpunished.

We hung out together, ordering dinner from room service—needing something more substantial than the buffet of candy Emily provided—and camped out on the floor. Nico and I had a beer or two, the girls enjoying their wine, while the other guys stayed true to script and rocked it hardcore with some Arnold Palmer.

Every time we thought the counter had bottomed out or gone as high as it was going to for the night, we were proven wrong. The reach went further and faster than that stupid status I'd posted, giving us numbers a Kardashian would get wet over. We'd left Earth's gravity hours ago, our trajectory firmly locked on outer space.

And as much as I wanted to pull Gillian into my arms and sleep with her by my side, I was content to know she was close. Satisfied we'd be having a private celebration later and happy to share the current one with all of the people who made it happen. That she was a part of it meant I got to throw in a few extra hugs without it looking suspect. Not that I really cared anymore. I wasn't sure what Emily knew, but the first opportunity I had, I was telling Nico.

Lucky for me I was given the chance early the next morning. Emily and Gillian disappeared into the bathroom in Emily's bedroom to shower and change—I let the joke slide that they went in together—while we fended for ourselves. Laying it out to my bass player and my friend that I was in love with the girl currently captaining our ship.

"I know." He smirked, flooring me just like Declan had. "Whatever makes you happy, man."

"If you knew, why didn't you say anything?"

Nico wasn't the kind of guy to keep his mouth shut. And while it had been Connor and I that had been the tightest, he had no problems giving me his opinion. I'd have imagined me sleeping with Gillian would have given him a lot to say, especially since the implosion of our last band had happened because of secret fucking. That it hadn't been me, seemed irrelevant.

"Because clearly you didn't want to talk about it. And to be completely honest, you've been writing and singing some of the best stuff I've ever heard. I didn't want to fuck it up and say something and rock the boat." He leaned in, keeping his voice tight between us. "Full disclosure, if you were sleeping with her dad and churning out the same material, I still probably wouldn't have mentioned it."

"That is fucking disturbing." I shuddered, relieved that the big reveal had been such a non-event. "But I want to make myself clear that I have zero tolerance when it comes to shit landing on her doorstep. Even though the truth is out there, you treat her with respect. Nothing's changed and as far as me and business are concerned we're two separate things. She has enough hesitation about taking us public, last thing she needs is people saying shit they have no right to comment on."

There could be no miscommunications as to what was acceptable, and her being in the middle of a shitstorm wasn't it. And as long as everyone remembered their manners and kept their noses out of it, then we'd have no problems.

"Dude, relax." He laughed, holding his hands up in surrender. "Firstly, I love Gillian. She's awesome, and if it came down between you and her, I would genuinely have to think about it. Secondly, I'd never do that. Your biz, is your biz and while I might give you a hard time, I'd never do that to her."

Nico was a lot of things, but lying son of a bitch wasn't one of them. So with our positions clarified we shook on it, me confirming with Declan and Austin that we kept it between us. No one had any objections, trusting me more than I probably deserved and genuinely happy for me and her.

And while I knew it was the calm before the storm—eventually everything needing to come out—I was going to enjoy the smooth sailing as long as I could.

27

Gillian

The band might have been surprised by their apparent overnight success, but market research didn't lie.

While the branding had yet to be finessed, the plain black background and white lettering was clean and compelling enough for people to take notice. That was before I'd even played the song, the handful of likes we'd achieved simply by launching the pages solely on their name alone. No explanation, no mission statement, and no idea as to who they were.

But once the music was out there, all bets were off.

Unprecedented growth boosted their new social media pages to respectable levels, my phone about to disintegrate under the strain of messages and calls. And it wasn't just industry people wanting the inside word, everyone from sports shoe companies to soda giants, making all kinds of offers and brandishing endorsements.

My father didn't share the same sense of excitement.

It shouldn't have been a shock to him that I'd done it completely my own way, but that was where we found each other. Him both angry and annoyed that I was the product of his DNA. Of course, he was quick to forget that Domination didn't become what it was now by everyone sitting around and chanting peaceful affirmations. No, he'd double-crossed his original investors, cutting them out of his first largest artist, which gave him the capital to buy them out. It had been shrewd and calculated, with zero emotion. But when I pulled a similar maneuver taken directly from *his* playbook, I was a renegade with my own agenda.

Ignoring the yelling—something that I was more familiar and comfortable with than his gratitude—I reminded him that unlike what he had done, he was still looking to make a sizeable return. Sure, not as much as I was going to make, my appointment as their manager *and* agent autonomous from Domination giving me a comfortable cushion. I wasn't even sure if Vaughan or any of the guys realized the clause buried on page three, the Domination label used purely for distribution.

But I wouldn't have traded anything, knowing it was not only the right thing to do for Vaughan and the band, but for me also. That he'd been so deliriously happy was just the icing on the cake.

In the days that followed we struggled to find our new normal. I pushed the band harder than ever before, slightly worried the creative process that had been working so well, would dry up when we went back to New York. And while technically my father had no say in what the band did or where they recorded, I was still contractually bound to Domination. If Warrick Duzan called me back into the fold, I had no choice but to go. Unless I was willing to resign and throw away everything I'd worked for.

But the nights with Vaughan were my saving grace, our little pocket of paradise where everything going on in his life and mine were pushed off to the periphery.

Just the two of us.

Being together.

It was our last night in Pittsburgh, his small apartment in Swissvale probably being upgraded by the time he got back. We'd made love and spent hours exploring each other's bodies like it was the last time. And for me, I wasn't sure if it was. But more than the orgasms he'd given me, I loved the way he held me. His arms wrapped around me tight, my head on his chest as I listened to his heartbeat.

"You packed?" His hand trailed down my shoulder, tickling my skin.

I pressed my lips to his chest, kissing it as I grinned. "You saw me do it, a more appropriate question would be have *you* packed?"

He laughed, the air between us sizzling as he cinched me in closer. "I've got everything I need, and whatever I forget, I'm sure Marcus can take care of."

Despite barreling into the unknown in the next few days, there was an ease between us. And that was going to be the hardest thing to give up.

If I could just slow down time, I'd wind it back to a crawl.

His lips kissed my forehead gently while his hand played in my hair. "The early feedback is good, isn't it?" The question surprising me as I tilted my head up to look at him.

It seemed I wasn't the only one who was nervous, our reasons obviously different.

"Vaughan, everyone loved the track, my phone hasn't stopped. Don't tell me you haven't noticed, I know you're not that humble or oblivious."

I didn't want to try to minimize his feelings, or make them seem invalid. And when it came to dealing with human emotions, I knew I needed work. But insecurity wasn't something I expected from him, not sure if it was masking something else.

"Are you worried about going to New York?"

I knew it wasn't his favorite place, not sharing my love for my city. But it wasn't permanent, free to go back home whenever he wanted.

He didn't answer, instead studying me closer than I liked as he opened his mouth. "Are *you* worried about going back?"

"No, not worried. I'm excited, looking forward to getting back home." I lied, not wanting to ruin the moment. "Honestly, it will be nice to have my own bed back." I laughed, hoping to lighten the mood.

"Can't say I'm not going to enjoy being in your bed with you. I'd fantasized about it last time, not sure I even got to see the inside of your bedroom before we left."

And therein lay the problem, him assuming we were going to pack and move our game of happy families across state lines.

So much for leaving that shit to deal with later.

Damn, it was going to suck.

"Vaughan, as much as I would love to have you, there's no way you can stay with me. I moved you into my apartment last time because you had a concussion and were a flight risk, no one would have assumed any foul play. But you have to know that can't happen when we go back. It would raise too many questions. Hell, I'm not even sure how we've gotten away with no one asking about us here. No one can honestly believe I'm still sleeping on your couch."

I'd been pleading ignorance, assuming everyone else was doing the same. Not one raised eyebrow, not one shady question and not one snicker thrown our way. They either suspected absolutely nothing or were keeping it to themselves, but even I had to admit that it looked "questionable" that I was still sleeping on Vaughan's pull out mattress when Emily was at a hotel.

"So what if people knew?" His body stiffened a little, the innocence and sincerity in his voice making my heart hurt. "What if people knew we were together?"

"Oh, Vaughan." I shook my head, counting the ways of how terrible it would be. "Not only will it risk my reputation but yours too. Are you ready for all the accusations of sleeping your way to the top? Or the under their breath jokes about being a whore? And trust me, that is some of the nicer stuff they could say. You don't even want to hear what they'll say about me."

Believe me, I'd gone through it a million times in my head. No matter how much time passed, it didn't look any better.

"And think about Nico, Declan and Austin." His sense of brotherhood surely wanted the best for them. "Think of what they'll say or what they'll think. I would hate for anyone to think that what we created was just a means to get you into my bed. Or you, a way to get into mine."

He hesitated, a flash of something—possibly regret?—passing through his beautiful green eyes as his finger traced my spine.

"They know." His focus didn't falter, his eyes locked on me and tilting my chin so I had no choice. "And no one cares."

My body froze, ice running through my veins as I was utterly blindsided by his words. I couldn't have heard it right, convinced I'd misunderstood him or he'd said something else.

He couldn't seriously mean that Nico, Declan and Austin knew we were sleeping together. That just wasn't possible.

"What do you mean?" I was conscious to get all the facts and not fly off the handle. Besides not really being my thing, I had never seen it done with any benefit. And getting emotional would only add to my trouble.

His eyes caught on mine, the apology written all over his face before he'd opened his mouth. Any doubts of our little secret having stayed that way were gone, his next breath confirming it.

"I mean, I told them. It came up with Declan accidentally but apparently he already knew. Then I thought it was better if Nico heard it from me, but he had already connected the dots as well. I hadn't planned it, honestly it just kinda happened. I have feelings for you, Gillian, and we work so close together they noticed. I figured it was better to just get it in the open. Trust me, they get it and they're totally fine with it. Even promised not to make you feel weird about it."

Like a bomb had detonated, I had no feeling in my body. My arms and legs felt like jelly, and I was thankful we'd been lying down. My head was only held upright by sheer force of will, my mouth unable to open as the ringing in my ears continued.

"How long?" I croaked out, my voice horse. "How long have they known?"

His hand reached out again, grazing my cheek while his arm stayed wrapped around me. I wasn't sure if it was his attempt to comfort me or he was worried I was going to leave, but he didn't let up an inch. "Since the day of the song, just over a week."

"A week?" The air left my lungs in a rush, not sure if I was mad, embarrassed or devastated, the trifecta crushing me from the inside out. "And you didn't tell me?"

"I knew you would get upset, and there was no reason to. Gillian, I'm in love with you, okay. I know we haven't really talked about it but this is the real deal for me." His fingers brushed the hair off my face, surprising myself I hadn't asked him to stop.

He was insane.

Crazy not only in thinking there'd be no accountability and everyone was going to be so *cool* with it. And crazy for thinking that he was in love with me.

"Of course I'm upset." I pushed against his chest, giving me the distance I wasn't sure I wanted. "Vaughan, you've made me look . . ." *pathetic, stupid, weak—take your pick.* "You should have told me."

My jelly legs found some traction and kicked back the covers, my body covered in goosebumps as the cool air hit my skin. I wasn't sure what I needed to do but lying down beside him wasn't it.

"Gillian, did you hear what I said?" He watched me scramble, my uncoordinated body not getting me further than the edge of the bed. "I said I'm in love with you."

There was that word again.

My attempt to ignore it hadn't helped. And clearly he wasn't going to let it slide, repeating it for the cheap seats in case they'd missed it the first time.

"Vaughan, I—" I had no idea what to say.

What I wanted was for him to say it again, kiss me and let me tell him that I loved him too. Or at least, I thought I did, nothing else I'd shared with any other guy ever coming close.

But I couldn't.

Like everything in my life, it wasn't simple. And I couldn't just forget I had responsibilities, pretend it didn't matter and hope like hell it worked out for us. My dad had been married so many times he wasn't even sure how many ex wives he had. And as for my mother, well who knew what became of her.

That wasn't even taking into consideration his ex-girlfriend who he'd apparently loved too. Oh, I didn't think he still had feelings for her, but wasn't it too soon to have those feelings for me? How did he know what he was feeling was love?

I refused to bow my head, to mumble in his chest like I was dying to do. He deserved to see my face, to have me tell it to him straight. The problem was the minute I'd locked eyes with him, the words I meant to say didn't come out.

"What about Lindsey?" I asked, not wanting to bring her up but feeling like I had to. Because clearly I had ruined whatever small slice of happiness we had and mentioning the woman who'd broken his heart seemed like a good way to do it.

He laughed, his thumb tracing my jaw. "What I have with you isn't even the same ballpark. I cared about her, stayed with her out of habit, but it wasn't anywhere close to how I feel about you. You could never be anyone's replacement, let alone hers. I love you, Gillian. It's you, and only you. And I hate I have history I can't change that makes you doubt that."

"I can't pretend this will just work out, Vaughan. I can't just snap my fingers and make it okay. There will be questions, questions about us I don't want to answer."

It was a cop out and I knew it, dragging it out a little longer because I couldn't commit and couldn't tell him to leave either.

He didn't let it go, staying right there in the moment as he whispered against my lips. "You still haven't told me how you feel, Gillian. I need to know if I'm alone in feeling the way I do."

I needed to say something.

Anything.

He deserved that.

But as my mouth opened, the lie ready, I surprised us both. "I love you too."

It was the first time I'd ever said those words, at least not trivially. I said I loved some shoes, an amazing lemon meringue pie and a dog when I was eleven. Even when Emily or her mother said it to me, my response was always just a "me too," feeling like it was bad luck to actually say the words. But I loved him, I did, and I wanted the chance to say it at least one time, even if I never got to say it again.

His lips spread into an elated grin, lighting up his face as his eyes blazed. "That's all I needed to hear." His mouth pressed against me, kissing me like his life depended on it. "We'll work out the rest."

"No." I hated the tremble in my voice. "This isn't something we can just work out. Vaughan, this is our lives and a decision that could change both of them."

"So what are you saying? That you love me but you won't be with me? Because you know how crazy that sounds?" He scrunched up his face in confusion, not understanding how I couldn't just skip into the sunset with him.

"No more crazy than pretending that us announcing our relationship isn't going to attract a backlash we might never recover from. It's bad enough the band knows, there can be no one else."

Contain.

It was either end it, thank him for the memories, or circle our wagons and stop the fallout. And I wasn't sure he was capable of the latter.

"Gillian, how long do you think we're going to last sneaking around? You already said I can't stay with you and clearly we aren't going to be able to see each other in public? What does it leave? A shady rendezvous at a cheap hotel?"

"Security cameras. No hotels."

"Then what?"

There was a warning in his voice, telling me that if I suggested we stopped seeing each other he was going to fight it. He wasn't going to let it go, no matter what I said.

"Do you know what's going to happen when we get back to New York?" I asked, wondering just how much thought he'd given it. "Whatever happened before, the attention, the phone calls, people following you around—multiply that by a thousand. Before you were just known, a news story, something people had heard about while scrolling through their feed. Now, you've got something to say and we're giving you one hell of a platform. And relationships?" I laughed, knowing the line of women had probably already formed and they hadn't even seen his face. "You'll barely have time to shower and sleep."

"I am not giving up on you, Gillian. All this talk, trying to make it seem like there is no other way, isn't going to scare me. I know this is real, Gillian. Because everything else and everyone else I was with before doesn't come close. It's too late; I've felt it, it's inside of me and I won't walk away from it."

God, he was so sure. So freaking positive that we'd make it through.

"It is easier if you do." Because clearly I was too much of a coward to do it myself.

God, I was so angry. So pissed beyond measure I hadn't told him it was over. It would have been better for both of us—the clean break—hopefully remaining friends. But instead, I had to be selfish, wanting whatever time I could get even though I knew it would be impossible.

He stroked my cheek, his charming smile never far away from his lips. "C'mon, baby. You know me. And when have I ever done it the easy way?"

It seemed neither of us was thinking straight.

"Fine, but don't say I didn't warn you."

test, or her trying to prove a point it wasn't going to be a walk in the park. But I didn't like it, the radio silence making me antsy as fuck.

"Where are we going?" I asked the driver, a little sick of being in the dark as the other guys climbed in the car.

"Photo shoot in Brooklyn," he called over his shoulder. "That's all the information I've got."

The mood in the car was electric, everyone still riding high from the online buzz. I'd even managed to sideline my unease, glad to be out of our hotel rooms. And a photo shoot had to mean good things, why else would they want photographic evidence unless we were going to be telling everyone who we were. The sooner the better as far as I was concerned, and it wasn't about the fame. It was about finally being able to be proud of what I'd done; hiding in the shadows never had been my forte.

We pulled up to a warehouse in Brooklyn, the driver telling us there was someone waiting for us inside. Sure, that sounded like every freaking gangsta movie ever made. Not that it stopped me or anyone else from going in, too freaking excited as we stepped inside and faced our new fate.

God.

She was beautiful.

The minute I saw her was like a punch in the nuts, the sharp intake of air making my lungs hurt. It had only been three days but it felt like an eternity, and I wanted to touch her more than my next breath.

Her head was down, her dark blonde hair tied back like it usually was when she was *on duty*, her beautiful golden eyes hidden. It didn't even matter what she was dressed in, her corporate black armor not doing its job.

"Gillian." Her name was like a fucking prayer, my feet not stopping until I was standing right in front of her. The rest of the band could've still been in the parking lot and I wouldn't have given a shit, too starved from not seeing her to stop.

She lifted her head, giving me a smile that didn't reach her eyes as she watched us walk in. We might have been in the same room, but I might as well have been back in Pittsburgh. The distance still there.

"Hey everyone, great to see you." She welcomed us—no hug because New York Gillian didn't do that—and shook everyone's hand, my hand hesitating on hers when she finally got to me.

"You think we can talk?" I asked, doing my best to keep my voice low. There was a photographer in the corner and a few other people around so I knew why we were going through the motions. But it didn't mean I wasn't going to try.

"Vaughan." She said my name like I was any other guy. "We're about to get started with the shoot, can it wait?"

Ha! Wait? Wait for when? She'd been dodging me for three days, when was it going to happen.

"No, it can't."

"Celine, can you please get the other three styled. I want the black jeans and the leather jacket for Vaughan. No shirt underneath." She addressed one of the women, talking about me like I wasn't standing right in front of her. "We need a few minutes."

With Celine and her posse happily playing dress up with the other boys, Gillian lead me down the hall. She didn't touch me, smile or give me any indication she wasn't going to rip my balls off the minute we were alone but I was hopeful. She opened the door on a small windowless office, waiting until I stepped inside before joining me and shutting the world out behind her. The light was already on, the bright halogen overhead flooding the small space, the glow hitting her eyes just fucking right so they looked like they were on fire.

I didn't think, too wired from her early indifference and our separation to be using my brain, my body firmly with its own agenda.

"Fuck I've missed you." I kissed her before she could react, pressing her against a wall as my body covered her. She opened her mouth, my tongue taking full advantage and not wasting another second, my hands on her face as I held her still.

"Vaughan."

That was it. Exactly how I wanted her to say my name, the breathy sigh stealing past her lips whether she wanted to or not.

She was liquid in my arms, her mouth fused to mine as her nails dug into my back. She'd been just as starved, wanting me as much as I did her.

"God, I want you," I cursed into her hair. "I fucking want you right now, right here."

I didn't care what was going on outside the door. If the place were on fire, I'd have let it burn down around us. Wanting to stay with her just like that, with her lips on me and her heartbeat thumping against my chest.

"We can't." She tilted her head, nailing me in the eyes. "Vaughan, I know this has been hard for you, but we can't just do what we want."

Hard wasn't a word I wanted to be hearing from her pretty pink lips, the rod between my legs rock solid since the minute we saw her. "Gillian, you can't keep avoiding me. I'm fucking dying."

Yeah, it was dramatic, fucking sue me. But it was no less accurate. And I hadn't realized how much until I walked in. Seeing her was a delicious torture I wasn't sure I could hate.

Her hands pressed against my chest, shaking her head. "It's been three days, you've barely had time to miss me."

"Oh, I beg to differ." I scoffed, wondering what arbitrary amount of time I was supposed to wait. A week? A month? Like when was I allowed to miss her? "It's not just the sex, we haven't even talked."

She shook her head, either not knowing what to say or not being able to say it out loud. "Vaughan, we need to go back."

"Okay." What was I supposed to do? Fucking beg? Force her to talk to me? I mean, she had to *want* to or what was the point? Maybe if I gave her some more time she'd come to the realization all by herself. The one where I wasn't going anywhere and we belonged together.

I kissed her again because I was only willing to make so many concessions and then pulled away. Those few inches already felt like they were too far, but I could play nice.

"Great, let's go get you ready for the camera. The fans are going to love you." Her lips spread into a smile I didn't believe as she moved back to the door. And just like that, she was walking away from me.

We went through the motions, Celine asking me to follow her into a dressing room where she handed me my approved outfit. It was nothing special, a pair of distressed black jeans and a black leather jacket and that was it. When I walked out, some other woman I didn't know was ready with a makeup brush and some product that apparently needed to go in my hair. Continuing my commitment to playing nice, I did whatever they asked. Not one word of complaint.

The rest of the guys were also dressed, taking their turn in the chair like I did and getting their hair and makeup done. Wasn't sure why we needed freaking powder and bronzer but clearly the man behind the camera knew better.

Wasn't real fond of him.

He had been chatting to Gillian while the four of us were getting "ready," their interaction one of familiarity. She was smiling, whatever he was saying obviously amusing as he picked up his camera and showed her something on the display. Clearly it was riveting, Gillian only giving it a glance for a second or two before turning her attention to us.

Better.

But not great.

Under the dickwad's—sorry, we hadn't been formally introduced so that's what I went with—direction we were posed against a solid black background as he snapped off a few pics. He'd move around, telling us to look off into the distance like a bunch of dumbasses as he continued to shoot. How he was going to get anything usable was beyond me.

Declan and Austin apparently knew the drill, though their past photo shoots were a little more milk-and-cookies than what we were doing. Still they gave the douchebag—still didn't know his name—what he wanted, each of us getting pulled aside individually and getting personal attention.

"Van, tilt your chin down."

"It's Vaughan." I eyed him hard but did as he asked.

Snap. Snap. Snap.

He paused, his camera tilted to the side as he waved his hand. "Maybe take the jacket off?"

I was about to tell him to go fuck himself—my limit for being nice due to expire—when Gillian stepped in front of me. Whatever I was about to say was no longer my priority, her hands reaching up to my shoulders and pulling down the jacket so it hung on my arms. Her fingertips made contact, my body staying still as she touched me. And if I could've made a room full of people disappear I'd have banished every last one of those assholes.

"Not all the way off. We're teasing, not giving them the whole show." She took a step back to inspect her handy work and I wondered what the hell she was thinking. Lord knows I only had one thing on my mind, my jeans getting tighter in the crotch as I hoped she'd do it again.

I didn't get to enjoy it long, the clicking of the camera starting the moment she'd stepped back.

"Yes, that looks fantastic."

Fuck you, asshole, no one asked your opinion.

"Vaughan, tilt your head and now think of something sexy."

There was only one thing I could think of and she was standing a few feet away. Our eyes connected, the heat passing between us until I dropped mine and did what the dipshit asked.

"Awesome. Got everything we need. You guys can go get changed." Our time being models coming to an end as he started to pack up.

"Man, I hope I don't look dumb," Nico complained, pulling off the tailored jacket they'd made him wear. "Seems like a lot of effort for a few photos."

"They'll be used for promotional work, album art," Gillian responded. "And I was watching the monitor while Gerard was taking them, you all looked perfect."

Firstly, *Gerard*? What kind of a jerkoff name was Gerard? And secondly, I wanted to press her against another wall and show her how much more *perfect* it could look.

"Going to trust you, Gillian." Nico chuckled. "But if I see myself on a billboard looking constipated, we're going to have words."

She laughed, the amusement animating her face as she bit her lip. A pang of jealousy washed through me, pissed that had been because of Nico and not me. "I promise, you will not look constipated."

She gave Declan and Austin similar words of praise and reassurance, letting them know how awesome the photos were going to look. But when she got to me, the smile dropped, apparently all the niceties used up. "Vaughan, you can follow me."

Nico, Declan and Austin each gave me a grimace of sympathy, the devil himself feeling her fucking chill all the way down in hell. She was pissed off, that was for sure, and I had no fucking idea why.

"Celine, have the car take the others back. They don't have to wait." The stare she'd leveled at the poor girl, making her jump.

"Sure, no problem, Gillian." She shot me a look of apology as she watched us walk out of the room.

"Gillian—"

"Vaughan, not a word," she warned, ignoring me as we continued forward. She didn't even bother to turn, keeping her eyes glued forward as every inch of her body radiated anger.

With no fucking clue as to why, I was left to make my own assumptions. Maybe someone had said something? Seen her mouth a little puffy when we left the office? We hadn't been in there long enough to suspect anything else, and surely no one had heard.

The door opened, a different office than the one we'd been in. It was smaller; the walls lined with archive boxes, six high, with a chair-less desk sitting in the middle. The slam behind us let us know we were alone.

Not going to lie, but I was a tiny bit turned on. Gillian fired up was something that excited me, and even if I didn't particularly know the reason for the latest rage, I couldn't help but be thankful for it. Her and me alone, the end result.

Her hands pushed against my chest, the force taking me by surprised as I stumbled back and hit a wall of boxes. My eyes wide as she came at me, her mouth attacking mine while her fingers tore at the stupid leather jacket.

"Gillian," I mumbled between kisses, ripping off the jacket and letting it drop to the floor. My hands free to roam her body like hers were roaming mine.

"I said not a word." She kissed my neck, her fingers busy with my fly. "Don't say anything."

If she wanted silence, I'd cut out my own tongue, just fucking thankful to be touching her and kissing her again. Besides, conversation was overrated, especially as she lowered my zipper and palmed my cock.

I swallowed the hiss, her hands feeling so good on me as I peeled off her layers. It wasn't easy, dexterity a challenge as her jacket and shirt hit the floor as I moved to her bra. Kicking off my boots, my hands left her for a second so they could yank off my jeans and boxers. I even dumped the socks, the whole effort achieved in record time.

She didn't stop, her grip around my shaft tight as I unzipped her skirt and worked it down her hips. Her panties also didn't stand a chance, the bastards pushed down her legs before I was able to appreciate the material. Not that I gave a shit, the secrets they were hiding more to my liking.

I worried I was being rough, my hands all over her as I palmed one of her boobs and kneed open her thighs. Everything about her was charged, her nipples hardening on contact as my fingers slipped between her legs. She was wet. Soaking and hot, needy as my thumb teased her opening.

A soft moan escaped from her lips, my fingers plunging into her as I continued to kiss her. I didn't care if the world fucking ended, there wasn't a chance I was stopping, watching her tits heave with short, sharp breaths.

Ripping her hands away from my cock—any longer and I was going to come in her hand—I sunk to my knees. She'd barely had a chance to register, my tongue fucking her core while I held her still. Her hips rocked, arching her back as I lapped her, one of her legs lifting and resting on my shoulder to give me better access. And I was fucking thankful, taking the gift and working her into a frenzy as my mouth did what my cock was aching to do.

"Fuck." She covered her mouth, trying to stop the scream as she rode my face, the sexiest woman I'd ever known coming so hard her legs started to shake.

I didn't stop, working every last tremor out of her as she held onto me. Her teeth sunk into her bottom lip, curses left unsaid as the last of the shudders left her body.

God, she was beautiful.

So freaking gorgeous especially like that. Raw, untamed—coming apart just for me.

But she didn't give me a chance to enjoy it, her leg off my shoulder as she joined me on her knees, apparently something else on her mind as we entered round two.

Her hands pressed against my chest, pushing me down to the floor and I wasn't about to say no. My head lifted, watching from my vantage point as her tongue swirled around my cock and then sucked it into her mouth.

FUCK.

My fists clenched at my sides, my eyes straining not to slam shut as she took as much of me as she could down her throat. It was magic, her lips, tongue and hands working like a Beethoven symphony and playing me to the edge of madness. Everything felt good, my balls rearing up tight as she sucked in hard.

I wasn't going to make it, torn between wanting it to go forever and needing to blow my load, I hovered in a state of sweet agony, waiting for biology to make the choice for me.

She pulled my dick from her mouth with a pop, holding it hostage while she panted. "I want you. I want you inside of me."

Holy.

Fucking.

Hell.

I couldn't think straight, nodding my head—or as close as I could manage—as my hands grabbed her, pulling her down on top of me. My lips found hers, wanting more of her mouth as I rolled her underneath me.

Her hips ground against my cock, arching her back is it hit her right where she needed, the little moans of pleasure threatening to jailbreak against her lips.

In one swift stroke, I sunk into her deep, filling her completely as I kissed her shoulder. She was heaven, hot and tight, my body needing a minute just to fully appreciate how amazing it felt.

Her core tightened around me and not moving was no longer an option, driving into her hard and deep with each pass. Out of control, I pistoned into her, dropping my mouth to her tit as I licked on her nipple.

She tilted her pelvis underneath me, the angle getting me in deeper as I thrust out of control. It was all I needed, able to work her clit with each swing of my hips.

Squeezing her mouth shut, her eyes flung open as she came hard, the waves rolling through her as she splintered apart. I wasn't far behind her, the pulses against my shaft pushing me over the edge, exploding into her in a heated rush. I couldn't stop, my hips continuing to rock as I spilled my load inside of her, every part of my body feeling it had been doused in gasoline and lit on fucking fire.

Oh.

Shit.

With my cock still semi hard inside of her, the realization of what we'd done became apparent. Any condom I might have had, would have been sitting in my pants. Not that it would have done me any good even if I had remembered, the pants I had been wearing were not my own. So instead of suiting up like I should have, I'd skipped that step and gone in bare. And as horrible as it sounded, I couldn't make myself regret it.

"Gillian, I wasn't wearing a condom," I groaned into her neck, wondering if she'd be sharing the same lack of regret.

She nodded, her fingers trailing up my chest. "I know, it's okay."

I had no idea what that meant. Okay—she was on birth control, okay—that she knew I'd be safe, or okay—that she was. *It's okay*, told me nothing, least of all that anything would be fine.

But as I bent down my head and kissed her again, feeling her warm in my arms, everything was indeed o-fucking-kay, at least right at that moment.

29

Gillian

I'd always prided myself on being smart, but clearly I'd made that judgment call way too soon. Because when it came to Vaughan, I left my intelligence and common sense at the door and let my mind be dominated by my vagina.

After sex on the floor—not my finest moment—he kissed me, and I felt guilty for what I'd done. I was supposed to be keeping my distance, trying to get him to see how much easier his life would be without me, and trying to get my head right. But he had a way of changing all of that.

If Gerald had been trying to capture pure sex through his lens, his objective was definitely met. Every part of Vaughan smoldered, the heat and intensity radiating off him like a nuclear weapon. And that was how we'd ended up having unprotected sex on a warehouse floor. Because he was hot, and apparently I was weak.

With no evidence or proof that he wasn't carrying some gross and highly contagious disease, I dismissed the concern. I knew I'd always been safe, and believed he had been too. Which just proved how dumb I was because I hadn't even bothered to ask. The almost impossible chance of pregnancy was the only thing I was certain of, my regimented use of birth control and regular cycle helping me dodge the bullet.

We'd waited until almost everyone was gone. Vaughan headed back to the changing room and got back into his clothes, while I took my time to make sure I didn't look like I'd just been fucked. I wasn't sure how successful I'd been, and not wanting to test the theory, we left before anyone still mulling around noticed.

As I drove him back to his hotel, the smile on his face told me I'd made a mistake. My moment of weakness wasn't going to be the amazing reunion he'd probably hoped. Nope, I'd used him. Used him to feel good in some stupid and selfish version of assisted masturbation. And loving him didn't make it any better, the fact I'd cared and still done it—knowing there wasn't a future for us—made it so much worse. Because I should have loved him enough to walk away, not fucking tormenting him with mixed messages.

He chatted in the car, excited about the album, the band and everything else. And I nodded and smiled in all the right places, not once telling him what was really on my mind. That I was terrified, feelings I wasn't used to and didn't fully trust rippled through my body and I had no idea what to do. Again proving how stupid I was. Dammit.

It was with a sigh of relief that he didn't kiss me goodbye, chuckling under his breath that there were security cameras and told me he'd see me later. I did my best to look him in the eye, not allowing myself to get off so easy and waved as he walked away.

I was so fucking lost.

The man I never expected, with a love I didn't think was possible, was walking away, and I wasn't sure I knew how to hold onto him and not give up everything I'd worked for. Everything I was.

And I'd thought I was smart.

Not even close.

Work was a welcome distraction. Growth on their social media accounts weren't showing any signs of slowing and "Rise Up" was now a hit by anyone's standard. Even my father who was still pissed at my "underhanded shit" had settled. He was too busy trying to take credit, and telling everyone the apple hadn't fallen far from the tree. It annoyed me more than it should, feeling myself getting angrier every time he claimed me going rogue had been his idea.

It had been two days after sex in the warehouse that I sat the band down ready for the reveal. I'd made a more conscious effort not to ghost Vaughan totally, the platonic contact seeming to satisfy him enough not to push harder.

"Why don't we just book a club to play a show?" Vaughan asked, wondering why the hell he and the band were back at the Brooklyn warehouse, their equipment already set up inside.

"Because a club can fit how many? A couple of hundred? When you go live and everyone sees you, it will be in the millions." I unlocked the door and let them in.

Each of them looked fantastic, flawlessly styled, a perfect embodiment of a rock star. They were so excited, itching to play and let everyone see who they were. And we'd put it off long enough.

There was a camera set up on a tripod, connected to a laptop and I logged on while they warmed up. Emily was back at Domination with IT making sure our connection didn't drop or the server didn't go down, and I'd already scheduled press releases to go out thirty minutes after we started. She had media kits with photos and details ready to be posted as soon as we were done, and I didn't doubt her phone was going to be ringing off the hook because mine was currently off.

Austin hopped behind his shiny new drum kit, while Nico and Declan plugged in their flash new guitars and basses. There was even a new mic stand, a silver state-of-the-art microphone sitting on top of it, waiting for Vaughan. They looked so happy, so freaking pleased as they high-fived each other and got ready to play, waiting for my signal.

And as I hit the button, nodding to them they were live and Vaughan announced to the world who they were and launched into their song, I just wanted to cry. Because as much as I was ecstatic for them, I was miserable for myself.

Everything I'd wanted to do at Domination, I'd achieved, culminating with Army of None. I'd proven I could work harder than any man, climbing my way up the ranks not because of my last name but in spite of it. I'd proven that I could spot talent, develop it and turn it into the next big thing. I knew when not to give up, when to take what everyone thought was a lost cause and give it another chance. Me. Not my father. ME.

But what had it cost me?

And why the hell wasn't I happy?

I swallowed my misery, the pride I felt combating the pain in my heart as they went right into a second song. All four of them beamed with delight as I gave them the thumbs up, the comment sections rolling so fast I couldn't even read them. And once the third and final song was played, we faded to black, leaving the audience wanting more as they said goodbye.

High-fives and congratulations were thrown around the awesome-foursome, super pumped at how well they'd sounded. In an hour, they wouldn't even be able to walk outside without someone taking their picture. And the success of that first song would be nothing compared to their first album.

"That was fucking amazing!" Vaughan punched the air, striding over with purpose as he took me in his arms and kissed me. His mouth on me before I'd even realized what he'd done.

"What are you doing?" I pushed him away, looking around and hoping the roadies hadn't come back in to pack up the equipment. Nico, Austin and Declan looked directly at us, not missing the fact their lead singer and their manager had been lip locked not more than a few seconds ago.

"It's just us, Gillian. No one else is around to see." Vaughan's hands slid seductively down my back. "I told you they know, and no one cares. I was just trying to celebrate, I wanted to share it with you."

"No, not in public." I eyed him hard, taking another step away. "Not like that."

The uneasiness crackled through the air, no doubt making everyone feel awkward. Nico was the first to speak, breaking the silence. "Hey, why don't we all go out to celebrate? Surely there's a club or something we can get into?"

Choruses of agreement peppered the air as I distracted myself with the computer. I was not only mad Vaughan had tried to force my hand, but hated he'd made me look bad in front of the others. I was just waiting for the moody female jokes, asking me if I was on my period, or why I was sensitive about kissing my fucking boyfriend in public.

"Hey Gillian, I'm sorry. I got caught up in the moment." Vaughan came up beside me, his apology sincere. "It won't happen again."

"Let's just talk about it later." I waved to the crew, ready to pack up the equipment. "I think Nico's idea is perfect, let's head to a club."

"Really?" He seemed skeptical, like he'd expected something else. "I thought we might go somewhere we can be alone and . . ."

I waved my hand dismissing his idea. "Don't be silly. It's your big night, you guys should go out. Pretty sure any club worth their salt will be happy to host you. If you guys aren't picky I can call ahead, make sure there's adequate security." Just like that I slipped into business as usual, putting aside my own messy emotions to deal with later.

"Sure." It rolled off his tongue like he was anything but sure. "Pick a place, whatever works."

He hesitated while I picked up my phone and made the call, a Manhattan nightclub called *Panic* only too happy to have *Army of None* as their VIPs. I smiled as I made the arrangements, nodding as they assured me they were not only equipped to deal with any crowd they might attract but had a separate private VIP area as well. Their assurances weren't necessary but gave me an excuse to stay on the phone a little longer, the rest of the guys ready to leave by the time I'd hung up.

"Everything's organized, let's get you all into cars." I directed them to the door, the Escalade with our driver, Tyler, still waiting outside.

Thankfully I wasn't the only one choosing ignorance, the rest of the band pretending like nothing had happened as they piled into the SUV. Too busy chatting and reliving the moments to worry it seemed, Vaughan looking at me expectantly as I went and sat beside Tyler. It made sense to give us a little extra distance, especially since he seemed to think that just because he didn't see anyone around that no one was watching.

When we got to *Panic*, I asked Tyler to stay close as I accompanied the guys into the club. Given a choice, a noise-filled place packed with people wouldn't have been where I wanted to be, but I still had a job to do. And since it had been so important to me in the first place—my job, my career—then I should at least do that considering I sucked at being a regular human.

We'd been in the club for only a few minutes when people started realizing exactly who they were. Camera phones came out, people stopping them and asking them for selfies, and women throwing themselves at them like polyester on a cheap suit. It wasn't unexpected, and part of the reason I'd brought them. My visual aid to demonstrate what Vaughan's life could look like so he could make an informed choice.

"Let's get them upstairs," a security guard shouted over the noise into my ear. "We can get a better handle on the crowd and escort them down later once everyone settles down."

"Great, sounds good." I nodded, stepping back and watching as two guys who wouldn't be out of place in a strongman competition, guided Vaughan and the band up the stairs to the VIP area.

Vaughan's eyes were on me, the tension rippling through his body saying all the words he'd left unsaid back at the warehouse. He hated it—or me—but he didn't say a word.

Once I'd made sure everyone had a drink in their hands— non-alcoholic for Austin and Declan—I knew it was my time to leave. The uneasy mood between Vaughan and me hadn't lifted, and I didn't want to be a downer on what was supposed to be a celebration.

"Hey, I'm going to go," I announced to the group, Vaughan's eyes flicking to me as his mouth formed a tight line. "Tyler will take you guys home whenever you're ready."

As I went to walk out, he grabbed my arm stopping me from leaving, his voice a low growl. "Don't go."

"I have to." I shook off his arm and tried to smile. "Be good."

As I walked away I had no idea what I'd meant. Those innoxious words open to all kinds of interpretation. Did I mean not get drunk? His tendency to turn to the bottle when faced with disappointment was his usual path. Or did I mean fidelity, not find someone else less complicated since our relationship was never fully defined. Maybe I'd become so weak I'd brought him to that club on purpose, waiting for him to make a mistake so I could say "ha, I knew it!" and have the choice made for me. God, I hoped I wasn't that pathetic, that my mind hadn't gone to a place so dark that I would do that to him.

I pushed through the crowd of people, torn between wanting him to come after me and hoping he wouldn't, unable to breathe until I'd stepped out onto the street. But he didn't come, doing what I asked of him for like the first time in forever as I hailed a cab and went back to my apartment alone.

"Hey." Emily was sitting on my couch, waiting up for me. "I saw the broadcast. They looked amazing, the internet has gone berserk."

I nodded, not needing the reassurance that I had done my job well. It was about the only thing I seemed capable of doing right. "I'm glad. Hey, can I ask you a question?"

"Of course." Her ready smile spread across her face as she tapped the seat beside her. "Sit, ask me anything."

"Do you think I'm making a mistake with Vaughan?"

I didn't usually ask people's opinion, especially not on personal stuff. But I was out of my depth, completely overwhelmed.

"It should be simple. He's a client, a relationship between us can't happen. So many complications, not to mention the danger of litigation if something went bad. But I love him, and I want to be with him. So the only responsible thing to do would be to recuse myself, sign him to another manager so there was a clear separation there. But I'd lose everything I've worked so hard for. I just don't know if I can walk away from either of them—my job or him."

"Oh, Gillian." She put her arms around me and pulled me into a hug. "You have to do what makes you happy. Even if it means giving something up."

"I should walk away." I shook my head, hating the words even though I was the one saying them. "He had one woman ruin his life, I won't be the second. I don't want there to be any doubt that he earned this on his own, or that he won extra credit because he was with me. He is so good, Emily. The best I've seen in such a long time and I don't want to tie him to this tragic in between. He deserves better. He needs to be spending this time happy, not fucking miserable with me."

I wasn't big on crying, my dad telling me when I was little that it solved nothing so it was pointless. But as much as I knew it wouldn't fix anything, I couldn't stop those tears from falling. If for no other reason than to prove to myself that I wasn't a robot. That I had a heart just like everyone else, capable of breaking just the same. But I wouldn't change my mind, knowing it was the right thing to do. Because as much as I was my father's daughter, I would do something he'd never done—put someone else first.

Not just ethically, but morally it was my only choice, and someday I hoped someone would do the same thing for me. Because I sure as hell deserved it too.

I didn't hold back, sobbing in Emily's arms like I'd never cried before, my emotions in pieces and I didn't know how to fix them. The inside of me felt like it had been ripped apart.

It was not how I'd imagined it.

There had been no break up.

No heated angry words that we couldn't take back.

And no screaming or lashing out or slamming doors.

Instead it was a tornado of feelings that I refused to hang onto, knowing it would eventually blow itself out. It felt cheap, like I had nothing to grieve, cheated out of being allowed to wallow because I'd simply chosen to walk away.

But it didn't hurt any less. Or make me feel any better, my invisible scars no less deep because I'd plunged the knife in myself.

So I cried.

Cried, knowing it solved nothing but allowing myself to do it all the same.

30

Vaughan

Three months ago, if I'd been sitting in the VIP section of a New York club celebrating my success in the music industry, there wasn't a chance I'd be able to wipe the smile off my face. Not like I hadn't imagined it, dreaming about peeling off hundreds and ordering bottles of Cristal, but it was far from magical.

Instead of partying with my girl, I was with two sober Christians and Nico. And that wasn't even the shitty part, Declan and Austin and their god-fearing lack of beer not a problem for me. And Nico was too busy flirting with a woman—he wouldn't have stood a chance with in regular circumstances—to be the pain he usually was. But no, my lack of enthusiasm and general surly mood was because Gillian had not only left but had been pissed off and distant. And yes, I knew it was because I'd tried to kiss her, the concern that some nobody who shouldn't get a say in either of our lives might have seen. But I was caught up in the moment, who could blame me? Still, better to let her cool off, and hopefully in the morning we'd either talk about it or fuck it out of our systems.

It only took a few hours before all of us got bored, heading back to the hotel to sit around and reminisce like a bunch of old men. Funny how shit turns out. Hoping and praying for stuff and when you finally get it, you're not sure you want it.

I went to bed alone, which wasn't something I'd done by choice. Not that there were any shortage of willing participants at the club, anxious to help me warm my sheets. But it wasn't lack of opportunity that kept my dick in my pants, but that my dick only wanted one woman. And having her not in the room didn't change his preference.

The dawn of the new day brought the promise of good things, and it sure as hell delivered when we opened a shiny new offer from Domination.

Warrick Duzan was still mildly pissed that his kid had pulled a bait-and-switch. But he didn't hold the grudge long because last time I checked he wasn't allergic to money. As Army of None's contract was only with Domination for one album, the son of a bitch wanted to get us all wrapped up for albums two and three before anyone else had any bright ideas. Smart, but arrogant, especially considering I'd learnt my lesson when dealing with him in the past. And I wasn't signing shit until I'd talked it over with Gillian. I wanted her to be beside me when I wiped that smug grin off his face and told him we'd look at other offers first. The secret knowledge that I was also fucking his daughter giving me a little extra pleasure.

I'd tried to call her through the night but went to voicemail, stopping myself from hitting panic stations because she'd done the avoid before. She'd text eventually, or call; the need to discuss business a motivating factor if nothing else.

But as the day wore on, my phone continued to be a non-stop hub of activity, but none of those texts or phone calls belonged to her. It wasn't until the next day when I started to get worried.

"Hey, Gillian, can you call me back."

I'd left enough messages on her voicemail to attract a stalking charge but added another for good measure. The lack of contact started to worry me a little, especially since Warrick had called me twice, wanting to know if there was anything else he could do. *No, dipshit, unless you can get the woman I love to talk to me there's nothing you can do.*

It wasn't until dinnertime that I got really concerned. I'd avoided being online, keeping myself busy with the boys as we continued to "celebrate." But when I finally did take a look, I saw she'd been posting, the social media accounts a flurry of activity. And sure, maybe it was her assistant Melanie back on the case now the band was no longer a secret. But I had to wonder, if she had time to answer a question from *SomeLikeItHotoo* then she had a spare minute to pick up the goddamn phone. Oh and if that wasn't enough, my newly created inbox was bursting at the seams, the amount of emails I was CC'd on staggering, and all of them from Ms. Gillian Duzan.

She'd certainly been busy, scheduling all kinds of appearances and interviews, our next few weeks booked solid judging by her impersonal group messages. No warmth, completely detached—with every single one of them ending with *Best, Gillian.* Just like that, she was gone. Slipping into business mode, with me relegated to the musician she didn't sleep with. Except when it was convenient for her of course, then she was happy to slum. And I no longer needed to ask her why she hadn't called, the *business* side of our relationship clearly the fucking priority.

Well, fuck that.

Wondering where the hell I'd left my balls in the past few days, I was done moping around and acting like a pussy. She wanted to play mind games, then she could knock herself out. I hoped she enjoyed herself all the way up there in her fucking ivory tower. But she wasn't going to get a free pass, and was going to have to deal with me one way or the other.

Throwing caution to the wind and probably looking for trouble, I went down to the lobby to try to get a cab. *Yeah. That wasn't happening.* The secret of our location was no longer a mystery with people loitering in the hotel, the crowd gathering across the street really not helping the cause.

"Shit." I sunk my hands into my jeans, a bunch of eyes glued on me as I walked to the concierge. I didn't like my options, but I was done sitting on my hands.

"Hi, hey, I'm Vaughan from—"

I didn't get to finish, the gray-haired dude dressed in a three piece suit smiling as he cut me off. "Of course Mr. Hale, I know who you are. What can I do to help you?"

Not sure if it was my extended stay or my YouTube hits responsible for the recognition but I was glad. Also excited that he had a current need to please, the request not something I was comfortable making. "Great thanks. So here's a strange one for you." I rubbed the back of my neck. "Can you please call Gillian Duzan and tell her that I'm drunk and disorderly."

His brow rose, my lucid speech and upright posture at odds with the information. "You're planning on drinking, Sir?"

"No," I laughed, wondering if it wasn't quicker to just get liquored up and play it out for real. "She's our manager and we're hazing her a little. You know, rock star stuff." *And if I ever said that shit again I was for real going to kick my own ass.* "We want to see how quickly she'll get here."

His hand hesitated on the phone, the mental to-and-fro clearly toiling away in his noggin. "Just you, Sir. Or the entire band?"

"Nah, just me." I chuckled. "We don't want to give her a heart attack."

I watched as he dialed, making eye contact as he said hello to her and recited the agreed upon script. He even improvised a little, saying I was disturbing guests but wanted to give her the chance to handle it rather than call security. And by the time he'd finished, he'd given an award-winning performance, an applause from me the least I could offer.

"That was sensational." I clapped, wondering if she was going to break the land-speed record hauling ass to the hotel. After all, she wouldn't want anything to happen to the *talent* now would she, her investment riding on us staying on the straight and narrow. "Seriously, you were perfect."

"Thank you, thank you." The old guy's cheeks getting pink, taking a small bow. "You know I did dabble a little in theatre in my younger days."

Thanking him for the effort, I slid over a fifty and shot him a forced grin. "Better get up stairs and play my part. Thanks again." And with a wave, I retreated into to the elevator and back into my room.

All I had to do was wait, her arrival imminent. And yeah, she could easily send some nobody to come, and stop me from being the evening's news but she wouldn't. Because if it was one thing I knew Gillian gave a shit about, it was fucking image, not looking too kindly on it if I tossed mine away after she'd put in so much work. So I kicked back, taking a seat on the couch and got a little "method" with a tiny ass bottle of Jack from the mini bar. One way or another, this shit was ending and I wasn't doing her any favors.

It was thirty minutes later when there was a knock at my door, her thunderous voice coming from the other side. "Vaughan, open the door."

About.

Fucking.

Time.

I strolled casually—not in any hurry—and let her stew in the hall for a little. Only fair since I'd spent the past two days in limbo, opening the door when I was good and ready.

God.

She was beautiful.

As much as I wanted to not feel the visceral response, and shut down my feelings, there wasn't a lot I could do when she was

They weren't even close.

My vocals from White Trash Circus were nothing like the track I'd laid down, the warmth and tone in my voice lacking from my early stuff. Never considered doing it another way, and yet in walks a bombshell with an attitude to match and she'd lit the path. Technically, I was singing so much better, and given the talent injection we'd received courtesy of Declan and Austin, it was an unstoppable mix.

Two black Escalades were parked on the tarmac waiting for us, the one the band got into taking us to a small boutique hotel on the Upper East Side.

Gillian and Emily slid into the other.

They met the band at the hotel, hooking us up with our rooms and keys but it was very obvious that moving forward there would be a distance I wasn't happy about. Yes, she'd told me I couldn't stay with her but surely when we were in my room we could at least spend an hour or two before she had to bail.

Nope.

Didn't happen.

The girls left us alone and that's where we spent the first few days. Working out in the gym, writing music in my room or Declan's, and trying to ignore the craziness online. Radios already had "Rise Up" on rotation, DJ's making predictions about us being the next big thing. And since being up loaded onto online retailers, it was roaring up the charts. People were spending their hard-earned cash buying the song without even knowing who we were, and didn't that just renew my faith in humanity. Music bought on its merit without the bullshit image attached to it.

It was a Monday—and three days after we'd arrived in New York—when the Escalades came back. Gillian wasn't taking my calls, but still responding to texts, giving me the same *sorry busy, talk soon* since the day we'd landed. Not sure if it was a

28

Vaughan

Flight back to Teteboro was completely different than when we left. Firstly, the jet was bigger, the extra seats filled up with two members who I'd already classed as friends. And secondly, I was motherfucking excited.

Yeah, I still thought the city was busy, overrated and not my favorite place to be, but my life was so freaking awesome, I no longer cared.

Gillian had tried to convince me the best thing for us to do would be roll back the clock to when we weren't sleeping together. Yeah, not fucking likely. I didn't give a shit how hard she thought it was going to be, it was going to be a hell of a lot easier than losing her all together. So whatever "conditions" she needed to add, we'd work through because me leaving her wasn't happening.

Even though the band knew about us, she kept her distance on the plane. She was with Emily, the two of them in deep conversation, while I sat with the boys as we laughed about the current online speculations about the identities of who was in Army of None.

standing in front of me. The need to kiss her was overwhelming, and I had to remind myself I'd been angry only thirty minutes ago.

"What the hell?" She pushed me inside, shutting the door behind her. "I've got to get someone to watch you 24/7 now? I don't need complaints from the hotel on top of what I already have to deal with. I thought you were past this shit."

She was mad, and I liked it. Because as much as I wanted to hold her, kiss her and have liquid her underneath me, I couldn't handle indifferent. So I would rather her be spitting fire, ready to hand me my ass than us sit politely and talk about my behavior.

"Nice to see you too, Gillian." I breathed into her face, backing her up against the wall. "Was beginning to think you were just going to send me your *best* in an email."

It was pricklier than I wanted to be, hating the tone I was using. But it was either that or go back to being a sap so I didn't have a lot of options. And maybe a small—fine a big—part of me liked to fight with her.

"This is about emails?" Her eyes were fire, blazing infernos and locked onto me. "Are you fucking serious?"

"No, I couldn't give a shit about the emails. It's about you and me."

It was about that time that she realized I was neither drunk nor disorderly, and she'd been lured under false pretenses. She looked around, her eyes searching the room before turning them back to me.

"Why did the hotel call me?" she asked, her hands on her hips, not moving an inch.

"Because I told them to."

"You shouldn't have done that."

"Yeah, well tough," I spat out.

In my head I reached out and kissed her, taking that pent up anger we both had and using it for something good. But I didn't touch her, not wanting to get back on the merry-go-round if she'd already made her mind up she was done.

She shook her head, fists white-knuckling at her side as I braced myself for whatever storm she was going to unleash. But as her chest rose and she took a breath, the fight in her washed away. "I did it for you."

I wasn't sure I'd heard it right, the words not making much sense. "What?" I asked, stepping closer even though it put me in the blast zone.

Her back that had been so straight, sagged, her voice lowering as she raised her hand, keeping me at a distance. "You need to let it go. You need to let *us* go. Vaughan, you—"

My head shook, having none of it. "No, don't tell me what I need. You want out, then own it. Tell me you don't feel anything for me and we'll call it a day. But don't make that choice for me."

Her eyes watered, tears pooling at the edges threatening to put out those infernos. "We can't—"

"Don't tell me we can't," I warned, hating myself for doing it but needing to hear the words. "Tell me you don't love me."

It was the first time I'd ever seen her cry, surprised that not only was it not as clear cut as I'd thought but that she'd let herself be vulnerable in front of me. I knew she couldn't help it, and if there was any way she could stop that she would. But the fact she was unraveling meant she felt something, and that was enough for me not to give up.

"Just tell me, Gillian. Open your mouth and say the words."

She closed her eyes, tears spilling down her cheeks as she wrapped her arms around her middle and shook her head. She was in agony, and I'd put her there and for that I hated myself.

I took another step, the need to touch overriding every other impulse as I reached out and pulled her into my arms. Her body crumbled against me, her face on my chest, wetting my T-shirt as she cried and I silently promised I'd never let go. "Tell me, baby. Tell me, you don't love me."

"I love you. I love you," she mumbled, the words hitting my heart with enough force to level a city. "This isn't because I don't love you, but because I do. I won't be the reason to screw up both our lives."

It didn't make sense, the idea she would screw up anything too unbelievable to even imagine. "Baby, what are you talking about? You're the reason this whole thing is even possible. If it wasn't for you, I'd still be in Pittsburgh probably living in my parents' basement, checking groceries at Sam's Club."

She tilted her chin and looked me in the eyes. "They will tear us both apart. My father. The public. The industry. Everything we've worked for. All of it. Gone."

"No baby, they won't. I won't let it happen."

As I made promises I had every intention of keeping, she broke it down exactly how her life had been. Sobbing into my shirt as she told me about what she'd had to do to prove herself to Warrick and the company, putting herself through the ringer just to show she belonged. It killed me, hearing her talk about wanting respect and acceptance, needing to show she was good at something because the asshole just didn't have it in his heart to love her. The bastard even had her on a contract, making her renegotiate every two years. Man, I fucking hated him. And finally she told of her dream, wanting to take over Domination, and having something she could call her own. My fucking heart breaking over all of it.

I was aware of the complications we were dealing with. The innuendo, the rumors and no doubt the world of heat she'd get from her dad. And I'd admit that I hadn't given it enough weight before, assuming we could be adults about it and move on. But what I hadn't considered—and was ashamed to admit it—was what it would do to her.

It was clear her dad wasn't the warm and fuzzy kind, and anywhere she'd gotten in life had been on her own back. And that was true for the company as well. And while I didn't give a shit what anyone said, the person who was supposed to love me didn't have the power to snap their fingers and take everything away. He was a vindictive fuck, proven time and time again by the way he treated everyone least of all his own kid, and I didn't doubt that if the mood took him, he'd cut her out all together. And while I'd like nothing more than to take her away, and make sure Warrick Duzan was out of our lives for good, it would mean Gillian would have to give up everything for me.

Wasn't going to happen.

The list of people who had hurt the woman in my arms was too high to count, and I wasn't adding my name to it. So if someone was making a sacrifice, it was going to be me. Doing what should have been a million times before, and no one else had seen fit.

"Gillian, I'm walking away," I whispered into her hair, kissing her as I clutched her tighter.

She nodded, sobs still wracking her chest. "I know, it's okay. We'll find a way to be okay."

"No baby, I don't mean from you." I chuckled, wondering how she could ever think after everything she'd told me that I'd just up and leave. "I'm not leaving you. Never. You want to leave, then you'll have to be the one to pull the trigger, not me. I mean the band. I'm walking away from Army of None."

Her fingers grabbed at my shirt as her eyes widened with terror. "What are you saying? Vaughan, you can't just walk away. Think of the band, of the money, the fame . . . it was your dream."

Was.

Past Tense.

I took her face in my hands, still wondering how the hell I got so lucky. "So what? You think any of that means shit to me if I have to do it alone? I'll be a million times happier being a nobody in Pittsburgh, writing tunes and playing to fifteen drunks at the corner tavern if it means I get to have you. I tasted my dream, baby, and what I have with you is so much better. I'm ready to leave it behind, as long as you're by my side."

"I can't let you do that."

I threw my head back and laughed. "Baby, what did I tell you about trying to tell me what to do. You know it's a lost cause. I'm a shitty listener and can't be told. So accept this is what's happening or file a restraining order, because as I see it, those are your only two options."

Not one regret either.

I'd miss playing with the guys, and I had no doubt we'd be friends for life. Not saying I was going to be joining prayer meetings with the brothers anytime soon or stop telling Nico he didn't suck, but I honestly wanted nothing but the best for them. And when the contractual obligations were done, and all the debts were paid, I'd do everything I could to help them find a decent replacement. It wouldn't be hard, the gig the kind that dreams were made of. Just not mine anymore. My dreams were different. And I had everything I needed right there in my arms.

Gillian

I'd always thought Vaughan dabbled on the periphery of sanity, but never believed he'd go all the way over the edge. But as he held me, promising me things I never even asked for, that was exactly where he'd gone.

Craziness.

Willing to give up a chance of a lifetime for . . .me.

It didn't seem real, the idea almost too impossible to even hold in my mind, my heart breaking and mending a million times over.

"Make love to me." I pulled him down to my mouth, needing to feel more of him. "Vaughan, I need you to make love to me."

He chuckled against my mouth, deepening the kiss as he lifted me off the floor. For someone who didn't like to be told what to do, he sure took direction well.

His lips stayed on me as he carried me to his bed, laying me gently on the mattress before slowly pulling away. I groaned, pouting as I tried to pull him back, his head giving a shake as he very deliberately peeled off his shirt.

Oh.

Okay.

"You like that, huh?" He laughed, tossing the shirt aside as he moved to his pants. He didn't hurry, his fingers taking their time as he unzipped, and slid his jeans down his legs, taking care of his shoes and socks and finally his boxers.

I craned my neck, his perfectly sculpted body completely naked and all for me. There were probably a million women who'd give their right arm for him, but every inch of those beautiful toned muscles were all mine.

"I like when you look at me like that." He crawled on the bed, turning his attention to my clothes, taking his time as he started with my shoes and then moved up my body. "I want your eyes on me exactly like that, all the fucking time."

His hands moved, maneuvering me completely at his will as he stripped me bare, kissing each inch of exposed skin. I wanted to participate, my fingers reaching for him and slithering down his chest as he kept his cock just out of reach.

"I want to touch you," I begged, my lips making contact with his neck. "Please."

"Do you now?" he teased, settling into the space between my legs, his hard-on rocking against my clit.

It felt amazing, the slow circle of his hips working his length against me as his mouth took mine. I stopped trying to think, stopped trying to move, stopped trying to control—surrendering everything as I let his body dictate the tempo. Every dip, rock, kiss, lick, touch—agonizingly slow as he worshiped me. I couldn't even talk, preferring for my mouth to kiss him instead and moan against his skin as he made me come.

He was gentle, unhurried and patient, taking extra care as he entered me, our bodies coming together as he looked into my eyes. And nothing had ever felt as good. The excitement built in my core as he took me again and again, not stopping until I was breathless, shattered and sated, whispering how much I loved him against his sweat-soaked skin. I loved him, with every single part of me, I loved him.

He came in a rush, his body smothering mine as he held me tight. I liked the way it felt, the weight of his body reminding me just how strong and powerful he was, my name chanted like a precious prayer as he filled me.

When our breathing slowed and the last shudders left our bodies, he held me in his arms like I was his world. And I knew I was no longer alone.

Neither of us spoke for the longest time, the outside world forgotten, as I let myself just be happy. It took so little effort when he was around, my heart beating a beat faster in celebration.

"What are you thinking about?" His fingers strummed my back as he kissed my forehead.

I sighed, the inevitable conversation needing to be had. "That I can't let you do it. I mean, as far as grand gestures go it's pretty freaking huge, but I don't want you to walk away. And not just because I worry you'll resent me later, but I worked my ass off to make it happen."

He laughed, pulling me in closer. "And you think *I* have a big ego. Well, we need to work something out because, Gillian, I wasn't joking. At the risk of wasting all your hard work, energy and time, I will walk if it's the only way for us to be together. And there isn't a chance I'd resent you, I don't care what you think."

I had no idea how he could be so sure, but it was clear he wouldn't be swayed. And lord knows he was stubborn, any hope of changing his mind not happening.

So there we were.

Everything was perfect, yet nothing was resolved, except that we were together.

And maybe for right at that moment—for the first time ever—I'd let that be enough.

"I love you, Vaughan Hale. And we will work it out."

We made love again a few times, ignoring his phone and mine and the few knocks at the door courtesy of his band mates. They'd scattered pretty quickly when we both told them to get lost, our shared voices coming from the bedroom enough for them to work out we were very much together.

I'd hated there had been so much secrecy, so much of my relationship with Vaughan hidden, and what that must have looked like. I knew what it was like to be kept in the shadows, to feel unimportant and I was so mad that I'd done that to him. No matter what the consequences were, I'd never treat him like a dirty little sidepiece ever again.

It was late when we finally showered and dressed, the world outside and everything in it only being able to be ignored for so long.

Vaughan went and got the rest of the band, both of us deciding that whatever happened with Army of None had to be a group decision. I waited in his room, checking out the contract on his coffee table, the letterhead one I was incredibly familiar with.

My fucking father.

Not content with enjoying the spoils of the band's first album—which hadn't even been released yet—he was already trying to tie them up with a low-ball offer. He hadn't told me, ignoring that I was acting as their manager and agent and going behind my back to undercut me. I swear if it weren't so tragic that he was my family, I'd have laughed at his fucking nerve. There was never going to be a time I trusted him, and I don't think there was anyone on earth he did. It was really kind of sad, that he had all that success, all the money and yet he was a paranoid narcissist who was completely alone.

Yeah, not what I wanted for me.

So what did I want? My fingers flicked through the contract as I tried to work it out, the band entering the room just as I had a crazy—I mean really insane—idea.

"Hey." Nico waved, sitting awkwardly on the chair opposite me. "Sorry about before, I didn't know you guys were . . . in a meeting." Not even trying to hide his smirk.

Declan and Austin grabbed chairs too, taking a seat in a makeshift circle, Vaughan taking his place right beside me in case there were any doubts. "So now would be a good time to let you guys know Vaughan and I are together."

"Is this opposed to the other time you were together?" Declan grinned. "Or the time before that when you were together?"

Whoever said working with animals and children was hard hadn't worked with musicians. "Okay, okay, smartass. This time we're just being honest about it."

"That doesn't mean you can run your mouth or give her shit," Vaughan warned. "I swear anyone who does will have me to answer to."

"Settle down, Vaughan. Only one who gave her a hard time was you." Austin chuckled, shaking his head.

Nico laughed, pointing accusingly at Austin. "Wow, and cock jokes dished out by the freaking virgin. Not as good as you pretend to be, are you?"

"I meant *difficult*, Nico. You know like you trying to play the bass part of something Declan wrote." Austin smirked, not taking the insult laying down.

"Hey!" Nico countered. "Why the hell are you picking on me? Jesus, you're all a bunch of ungrateful ingrates. I'm the heart that keeps this band together."

Vaughan yawned, trying to look bored as he hid his grin. "No one gives a shit about the bass player, Nico. Not sure how many times you have to be told."

It was both hilarious and heartwarming to watch, the amazing group of men who in such a short amount of time had become so close. And in my own way, I loved them. Not the same way I loved Vaughan, but I cared deeply for each one of those guys. Wanting nothing more than to see every single one of them reach their full potential and stand back in awe when they did.

Which was why I couldn't let them go.

Vaughan had started to speak, his throat clearing as he opened his mouth. "So guys, I'm going to do this album and then—"

"We're going to switch labels." I cut him off, not letting him finish. His eyes swung to me, confused about what I was saying since it wasn't what we'd discussed.

"What I mean is." I went on, needing to get the idea out of me before I exploded. "I'm going to leave Domination. I'm handing in my resignation and giving them my notice. Warrick will probably walk me, not wanting me to hang around so I expect I'll be done sooner than later."

"Gillian, you can't leave. That's been your whole life, you've worked your ass off." Vaughan was ready to argue, talk of him quitting the band still in danger of making an appearance.

"You're right. I have worked my ass off, which is why I'm leaving. I deserve more, and I'm not hanging around hoping to get the leftover crumbs."

"So where does that leave us?" Declan asked, probably wondering if I hadn't screwed them over, my relationship with Vaughan no longer the biggest issue.

"They are the distributor. Nothing more. There's no way they'll turn their backs on you, not when there is so much money on the table. My dad is a coldhearted prick but he has never walked away from a lucrative deal. Besides, the contract is watertight, not even their fancy in-house counsel can get out of it."

"Does that mean we're shopping around for another label?" Vaughan asked, my separation from Domination not solving any *future* problems. Other than I'll finally be away from that toxic environment, not that it helped them.

"Yes and no." I grimaced, hoping and praying they went for it. "What about we set up our own label? We use the profit from this album, each of us putting in an equal share and do this on our own. We become partners."

Austin threw his hands up in the air. "What do we know about setting up a label?"

"You don't have to, that's why you have me. I've literally been training for this my whole life, and if you trust me, I know I can do this. And I don't expect any freebies, you guys will join me and together we'll form the board. All major decisions are voted on, a majority needed and I am sinking in cash as well. I will not let it fail."

Never in a million years had I imagined leaving my dad's company and setting up my own in direct competition. Apparently neither had he, the non-compete clause missing from my contract every time I signed. I guess we'd both assumed eventually when he either deemed it so or died, that I'd take over so it seemed unnecessary. And thank the Lord for that.

But if there was one thing I could do, it was running a label. And setting one up—that I was actually a part of—and watching it grow, was something that got me excited. It wouldn't just be a job, it would be an investment, in myself as well as the industry.

"Guys, I promise you. We can do this, and we can be competitive. That seven-figure deal my dad offered was conservative, nothing like the kind of money you're going to make. And think of how much easier it will be with complete artistic control. I'll hire the best sound engineers, the best artists, the best—"

"Gillian," Vaughan cut me off, raising his hand. "We know. And there isn't a doubt in my mind that anything you do is going to be amazing. And I sure as hell don't need any more convincing. So, in the spirit of how things are going to run with this band moving forward, I say we open in it up for a vote. Majority rules."

"Okay." I nodded, feeling so nervous I felt like I was going to throw up. It was a huge decision, asking them to not only trust me with their money but also their career, gambling everything on just my word.

"Everyone who thinks we should fuck the man and start our own label, raise your hand." Vaughan raised his, my heart in my throat as I watched Nico, Declan and Austin unanimously join him. "Looks like the board's made its first decision." He shot me a wink. "You don't need to vote, since we've already outnumbered you."

I laughed, pushing playfully against his chest. "Great. So that's how it's going to be. You guys outnumber me and I don't get a say."

"Hey, don't try and change the rules now, Gillian. Take backs aren't allowed." He pulled me close, kissing me right on the lips with everyone watching.

I didn't even care we had an audience, too deliriously happy to think about anything else other than him, us, and the band. "No take backs," I promised, kissing him right back.

Declan coughed, clearing his throat. "Guys, seriously, anytime you want to remember we're still in the room that would be awesome."

"Okay." I laughed, tearing myself away from Vaughan's mouth. And it sure as hell wasn't easy. "Let's get to work."

I grabbed my phone and called Emily, telling her to get my laptop and haul ass to the hotel. She had no idea what was going on, but agreed without too much argument, me promising to tell her everything the minute she arrived. I could tell she was nervous, having seen me fall apart and no idea if when she arrived it was a situation that was worse. But no matter what happened, when I needed her, she'd be there. And I hadn't realized how much I needed her, especially now.

"You good?" Vaughan asked, putting his hands around my waist and pulling me close. "Emily bringing everything you need?"

"No, but everything I need will be in this room when she gets here. So yeah, I'm good." I hugged him back.

"Still here," Declan called out from the couch, Nico and Austin chuckling along with him.

"Well then buckle up, buttercup." Vaughan called over his shoulder. "Because I'm going to kiss my girl and there isn't a man alive who is going to stop me."

"Kiss me, Vaughan. Let everyone see."

I was done hiding. Done compromising and mostly done settling. I'd thought I'd had my future mapped out, knowing exactly what I wanted and where I needed to be. And then some random guy with a bad attitude, insanely gorgeous green eyes and the most amazing heart tossed my plan out the door. But I had something better than a plan, I had something I'd never really had before, something that meant I'd never fail again.

I had a family.

And I wasn't ever letting them go.

EPILOGUE

Vaughan

"Let me tell him, Gillian, you owe me."

When it came to kick ass news, the hits hadn't stopped. Every single time I turned around it seemed like it was raining fucking rainbows and unicorns, the last twelve months nothing short of miraculous. Not that I'd admit that to Declan and Austin, they didn't need any more encouragement.

When Gillian quit her job at Domination her dad let her know her notice wasn't required, marching her out the door like a shoplifter at the mall. Not that we cared, our sweet revenge coming a few months later after we'd formed *Rise Up Records*, the news sending the old man to the hospital.

Literally.

As in he actually had a heart attack and ended up in the emergency room.

Yeah, it wasn't very nice of me to be happy about it—the bad karma I was apparently attracting going to come and eventually bite me in the ass—but I was trying to tell everyone it was a good thing. The heart attack proving he'd actually had one, because up until that point no one had been sure.

Anyway, even though everyone told Gillian she didn't have to, she went and saw him in the ER and some of their shit was sorted out. Not everything because that was like ten years worth of therapy and to be honest I didn't think he had it in him. But for the most part he was trying to not be a completely selfish dick, even remembering her birthday.

Him finding out we were together had been another stellar moment. Warrick Duzan had looked at me like he wanted to pull out my spleen and use it as a hood ornament when Gillian had told him we were dating. And he wasn't shy in telling her she was throwing her life away. So I'd like to think I was partly responsible for the heart attack too since it had happened just before the news of the label. Let's just call it a team effort and leave it there, my cup over filling with freaking awesome because we didn't have to hide anymore.

Sure people said shit—stuff about her, stuff about me. But they were really quick to shut their goddamn mouths once the album was released and we went platinum in a week. Not bad for a bunch of nobodies who were apparently a one-hit wonder. And all those sons of bitches who had criticized or hated on us got to eat their words, some of the bastards even trying to be our friends. Funny how that happened, cue my lack of fucking surprise.

So the band was unstoppable, we released hit after hit and even did a three-month domestic tour. Me—the luckiest bastard alive—got to have my girlfriend along for the ride on account she was also my boss. Or maybe I was her boss. We never did work out who was in charge of who, and it was probably for the best. Whatever the deal was, it worked, the money and offers coming in so fast we needed to hire extra staff.

Emily was part of the team of course, saying she was only temporary until she got her shit together to open a bakery. But I'd tasted her cooking and to be honest, I think we were doing the world a favor, saving them from the food poisoning.

Connor and Lindsey lasted exactly seventy-one days. I knew the exact number because Lindsey called me crying and telling me what a mistake she'd made. Connor had broken up with her—cue my complete lack of surprise—when he couldn't give her the "attention" she needed. I'd like to say it felt good to know it had fallen apart, but it didn't really. To be honest, I didn't really care either way, which made me feel like a bit of a dick when I told her so. She wasn't too pleased, cussing me out before I eventually hung up. She was no longer my concern. Much like Connor wasn't when I saw him one night at a bar. He looked at me across the room but didn't approach, and I was cool with the way things were. No need to invite drama. Besides, last I'd heard he'd given up guitar and was working for a cable company. That was pretty much enough punishment for anyone.

As for my parents, they did a complete one-eighty and hadn't stopped singing Gillian's praises. Not that it had always been that way, but once they saw how much I loved her and how happy I was, they'd quickly come around. And once they'd found out that Gillian hadn't much of a family growing up, they'd taken it upon themselves to adopt her as their own. Took a while for Gillian to get used to it, the attention not always welcome or convenient but she never once complained. Not only that, but she treated my folks like they were crown royalty, constantly calling them and sending them updates whenever we were on the road or in the studio. And my brother and sister, they loved her as well. To bad if she wanted to keep Emily as her only sibling because she wasn't getting much choice in the matter. Hell, they hadn't even bothered to talk to Lindsey the entire time we dated. And, yet with Gillian, they were constantly bombarding her with texts and calls. Even without me in the equation, they'd grown pretty fond of her, and lucky for them there wasn't a chance I was ever letting her go.

And life was pretty fucking sweet. We'd even started working on our second album, the first one entirely on our own deal.

It felt motherfucking amazing to literally not give a shit what anyone thought, the only people who got a vote were the three other guys in the band and the woman that I loved.

Wow. Didn't hate saying that, literally needing to remind myself how lucky I was every single day so I didn't ever fuck it up. There were a lot of things I'd be able to muddle through, but losing Gillian wouldn't be one of them.

"Gillian, you have to let me do it. You got to tell him we were fucking."

She eyed me hard like she always did when she disapproved, but knew I was going to eventually get my own way. How could she say no to me, I was freaking irresistible.

"Vaughan, his heart is still not the best and his wife is filing for a divorce. I want to make sure we break the news to him gently."

The fact she gave a shit at all about Warrick was a testament to how amazing she was. Not sure I'd have been so generous, and still wasn't sure he'd deserved it.

"So I'll be gentle. C'mon, baby." I brushed my lips against hers, teasing her with my mouth. "Let me."

She sighed, opening her mouth and letting me kiss her exactly how I'd wanted, a low moan rumbling up her throat. "Okay."

"Yes!" I kissed her again before sinking to my knees and pressing my mouth against her flat belly. "Hey sweet baby, we're going to go tell grandpa you're coming and watch him turn fucking gray."

"Vaughan." Gillian rolled her eyes, groaning—and not in a good way.

"I didn't mean to say fuck, it just slipped out. I promise I'll get better before he or she is born. I've even got a swear jar with the virgins." I crossed my heart, committed so my kid's first word wouldn't be an obscenity.

"Firstly, you need to quit calling them virgins. It's not nice." She pulled me to my feet, her hands gently pressing against my chest. "And you know I'm not angry about the *fuck*, it's the other thing."

I laughed, kissing her neck. "Well it's a little late to be worried about fucking, considering that's what got you into this mess."

"Vaughan," she laughed. "Be serious."

"Okay, okay. I'm serious." I took her face in my hands and looked into her perfect golden eyes. "I'm not going to rub your dad's nose in it, but I'm not going to pretend I'm not ecstatic that you're carrying my baby. And while we're on the topic of being serious, when are you going to agree to be my wife? You've been wearing that engagement ring for months, you aren't getting cold feet are you?"

"Vaughan, I have a financial and personal investment in the company we share, am living with you in a house we bought together, in a city that I wasn't born in, with your baby inside of me." She took a breath. "It's a little late for me to be having cold feet."

She was right about that. She hadn't even fought me when I said I wanted us to live in Pittsburgh, signing right beside my name on the title of our new house in Fox Chapel. I think it was good for her, the clean break. But she'd been dragging her feet on the marriage thing, telling me there was no hurry and we were too busy with the band and the business. I didn't see how hard it was to go down to the courthouse and take care of it, wanting to call her my wife like my life depended on it.

"So marry me, Gillian. Just put me out of my misery and make an honest man of me." It was the only thing left on my wish list, the last box I needed to tick.

Her fingers reached up, tracing my jaw as she gave me a smile. "Let me be the one to tell my dad about the baby and I'll marry you right now."

Goddamn it.

She was good.

But you know what, I didn't care. Because the way I saw it, there were no drawbacks to my deal. I had the dream and the girl, so I really shouldn't be so greedy.

"Okay, you tell him."

"You sure?" she asked, not believing I'd given in so easily. "You're going to be okay not watching grandpa turn gray?"

"Yep, because marrying you is more important than sticking it to him." I kissed her nose, and turned and grabbed my keys. "A deal is a deal, now let's go get that marriage license."

Ironically, that slip of paper wasn't going to change a thing between us. Because I didn't need the state of Pennsylvania—or anyone else for that matter—to tell me we were going to be together forever. But I never wanted to put a ring on a girl's finger before and liked the idea of her having my last name. Hell, she didn't even have to change it, keeping Duzan if she'd preferred. But we weren't hiding anymore, it was the last piece missing.

"Let's go get the marriage license, husband." She shot me a smile. "I've made you wait long enough."

What she didn't know is that I would have waited forever, because there were no other options when it came to her. She was my first and last, and my only. And I would spend the rest of my life making sure she knew it. She deserved that, and it was my freaking privilege to give it to her. And as for telling her dad, yeah, I'd give her that. Because when my son or daughter was finally born, it would me who called Grandpap Duzan with the happy news.

Sucker.

"Come on, baby. Let's give the reporters something new to write about."

THE END

To keep up to date with all T Gephart's news, appearances and releases, please subscribe to her mailing list.
http://eepurl.com/bws5Av

Also please consider leaving a review
on your retailer of choice. They help the author
and future readers and we're all eternally grateful.

ACKNOWLEDGEMENTS

Thank you to my amazing family Gep, Jenna, Liam and Woodley, who not only support and love me but remind me that being normal is for losers. We're the best bunch of crazies I know, and I wouldn't want it any other way.

Big thanks to my extended family and friends who are sometimes ignored due to deadlines and crazy commitments. Thanks for understanding and loving me anyway.

Thanks to Gayle Williams who is going to be my right-hand woman. #TeamAwesome is ready for you.

Thanks to the Team Brower—Kimberly, Aimee and Caroline. Rock stars! Love you all.

Thanks to Nichole Strauss from Insight Editing who "tries" to rein in my crazy. A for effort! Seriously, thanks for your patience, flexibility, kindness and of course, your hard work that make my words shine. We make a good team.

Thank you MK for reading my words when they are still rough and vulnerable. You are so respectful, insightful and caring. Can't imagine publishing a book without you reading it first.

Thank you to Elaine York from Allusion Graphics LLC Publishing and Book Formatting. How exciting, our first one! Thanks for making my words pretty and being so understanding. Looking forward to many more projects.

Thanks to the most amazing cover designer in the world, Hang Le. Girlfriend, I can't even. This one is special. You never cease to amaze me, I love every project we work on together. Seriously, you make me look good.

Thank you to my proofreaders Lisa B, Jackie R and Rosa who are beyond awesome. Your sharp eyes are incredible, and I love each of you find something different.

Special thanks to my author friends who make me feel so welcome and loved. I love reading all your work and am giddy beyond belief you read mine. FYI I'll still send you those random emails until you file the restraining order, because that's how I roll.

A MASSIVE shout out to all the bloggers, reviewers, bookgramers, group admins and promoters, who read, promote, review, and share my work. Some of you do it completely unsolicited, straight from your heart and love for my work. I'm constantly surprised, humbled and honored by everything you do. Thank you so much.

Thanks to Jessica and Team InkSlinger for harnessing release day madness.

Thank you Liz, MJ and Jillian at 1001 Dark Nights.

THANK YOU TIMES A MILLION to the T Gephart Review Crew and Entourage. Thanks so much for all your love and support. Thanks to Michelle Clay and Annette Brignac who wrangle the review crew and put in so much hard work.

And my last and biggest thank you goes out to YOU. Not sure if this is your first book or you have read everything I've ever written, but I love and appreciate every single one of you. Thanks for reading, enjoying, reviewing, sharing, and choosing my book out of the literal millions of choices out there.

ABOUT THE AUTHOR

T Gephart is a *USA Today* and International bestselling author from Melbourne, Australia.

With an approach to life that is somewhat unconventional, she prefers to fly by the seat of her pants rather than adhere to some rigid roadmap. Her lack of "plan" has resulted in a rather interesting and eclectic resume, which reads more like the fiction she writes than an actual employment history. She'd tell you all about it, but the statute of limitations hasn't expired yet. But all those crazy twists and turns have led her to a career she loves—writing romantic comedy.

When she isn't filling pages with sassy and sexy characters with attitude, she's living her own reality show in the 'burbs of Melbourne with her American husband, two teenage children, and her fur child—Woodley.

She loves adventure, to laugh, travel, and strives to live her life to the fullest.

CONNECT WITH T

tgephart.com
Facebook - www.facebook.com/tgephartauthor
Goodreads
Twitter - twitter.com/tinagephart

Books by this Author
The Lexi Series
Lexi
A Twist of Fate
Twisted Views: Fate's Companion
A Leap of Faith
A Time for Hope

The Power Station Series
High Strung
Crash Ride
Back Stage